**Georgiana felt a strange tremor ripple through her, and raised her eyes to discover a tall gentleman standing in the doorway leading to the larger salon.**

Dressed in the impeccable style advocated by George Brummell himself, and with black hair cropped short and artistically arranged in the windswept look, he seemed to make nearly all the other gentlemen present appear slightly ill-groomed in comparison.

So striking was the change in appearance that Georgiana didn't immediately appreciate precisely who it was. Only when stark recognition on his own part replaced affectation, and those unforgettable dark eyes stared fixedly in her direction, did she know for sure. Then she very nearly forgot the movements of the dance, almost disgraced herself by missing a step, when heavy lids lowered and a look of such contempt took possession of those rugged features, a moment before he swung round on his heels and walked away…

**Anne Ashley** was born and educated in Leicester. She lived for a time in Scotland, but now makes her home in the West Country, with two cats, her two sons, and a husband who has a wonderful and very necessary sense of humour. When not pounding away at the keys of her computer, she likes to relax in her garden, which she has opened to the public on more than one occasion in aid of the village church funds.

**Previous novels by the same author:**

A NOBLE MAN*
LORD EXMOUTH'S INTENTIONS*
THE RELUCTANT MARCHIONESS
TAVERN WENCH
BELOVED VIRAGO
LORD HAWKRIDGE'S SECRET
BETRAYED AND BETROTHED
A LADY OF RARE QUALITY
LADY GWENDOLEN INVESTIGATES
THE TRANSFORMATION OF
  MISS ASHWORTH

*part of the Regency mini-series
  *The Steepwood Scandal*

# MISS IN A MAN'S WORLD

Anne Ashley

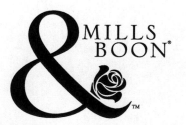

First published in Great Britain 2011
by Mills & Boon, an imprint of Harlequin (UK) Limited,
Large Print edition 2011
Eton House, 18-24 Paradise Road, Richmond, Surrey TW9 1SR

© Anne Ashley 2011

ISBN: 978 0 263 21866 4

**LP**

Harlequin (UK) policy is to use papers that are natural, renewable and recyclable products and made from wood grown in sustainable forests. The logging and manufacturing process conform to the legal environmental regulations of the country of origin.

Printed and bound in Great Britain
by CPI Antony Rowe, Chippenham, Wiltshire

# MISS IN A
# MAN'S WORLD

# *Prologue*

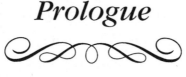

The firelight flickered across the Dowager's face, making her appear more intimidating than usual. Even her staunchest supporters, her closest friends, would never have called her a beauty; not even five decades before, when she had surprised so many by her betrothal to the sixth Earl of Grenville, thereby achieving a truly splendid alliance. Nonetheless, not even her severest critics, and there had been numerous of those during her lifetime, would ever have stigmatised her as the least light-minded, or as a woman who had failed in her obligations. On the contrary, she had been renowned throughout her adult life for putting duty first, even if this had meant going against inclination. She had always been steadfast in her resolve, a veritable pillar of strength to all those who had come to rely on her support and good sense down the years.

Yet today, finally, after seeing the last of her six

children placed in the family vault, much of that zest for life, that spark of determination, had faded from her eyes. Much, it was true, but not quite all, as the only other occupant of the comfortable parlour discovered when the Dowager finally ceased her silent contemplation of the glowing fire in the hearth and raised her head.

'I do not make this request of you lightly,' she revealed at last. 'I appreciate there is a very real possibility that you might be putting your own life in danger by agreeing to my request, should the person responsible for my son's death discover your quest. But the truth of the matter is there is no one I trust so implicitly.' The Dowager gave vent to a wheezy half-chuckle. 'A sad admission for someone of my advanced age, whose acquaintance over the years has been extensive, and yet, it is true. Should you accede to my request, I know you will do your utmost to discover just what my son meant.'

'And you are sure, ma'am, that he said, "No, not a stranger… It could only have been…one of the five. One of them must have been involved"?'

'Quite sure. It is something I am unlikely ever to forget, as they were among the last words he ever spoke to me. But, just what he meant by them, I have no notion. My son's acquaintance was vast, much larger than mine. He might have been referring to any number of different people—peers of the realm, members of the government, high-ranking officers in the army or navy. Or maybe even a secret society. Who knows? But when I do know for certain, that will be the moment to take matters further. Until such time, it would be best if the world continues to believe my son died at the hands of unknown assailants. Which, of course, is most definitely the case... But the one I am determined to bring to justice is the person who organised the attack.'

The silence that followed was broken only by the ticking of the mantel-clock, and the crackling of logs in the hearth, until the Dowager's companion finally said, 'It is still your intention to remove to Bath in a few weeks, is it not? That will give me time to ponder on how best to discover what we both dearly wish to know. Delay writing to your good friend Lady Pickering in London. Involving her might not be the ideal solution. A better way might yet occur to me, my lady.'

# Chapter One

*Spring 1802*

'Why don't you change your mind, Finch, and spend a week or two with Louise and me? You know how very fond of you she is. Why, she has come to look upon you as a brother! She will adore having you to stay.'

Viscount Fincham regarded his companion from behind half-closed lids. Anyone studying him might have been forgiven for supposing he had been on the verge of sleep during the past few minutes, for he had not uttered a single word since seating himself by the window in the crowded hostelry. Nor had he attempted to sample the tankard of ale the landlord had placed before him. None knew better, however, than the gentleman seated opposite that behind that languid air of blissful unconcern lurked a razor-sharp intellect, an astuteness that was frighteningly keen and occasionally quite disturbing.

An expanse of fine lace fell over one long-fingered hand as the Viscount reached for his tankard and finally sampled its contents. 'You are in error, my dear Charles. Being heartily bored with life at present, I should make sad company for Louise. Or anyone else, come to that. Besides which, your darling wife has enough to contend with. She would not choose to put up with my megrims so close to her confinement.'

Knowing better than to attempt to persuade his friend to change his mind and accept the invitation, Charles Gingham merely said, 'What you need, old fellow, is what I've been blessed to have these past years—the love of a good woman.'

White, even teeth showed behind a wickedly flashing smile. 'Evidently you forget I have one already. Caroline is, without doubt, the most skilful I've ever had.'

Charles gave vent to a derisive snort. 'I'm not talking about your birds of paradise, Ben. Good Lord! You've had enough of those down the years. And not one of 'em has meant so much as a groat to you, if I'm any judge. No, what you need is a wife, a lady you will love and cherish, someone who will give your life a new direction, some purpose.'

This time the Viscount's smile was decidedly twisted, revealing more than just a hint of cynicism. 'I hardly think that is ever likely to happen, my dear friend. No, perhaps in a year or two I shall marry, if only to beget an heir. After all, a fellow in my position is never short of candidates for a wife. I have the hopeful little darlings parading before me with tiresome regularity every Season in the Marriage Mart. I'm sure if, and when, I take a serious look I shall find at least one female who will meet my exacting standards—divinely fair, impeccably mannered and dutifully biddable.'

Charles Gingham stared across the table, a hint of sadness in his expression. 'Do you still ponder over what might have been? I know I do. If I hadn't dragged you across to France with me all those years ago, you might now be a blissfully contented married man.'

'Do not do offence to your feelings on my account, Charles,' the Viscount urged him, once again sounding distinctly bored with the topic of conversation. 'Your sympathy is quite misplaced, believe me. Charlotte Vane, that was, no longer enters my thoughts. She chose to overlook the understanding

between us, and marry Wenbury. Had she chosen to
await my return from France, she would undoubtedly have eventually become my Viscountess. My
brother's untimely demise was a shock to everyone, not least of all to me. I neither grudged him
his superior position in the family, nor craved the
title for myself. Fate decreed that I should inherit,
however. Had he produced a son, not a daughter, I
should have been more than happy to run the estate
until my nephew came of age. I would be a liar if I
said I do not now enjoy the agreeable benefits the
title has afforded me, because I do. And I believe
I have carried out my duties with diligence, and
consideration towards all those who look to me for
their livelihood. I also believe I have a duty to marry
one day. But let me assure you that love will never
enter into the equation. So long as my future bride,
whoever she might be, conducts herself in a ladylike manner at all times, and provides me with the
heir I desire, she will not find me unreasonable or
exacting in my demands. For the most part she may
go her own way, as I fully intend to go mine.'

Charles was appalled by such blatant apathy, and
it showed in his expression, and in his voice as he
said, 'I cannot believe you would be so indifferent
to the lady you should one day choose to marry.

You might fool most all the ton into believing you're cold and indifferent, but you'll never persuade me. I know how much Charlotte Vane meant to you. I know what you're capable of feeling.'

'Was capable of feeling,' the Viscount corrected in an ominously quiet tone. 'Unlike you, Charles, I am no longer a romantic. I leave all that nonsense to the numerous poets of the day. I do not look for love in marriage. Dear Lady Wenbury taught me a very valuable lesson eight years ago. I've learned to guard against the—er—more tender emotions. No, I shall be content with a female who behaves at all times with propriety and fulfils all her obligations as my Viscountess.'

No one could have mistaken the note of finality in the deep, attractively masculine voice, least of all the gentleman who had had the honour of being one of the Viscount's closest friends since the far-off days of their boyhood, and so Charles wasn't unduly surprised when his lordship tossed the contents of his tankard down his throat and rose to his feet, announcing that they had best leave, or risk missing the start of the mill.

The market town was a hive of activity. Not only was there a prize fight being staged in a field on the outskirts of the thriving community, there was also a horse fair taking place in an adjacent meadow. Visitors wishing to enjoy one or both attractions were making their way along a crowded main street, their ribald comments and guffaws of merriment mingling with street hawkers' cries as they attempted to sell their wares. So it wasn't wholly surprising that his lordship, leading the way out of the inn, quite failed to detect that single cry warning him of possible danger. It wasn't until someone cannoned into him, thereby successfully thrusting him back against the inn wall, out of harm's way, that he realised one of the drayman's large barrels had come perilously close to doing him a mischief. He watched it roll harmlessly by before turning his attention to the youthful rescuer at his feet.

'Good Lord, Ben! Are you all right?' Charles enquired, emerging from the inn just in time to witness the incident.

'It would appear I fared rather better than my gallant deliverer here,' his lordship responded.

Clasping a hand round a far from robust arm, his lordship then helped the youth to his feet, and saw at once a small quantity of blood trickling down the stocking below the left knee. 'Here, take this, lad!'

After having thrust a square of fine lawn into a surprisingly slender hand, his lordship watched as the youth tied the handkerchief about his leg. 'Are you hurt anywhere else?'

'N-no, I do not believe so, sir,' a gruff little voice answered, before the youth retrieved his tricorn from the dusty cobbled yard, and raised his head at last.

Taken aback slightly, the Viscount found himself blinking several times as he gazed down into the most vivid violet-blue eyes he'd ever seen; framed in long black lashes, they were remarkably striking, and quite wasted on a youth.

Drawing his own away with some difficulty, he requested his friend to locate the landlord's where-abouts, and then returned his full attention to his unlikely rescuer. 'Do you live locally? If so, my car-riage is at your disposal, and my groom can return you to your home, as soon as the landlord's good lady wife has seen to your hurts.'

'There's no need to trouble, sir. 'Tis naught but a scratch,' the boy protested, but his lordship re-mained adamant.

'It's the very least I can do, child, for someone who selflessly saved me from possible injury. Ah, and here's the very man!'

Tossing the landlord a shiny golden guinea, he bade him take care of the boy by providing whatever his youthful rescuer might request. In view of such generosity, mine host was only too willing to comply, and ushered his somewhat reluctant young customer toward the inn's main entrance, leaving the Viscount staring after them, his high forehead creased with a decidedly puzzled look.

'What's amiss, Ben? You're not hurt yourself, are you?'

'What…?' His lordship managed to drag his mind back to the present without too much difficulty. 'No, not at all, Charles,' he assured him, as they set off down the road. 'It's just that young lad… Did you notice his eyes, by any chance?'

'No, can't say as I did. Why, what was wrong with 'em? Not crossed, were they?'

The Viscount frowned yet again. 'No, there was absolutely nothing wrong with them at all… They were perfect, in fact! Perhaps the most striking I've ever seen in my life.'

'No doubt he'll turn a few fillies' heads, then, when he's older,' Charles suggested, fast losing interest in the topic, for his attention had been well and truly captured by something he considered far more diverting. 'Looks as if the mill's about to start. Let's see if we cannot attain a good vantage point.'

By the time Viscount Fincham had returned to that certain well-kept hostelry, late that same afternoon, he too had successfully thrust the incident earlier in the day, and his youthful rescuer, to the back of his mind. After taking leave of his friend, who lived a mere mile or so the other side of the thriving community, his lordship didn't delay in heading back to the capital.

As his well-sprung travelling carriage picked up speed, leaving the habitation far behind, Lord Fincham stared absently out of the window, and was considering how best to entertain himself that evening, when he caught sight of a solitary figure, carrying a somewhat battered portmanteau, trudging along the road. Just what it was about the person that instantly captured his interest he was for ever afterwards to wonder. It might have been the set of the slender shoulders, or the brief glimpse of a slightly worn and faded tricorn that struck a chord of memory. All his lordship did know was that he had instinctively reached for his silver-handled walking stick in order to beat a tattoo on the conveyance's roof, without giving the matter a second thought.

His head groom responded in a trice, and as the carriage drew to a halt his lordship let down the window, and leaned out in order to watch the solitary figure's approach.

As the youth drew closer, surprised recognition was clearly discernible on the young face. 'Great heavens! Why, if it isn't you, sir!'

The boy was more dishevelled than the Viscount remembered. His clothes were now liberally covered in dust, and there were streaks of dirt across his face. He looked decidedly weary, too, as though he had been walking for some considerable time.

A surge of annoyance—borne, he could only suppose, of a guilty conscience—suddenly assailed him, and Lord Fincham found himself saying more sharply than he had intended, 'Well, don't just stand there, leaving my horses champing at their bits, lad!'

There was a moment's hesitation before the youth clambered inside and settled himself opposite, placing the portmanteau carefully on the seat beside him, as though it contained all his worldly goods.

Which was possibly the case, the Viscount ruminated, before his youthful companion asked where he was bound. 'More importantly, what is your destination?' his lordship enquired by way of a response. 'When we—er—bumped into each other earlier, I assumed—quite wrongly, I should imagine—that you resided in the market town.'

'Oh, no, sir! I was merely exploring the place while I awaited the arrival of the stagecoach to London.' A rueful expression flickered over delicate features. 'Unfortunately, the innkeeper's wife was so very obliging. Not only did she attend to my slight hurts, she also insisted I had something to eat when she learned I hadn't had a morsel since breaking my fast early this morning. I'm afraid I simply couldn't resist the offer of sweet game pie and a bowl of broth, and returned to the coaching inn on the other side of town only to discover the stage had departed some thirty minutes previously. The innkeeper there told me of a carrier he knew on the outskirts, but by the time I'd located the premises the carrier had long since departed for the capital, so I decided to continue walking until I found a suitable inn where I might put up for the night.'

'In that case, your luck's in, child, for I am bound for the metropolis myself, and can take you wherever you wish to go.'

'Oh, thank you, sir! That would be most agreeable!'

The smile that accompanied the response was so enchanting that his lordship was quite startled by it. Then the astounding possibility that had momentarily occurred to him at their first encounter once again crossed his mind.

Leaning back against the velvet upholstery, he studied his youthful companion beneath half-shuttered lids. Hair, every bit as black as his own, was confined at the nape of a slender white neck with a length of ribbon. Beneath the tricorn hat the delicately featured face turned slightly, thereby offering him a perfect view of a profile that boasted high cheekbones, a small straight nose, a sweetly shaped mouth with a slightly protruding upper lip, and a perfectly sculptured little chin. Although a frock-coat of good quality adequately concealed the upper body, there was no mistaking the slender straight limbs beneath the knee-breeches and soiled stockings.

'You have yet to inform me precisely where you are bound, child,' his lordship reminded his companion, with a satisfied half-smile, as he drew his eyes away from narrow feet shod in buckled shoes.

Those striking orbs once again turned in the Viscount's direction. 'Oh, if you could just set me down at some respectable inn, sir, I would be immensely grateful.'

'Would you, indeed,' his lordship purred silkily, as he once again cast a speculative glance over his companion's trim form. 'Yes, I feel sure we could come to some mutually—er—satisfactory arrangement,' he added, before he watched one slender hand delve into the portmanteau and draw out a surprisingly bulging leather purse.

'What would you consider adequate largesse, sir?'

For several seconds his lordship didn't know whether to feel amused or annoyed. The chit couldn't be serious! Surely she wasn't so naïve as to suppose he was suggesting payment in cash? Or was she?

For several very good reasons Lord Fincham had learned to be mistrustful of the fair sex. Yet, for some obscure reason, which escaped him entirely, he was prepared to give the intriguing little minx opposite, for he no longer doubted her true sex for a moment, the benefit of the doubt. Furthermore, if she wished to continue the charade, then he'd play the game, for the present, at least.

'Put the purse away, child!' he ordered, once again more sharply than he had intended, simply because, had the truth been known, he was annoyed with himself for his own indecisiveness where this girl was concerned. 'I require no payment,' he said more gently. 'In view of the service you rendered earlier in the day, it is the very least I can do.'

Even as he said this he was having renewed doubts about their earlier encounter. Had it been all as innocent as it had seemed? Or had the whole incident been very carefully staged by one of his degenerate acquaintances as a jest? For reasons that escaped him entirely, he was once again prepared to give his companion the benefit of the doubt.

'But as we shall be bearing each other company for the next hour or so, I'd best introduce myself. I am Fincham, Viscount Fincham.'

When she betrayed neither surprise, nor, indeed, any outward sign of discomposure at being in the company of such a distinguished peer of the realm, doubts again assailed him. She must surely have known who he was?

'And you are?'

A slight hesitation, then, 'George, my lord George—er—Green.'

The Viscount successfully suppressed a knowing smile. 'Well, Master Green, are you sure you wouldn't prefer me to convey you to a relative or friend in the metropolis?'

'Positive, my lord, for I have neither residing there. But if you could, as I mentioned before, deposit me at some respectable inn, which is not too expensive, I shall be for ever in your debt.'

The hopeful expression was unmistakable. Was she the most accomplished actress who ever drew breath, or in earnest? He remained frustratingly undecided. 'I might,' he at last conceded. 'But first I should very much like to know why you wish to visit the capital?'

The response was prompt enough. 'In order to find employment, my lord.'

He raised a decidedly sceptical brow at this. 'Indeed? And what type of employment are you hoping to attain?'

Slender shoulders rose in a shrug. 'I hadn't really considered. Maybe a situation in service might suit my purpose best—a footman, perhaps.'

Again his lordship cocked a sceptical brow. 'How old are you, child?'

Delicate lids lowered. 'Fifteen, my lord.'

Clearly an untruth. Moreover, one that had been uttered most unwillingly, unless he much mistook the matter. Interesting…yes, most interesting.

'A little young for a footman, then,' he suggested,

still willing to play along with the subterfuge. 'A page, perhaps?'

'A page,' she echoed, seeming to consider the possibility. 'Yes, that might serve very well.'

Dear God, she couldn't be serious! Her sex would be uncovered in a trice! If she wasn't in the employ of some prankster, and engaged to entice him into committing some act of folly, then he had possibly done more harm than good by suggesting what he had.

Settling himself back against the plush velvet squabs once more, his lordship experienced a rare pang of conscience, simply because he still couldn't quite make up his mind about his intriguing travelling companion, which was most unlike him. He was renowned for being a shrewd judge of character, and although it would be true to say he didn't make snap judgements about people, his first impressions, more often than not, turned out to be accurate.

But young George Green had him well and truly puzzled. Speech alone suggested the chit didn't come from the lower orders. He strongly suspected, too, that she had received a well-rounded education. So what on earth did she imagine she was doing indulging in such an escapade? If she wasn't in disguise as a jest, then there was every likelihood she had run away from home, possibly fleeing some form of persecution, or even an arranged marriage that was not to her taste. If he had any sense at all, he told himself roundly, he would do what she asked, and just deposit her at the first respectable hostelry they came to in the capital! Yet, even as this most sensible course of action crossed his mind, he knew he would not act upon it.

He found himself studying her intently again. Yes, dressed appropriately she would undoubtedly make a damnably pretty girl... No, an extremely lovely one, he corrected silently. She was certainly older than fifteen... Eighteen, or maybe nineteen, he decided. And definitely no sweet simpleton, if he were any judge. She knew precisely what she was doing, too. There was some definite purpose in this outrageous charade of hers. He'd stake his life on it! One thing was certain, though, he found her and the situation intriguing and highly diverting, something he hadn't experienced in many a long year. He was determined to discover who she was and, more importantly, just what she was!

'I am pleased to discover you are not garrulous by nature, Master Green. None the less, I believe a little conversation would be permissible, even between virtual strangers.'

This succeeded in bringing to an end her intense study of the passing countryside. 'I do beg your pardon, my lord—only, I've never visited the capital before, and am finding the landscape quite interesting.'

'I, on the other hand, have travelled this route on numerous occasions and find it faintly tedious,' he countered, 'and should much prefer to discover a little more about you.'

There was no mistaking the guarded look that took possession of those enchanting features, but his lordship chose to disregard it. 'Why, for instance, do I find you alone in what, by your own admission, is a foreign part of the land? And why are you not accompanied by a relative?'

'Both my parents are dead, my lord.'

He found himself readily accepting the truth of this statement, possibly because her gaze had been so unwavering. Yes, already he was well on the way to knowing for sure when she was spinning him some yarn and when she was not.

'And is there no one else responsible for your well-being, child…? No distant relative or guardian?'

'No, my lord.'

Now, that was most interesting, for if she had continued speaking the truth, and he was inclined to believe she had, it must surely mean that she was somewhat older than he had first imagined, at least one-and-twenty. It possibly meant, also, that she was not running away from some arranged marriage that was not to her taste. Which instantly begged the question of what lay behind the outrageous escapade? With every passing mile his lordship's curiosity was increasing by leaps and bounds!

By the time the carriage had drawn to a halt before a certain much-admired residence in Berkeley Square his lordship had decided on his immediate course of action. His intriguing companion, on the other hand, did not betray any outward sign of being at all impressed by her surroundings when she alighted in his lordship's wake. In fact, when she discovered it was none other than the Viscount's town house they stood before, she appeared decidedly ill-at-ease, not to say a trifle annoyed.

'But I thought you said you would deposit me at some respectable hostelry, my lord?'

'I cannot recall agreeing to any such thing, child,' he countered, favouring her with one of his haughtiest stares. 'I can, in due course, arrange for one of my servants to direct you to just such an establishment, if it is what you wish. First, I have a proposition to put to you. But not here in the street, where the world and his neighbour are at liberty to view proceedings.'

His lordship did not trouble to discover whether his youthful companion was prepared to follow him into the house. When the front door miraculously opened, even before he had made known his arrival by beating a tattoo using the highly polished brass knocker, he strolled languidly into the hall, handing his outdoor garments to the high-ranking retainer who had served him diligently from the moment his lordship had unexpectedly come into the title.

'Bring claret and two glasses into the library, Brindle, and inform Cook I shall not be going out again this evening,' and so saying he led the way into the book-lined room, fully aware that he was being closely followed by his newest acquaintance.

Choosing not to acknowledge her presence until he had closed the door so that they could enjoy privacy, he then turned to study her. Although she had removed her hat, she had chosen not to hand it over to the butler, and held it securely against the portmanteau in her right hand. Which instantly revealed two things—firstly, she was alert to the correct forms of behaviour; and, secondly, she remained decidedly ill at ease. When she blatantly refused the offer of a seat, he did not force the issue and merely made himself comfortable in a winged-chair, while all the time studying her closely as she, in turn, considered the painting taking pride of place above the hearth.

'That is your family, is it not, my lord?'

'Indeed it is, child. The tall gentleman had the felicity to be my sire. My mother, although no beauty, as you can perceive for yourself, was possessed of much wit and charm. I am the younger child, holding the dog.'

He watched fine coal-black brows draw together. 'My condolences, sir. I trust your brother's demise was not recent?'

Clearly the chit took no interest in the goings-on in the ton. 'He died after taking a tumble from his horse some eight years ago.'

What she might have chosen to reply to this he was never to know, for the door opened, and her attention immediately turned to the rigidly correct individual who had served the Fincham family for very many years.

'You may leave the tray, Brindle. We shall help ourselves. I shall ring when I require you again. In the meantime, I do not wish to be disturbed.'

The major-domo was far too experienced to betray

even a modicum of surprise over his master's most unusual companion, and merely bowed stiffly before leaving the room and closing the door almost silently behind him.

'Come here, child,' his lordship demanded, and then sighed when the order was blatantly ignored. 'I assure you I have no intention of doing you a mischief. I merely wish to look at your hands.'

Gracefully arching brows rose in surprise. 'My hands, sir! Whatever for?'

The Viscount cast an exasperated glance up at the youthful face. 'Be warned that should I decide to offer you employment—against my better judgement, I might add—I shall expect my every request to be obeyed without question. Now, come here!'

This time he succeeded in achieving a favourable response. Lightly grasping the member held shyly out to him, he felt for his quizzing glass and through it studied slender tapering fingers and short clean nails. 'As I suspected, you are not accustomed to hard labour.'

Releasing the finely boned wrist, he reached for the decanter conveniently positioned on the table beside his chair and proceeded to pour out two glasses. 'As I cannot imagine you have quenched your thirst for several hours, you may sit yourself and join me in a glass of wine.'

Although her expression clearly revealed a hint of speculation, there was nothing to suggest that she might have considered it in the least odd to be asked to partake of refreshment in the company of an aristocrat, which succeeded only in intriguing him still further.

'Were you truly in earnest when you declared you were in need of a servant, my lord?' she asked, before sampling her wine in a very ladylike manner.

'I should not otherwise have said so, child. But before we come to any firm arrangement, I shall need to know a little more about you. Firstly, from whom did you acquire an education?'

There was no mistaking the mischievous little smile before she said, 'From the former rector of our parish, sir. My mother was his cook-housekeeper for a number of years, and—and he had a fondness for me.'

'And your father?'

'I never knew him, and he never knew of my existence. He was a soldier, sir, and died in the service of his country shortly after I was born.'

Studying her above the rim of his glass, his lordship considered what she had revealed thus far. She might well have told him the absolute truth. But it was also possible that if she was indeed the bastard daughter of some person of standing, her mother might well have spun the yarn about a deceased father in order to maintain the appearance of respectability. Undeniably the girl had a quiet dignity that was not feigned, and that certainly suggested she believed her parentage to be above reproach. Which made lending herself to such a start even more surprising!

Deciding to refrain from questioning her further for the present, he said, 'I am satisfied you could perform the duties of a page. If you should choose to avail yourself of the position, I shall have a new set of clothes made for you on the morrow.'

She betrayed no sign whatsoever of being delighted by the offer. In fact, if anything, there was a hint of mistrust as she asked, 'But why should you require a page, sir? Are you married?'

'And what has that to say to anything, pray?' He cast her a look of exasperation. 'No, I am not, as it happens. Why do you ask?'

There was a suspicion of a twitch at the side of the perfectly shaped mouth again. 'Well, because it's usually ladies who engage pages, sir.'

'Not always,' he countered, and then smiled grimly.

'And that is one of the reasons why I'm prepared to engage your services. I feel the most overwhelming desire to annoy a certain acquaintance of mine. He shall find it quite irksome when he sets eyes on you for the first time.'

'Shall he, my lord?'

'Most definitely, child! And now you may begin your duties by tugging the bell-pull, there, by the hearth.'

Taking her immediate compliance to his request to mean that she had accepted the post, he sat quietly, considering his latest responsibility until the summons was answered, and then turned his attention to his major-domo.

'The child you see before you, Brindle, is my new page.'

Not even by so much as a slight raising of one greying brow did the butler betray surprise, even though there had never been a page employed in the household for as long as he had been in service with the family.

'Is there a spare room in the servants' quarters?'

'Not one that isn't presently occupied or used for storage, my lord. He could share with the boots for tonight, I suppose, or perhaps it would be best if he doubled up with James, the footman. His room is slightly larger.'

The Viscount frowned heavily. 'No. For the time being he may use the small room my niece occupies when she stays here.' Once again he looked directly up at his butler. 'Now, pay attention, Brindle. Tomorrow, I wish you to take the boy out and buy him a new set of clothes, and whatever other little necessities he might need. In the meantime he is to be fed and you are to arrange for a hipbath to be taken up to his room, where you are to leave him until he rings for it to be taken away. Is that understood? He is also to have his supper up there on a tray. Do not rouse him in the morning. I dare say he is possessed of wits enough to find his own way down to the kitchen.'

'Very good, my lord. Will there be anything else?'

'Yes, you may allow Ronan to bear me company for the rest of the evening.'

His lordship acknowledged with a mere nod of his head the shyly spoken 'goodnight' from his latest employee. So deep in thought did he quickly become that he was hardly aware when the door opened softly a few minutes later; it was only when his favourite hunting dog came gambolling across the library towards him that he came out of his brown study long enough to return the affectionate greeting with a pat.

'Am I being foolish beyond measure even to consider housing the chit, Ronan?' Lord Fincham murmured, his mind having quickly returned to the enigma besetting him at the present time. 'After all, she is nothing to me.'

The dog, now happily settled on the carpet at his master's feet, merely cocked an ear, while his lordship smiled grimly. 'It cannot be denied, though, the minx has certainly succeeded in pricking my conscience. No mean feat, old fellow, I can tell you! But am I being foolish to give her the benefit of the doubt?' He considered for a moment, before acknowledging aloud, 'I did the same over you, of course, some three years ago, when the gamekeeper assured me you'd never make a decent gun dog. You have more than repaid my belief in you. Will she do the same, I wonder?'

His lordship gazed down lazily at his favourite dog. 'It will be interesting to see how you react to the boy-girl who will be sleeping in my niece's bed. After all, you are not overly fond of many people, are you, boy? But, firstly, I must satisfy myself that she is indeed the innocent she appears to be. No doubt some scheme to do precisely that shall occur to me before the morrow. Yes, I shall use the night hours to consider.

'Then we shall see '

# Chapter Two

It was Lord Fincham's custom to rise late in the mornings when residing in town and the following day proved no exception. Every member of his household, not least of which was his personal valet, was awake to his lordship's every desire and need. Consequently, his hipbath awaited him in the dressing room the instant he had broken his fast and had risen from the large four-poster in the master bedchamber.

Unlike so many of his contemporaries, his lordship had always been a champion of personal hygiene. Eschewing the use of strong perfumes in order to mask unpleasant odours, he had always bathed regularly, something which was becoming increasingly popular since the arrival of that astute arbiter of good taste, George Bryan Brummell, on the London scene a couple of years or so before.

The Beau had set a fashion in gentleman's attire

that many of the younger members in society had quickly attempted to ape—with varying degrees of success, it had to be said. Perhaps because he was so resolute and too discerning a gentleman to be influenced by the latest affectations, Lord Fincham had yet to adopt the less flamboyant styles of dress advocated by Brummell.

He continued to wear silks, velvets and brocades, and an abundance of lace. His wardrobe boasted many fine coats in a range of vibrant colours and in richly embroidered materials. He favoured, still, knee-breeches, and his hair remained long and tied back at the nape of his neck with a length of black velvet ribbon.

In fact, it was only his lordship's hair that had ever caused his pernickety valet the least consternation. Not once in the eight years he had served the Viscount had Napes had recourse to a powder box. Nor had he ever persuaded his master to don a wig. In every other respect, however, Napes could find no fault with his lordship, and was secretly so very proud to have the dressing of a physique that was truly without flaw. Shoulders, chest and waist were perfectly proportioned and long legs were so straight and well muscled that no artificial aids to correct the tiniest defect had ever been employed.

After washing his own hair, his lordship allowed Napes to pour a pitcher of warm water over his head, and then leaned back, happy to relax for longer than usual as he had nothing planned for what little remained of the morning. For a moment or two he absently studied the valet's progress, as Napes went about the dressing room collecting various discarded items of clothing, before his mind returned to the matter that had so occupied his thoughts during the early hours before sleep had finally claimed him.

'Tell me, Napes, have you had the felicity of making the acquaintance of the most recent addition to the household staff?'

'Indeed I have, my lord,' he answered in a flat tone that betrayed his complete lack of interest in the new arrival.

His lordship wasn't unduly surprised by this indifference. Only in matters of dress did his valet betray the least animation. 'Has the boy broken his fast?'

This did cause the valet to betray a look of mild surprise. 'I believe so, my lord. He was in the kitchen with Cook earlier, chattering away about something or other. Will there be anything else, my lord? If not, I shall take these soiled items down to the laundry and return presently with clean linen.'

Through narrowed eyes his lordship followed the valet's progress across to the door. 'Yes, do that, Napes. But send the boy up with the linen, and then return yourself. I rather fancy indulging in a long soak this morning.'

It was some ten minutes later before there was a slight scratch on the door. Experiencing a sense of grim satisfaction, his lordship bade enter, and then watched the most recent acquisition to his household take a step or two into the room, before stopping dead in her tracks. Violet eyes, betraying a marked degree of mingled embarrassment and doubt, widened noticeably, before lowering to consider some imaginary spot on the floor.

'I—I'm s-sorry, my lord. Mr Napes quite failed to mention you were still at your ablutions. Where shall I put these?'

'Oh, just put them down anywhere, child, and pass me the towel,' he responded with supreme unconcern, while quite deliberately raising himself slowly from the concealing waters of the hipbath. 'Look lively, lad!'

The mild rebuke was sufficient to regain the page's full attention. Then a look of fascinated horror, not to mention utter disbelief, gripped delicate features as those striking orbs remained glued to a certain portion of his lordship's anatomy located between the waist and the knees. A stifled exclamation of alarm quickly followed, the pile of recently laundered shirts was tossed in the air and then fell to the floor as though so many worthless rags, a moment before Master Green fled the room as though the devil himself were nipping at her heels.

Highly amused by the outcome of his little experiment, his lordship gave vent to a roar of appreciative laughter, uncaring whether it could be heard or not by his unconventional and highly discomposed young page.

'That,' he murmured, as he wrapped himself in a huge towel and wandered through to his bedchamber again, 'was most illuminating. Though not particularly flattering, now I come to consider the matter. I've never had any unfavourable comments about my manly attributes before!'

'Beg pardon, my lord.' Like a cat on the prowl, Napes had slipped silently into the room. There was in his eye a watchful look, as he made his way towards the dressing table where his master sat, running a comb through his damp hair. There was a suggestion, too, of peevishness about the valet's mouth.

His lordship could hazard a fairly shrewd guess as to why his valet felt aggrieved, but chose not to pander to the excellent dresser's feelings of wounded pride at having had an underling usurp his exalted place in the dressing room and raised one hand in a dismissive gesture. 'Merely thinking aloud, Napes,' he assured him, and then watched as the servant disappeared into the adjoining room.

The strangled cry that quickly followed came as no great surprise to his lordship either. Nor, it had to be said, did the subsequently voiced strictures on allowing unskilled menials to handle clothing of such fine quality.

'For heaven's sake, calm yourself, man!' his lordship ordered. 'The confounded garments aren't ruined.'

'None the less, my lord, the boy must learn to take more care of your belongings if…if you wish him to share my duties. He should be punished for such tardiness.'

When this advice was followed by a decided sniff, his lordship raised his eyes ceilingwards. 'Be assured, Napes, the child was not hired to replace you, or to relieve you of any of your duties. I merely wished to satisfy myself over—' His lordship checked abruptly. 'I merely wished to satisfy myself that he had slept well. All the same, your remarks are timely,' he added, staring thoughtfully into the glass before him, as he confined his long hair at the nape of his neck with a length of ribbon. 'Ring for Brindle!'

Whilst awaiting the arrival of his major-domo, the Viscount proceeded to dress himself. Although he allowed his valet to remove the smallest of specks from his clothes and polish his boots and shoes to a looking-glass shine, he preferred, with the exception of his coats, to don his own garments, and always tied his neckcloths himself.

'You sent for me, my lord,' the butler said, entering the room in time to witness the valet assisting his lordship into a coat of dark green velvet.

'I did, Brindle.' He turned, favouring the high-ranking servant with his full attention. 'Mark me well… No one, and I mean no one, is to lay violent hands on my new page. If the child commits any slight misdemeanour…' he couldn't resist smiling to himself '…and I suspect he will commit many, you, and you alone, are to guide him in a gentle, understanding way. If he should seriously transgress, you are to inform me and I shall deal with the matter personally.'

He paused for a moment before adding, 'I shall be

most displeased if I discover my orders have been disobeyed over this matter. Is that understood?'

'Perfectly, my lord.'

'And you, Napes…?'

'Yes, my lord.'

'Good. Now you may be about your duties. And you, Brindle, locate Master Green's whereabouts and request him to await me in the library.'

Although the butler automatically bowed and withdrew, his face wore a decidedly thoughtful expression as he made his way down the back stairs to the kitchen, where he found the page happily assisting the cook to shell peas at the large table.

The youth had been there for most of the morning, chattering away quite knowledgeably about various domestic practices to Mrs Willard and helping her out where he could. Clearly the cook had already taken a keen liking to the boy. Perhaps the lad had aroused her motherly instincts, for generally she ruled the kitchen with an iron hand and would brook no interference from anyone. The scullery maid and the boots knew well not to get under her feet and she wasn't above giving the youngest footman a sound box round the ear, if he happened to catch her in a bad mood. Yet Master Green, seemingly, could do no wrong in her eyes.

And it had to be said the child was no harum-scarum guttersnipe, Brindle considered fair-mindedly, as he made his way towards the large wooden structure taking pride of place in the centre of the room. Not only was the lad well mannered, he spoke, amazingly enough, in a very genteel fashion. Yes, Master Green was something of a mystery.

'You are to attend his lordship, child.'

There was a suspicion of alarm in the eyes that were raised to the butler's impassive countenance. 'Not in his bedchamber, I trust?'

'It isn't for you to question where his lordship wishes to see you!' Napes admonished, entering the kitchen in time to hear the decidedly nervous response.

A considering look took possession of those striking eyes as they followed the valet's progress across the large room, before it was vanquished by a knowing twinkle.

'Ah, but you see, Mr Napes, I have no desire to trespass on your domain. I think any skills I might have lie elsewhere, perhaps even here with Mrs Willard.'

'Oh!' The valet looked taken aback for a moment, not to say slightly relieved. 'There's no need for you to worry yourself on that score, my boy,' he assured, noticeably less sharply. 'His lordship demands you await him in the library.'

'Not quite, Mr Napes,' the butler corrected when the page had left them. 'He requested the child await him in the library... Requested, mark you.'

'Well, that do seem strange, Mr Brindle,' the cook declared, as the butler, continuing to look perplexed himself, joined her at the table. 'Mind, the child do have winning ways, I'll say that for him. Perhaps his lordship has a fondness for the lad.' She gave a sudden start. 'Oh, my gawd! You don't suppose...?'

'That possibility assuredly crossed my mind,' the butler admitted, following Cook's train of thought with little difficulty. 'But, apart from the hair, the child bears no resemblance to his lordship from what I can see. Nor the master's late brother, come to that. Besides which, I would have thought he was rather too old to be an offspring of his lordship's.'

'Not only that, Mr Brindle, the master were so good natured in his youth,' Cook reminded him. 'Never a breath of scandal attached to his name in those days. It was only after he came back from France and discovered what Miss Charlotte had gone and done that changed him.

'A bit before your time, Mr Napes,' she explained,

when she chanced to catch him frowning down at her, looking bewildered. 'Miss Charlotte were a close neighbour's daughter. She and Master Benedict were childhood sweethearts, inseparable they were back in them days. His brother only wanted Master Benedict to finish his studies up at Oxford, then he were happy to give the union his blessing and set Master Benedict up in a nice little property a few miles north of Fincham Park, with a nice bit of land attached to it, too. Well, no sooner does Master Benedict finish his studies than he goes jaunting over to France to help his friend Mr Gingham rescue a cousin, or some such. Wicked goings on over there at the time, Mr Napes, murdering all their betters. Wicked it were!

'Master Ben were away quite some few weeks, I seem to remember,' she went on, quickly returning to the point of the story, 'and when he came back he discovered Miss Charlotte had spent some time in London with an aunt or some such, and had upped and wedded Lord Wenbury.' She shook her head sadly. 'He were never the same after that, were he, Mr Brindle? Cold, he became, cold and distant.'

'He certainly became less approachable,' the butler was willing to concede. Then he shook his head. 'But that child seems to have stirred something within him again. I swore I heard him laughing earlier, shortly after I'd shown the lad where his lordship's dressing room was located, and I was about my duties on the upper floor. I haven't heard him laugh like that in many a long year.'

'But where did the young fellow come from, Mr Brindle, that's what I'd like to know? Ever since he came into the title, his lordship has always trusted your judgement when it comes to hiring staff,' Cook reminded him. 'So I don't think he came from any agency.'

'I'm sure he didn't. Just as I'm convinced he's never been engaged in service before. All I can tell you is his lordship brought him back with him yesterday. No doubt the young fellow will reveal more about himself when he comes to know us better.'

His lordship, seated at his desk in the library, was of a similar mind, and had decided not to bombard his unusual page with questions, but to bide his time in the hope of discovering more.

Only just detecting the light knock on the door, he bade enter and watched the girl come shyly into the room. The glance she cast him was brief in the extreme, before she resolutely stared at the floor, her heightened colour visible even from where his lordship sat. Clearly she was still highly embarrassed over the incident in the dressing room. But it was no more than she deserved! his lordship decided, hardening his heart.

'Come in and close the door, child, I wish to discuss your duties with you... No, over here,' he added when she remained where she stood. 'I have no intention of shouting and becoming hoarse.

'You may sit yourself down,' he invited when she had finally managed to edge her way across to the desk, though seemingly still unable to meet his gaze.

Wisely, she had betrayed a certain wariness towards him from the first. Clearly she mistrusted him now, and he didn't like it—no, not at all. If he was ever to discover the truth about her present circumstances he would, quite naturally, need to win her complete confidence. He was determined to do so and not merely in an attempt to satisfy his curiosity.

'I understand from my valet that you managed to find your way down to the kitchens this morning. I assume, therefore, you realise there is a dog in the house.'

At long last she met his gaze, albeit briefly. 'Yes, sir—Ronan.'

'Ah, so you have become acquainted already—
good! I hope you got along. He is not always at
his best with strangers, especially those of a young
age.'

'He was all right with me. I gave him a bone,
which helped, of course. Your cook wasn't best
pleased, because she wanted it for the stockpot.
But she forgave me when I offered to help shell the
peas.'

Never in his lordship's entire life had a servant
ever attempted to regale him with a catalogue of
goings-on below stairs. Yet this outrageous little
madam seemed to consider it the most natural thing
in the world! Far from annoyed, he was both amused
and intrigued by her attitude and decided to tease
her a little.

Leaning back in his chair, he feigned a look of
amazement. 'I never realised until today that peas
came in shells. I thought only oysters and certain
other sea creatures arrived at the house in such hardened coverings. Which only goes to prove one is
never too old to learn.'

It was only by exercising the firmest control that
he prevented himself roaring with laughter for the
second time that day at the look of mingled disbelief and dismay he received. Even so, he couldn't

prevent his shoulders shaking in his effort to contain his mirth, which instantly alerted his engaging companion to his true state of mind.

'You were jesting, of course,' she said, with just a trace of peevishness in her voice.

'Indeed, I was, child,' he confirmed. 'But not about Ronan. I am delighted to hear you both took a liking to each other, because I wish you to take charge of him for most of the time, when he isn't with me. Take him out for walks, but keep him on the leash whilst anywhere near traffic. I should not be best pleased if harm came to him. And for pity's sake do not release him in Green Park anywhere near the grazing cows! I do not wish to suffer a visit from the authorities informing me that you have stampeded the herd.'

She gurgled at this, a delightfully infectious sound that brought an answering smile to his own lips. Striking eyes then appeared to consider him intently for a long moment before lowering and staring down at the desk.

'And are those my only duties, my lord?'

'No, I shall require you to accompany me out from time to time.'

An arresting look flickered across delicate features. 'Shall you, sir?'

'Of course, otherwise I shouldn't have said so,' he returned, reaching for his quill in order to begin his correspondence. 'But until you have acquired new clothes, you may concentrate your efforts on looking after Ronan.'

'Very good, my lord.' She rose from the chair and went over to the door. 'I shall begin by seeing if I cannot persuade Mrs Willard to allow him in the kitchen from time to time. She usually shuts him away in the scullery during the day, I believe.'

'Is that so?' Lord Fincham responded absently, reaching for a sheet of paper while gazing across at the door. 'And who might Mrs Willard be, may I ask?'

He received a look of mock reproach. 'For an educated man you are sadly ignorant about many things, my lord. She's your cook, of course!'

'A word of warning, Master Green,' the Viscount said, oh, so softly. 'I am not above taking a birch rod to impertinent young cubs.'

Clearly the threat left her unmoved. He received a further gurgle of infectious laughter in response before he was left alone in the room. Although he shook his head, wondering at himself, he couldn't resist smiling again. 'I must be mad to tolerate such an impudent minx under my roof,' he muttered. 'Either that, or I'm entering upon my dotage!'

It was four days later before his lordship gave orders for his page to accompany him out. At nine o'clock precisely he descended the staircase to find his most recently acquired servant pacing the chequered hall, awaiting his arrival. Dressed in severest black livery, trimmed only with a fine silver braid, and with a cascade of white lace foaming below the pointed little chin, she appeared every inch the aristocratic gentleman's pampered page. Only when she heard his footfall and glanced up, those magnificent eyes shining, and those perfectly lovely lips parting in a spontaneous smile, was he reminded of her true sex.

She won no answering smile from him this time, only a brief look of mild concern. 'Yes, you look very well. You may follow me out to the carriage.'

'Am I to sit upon the box with the groom, sir?'

'No, you are not. You are to sit inside with me, for there are certain matters I must discuss with you.'

For the briefest of moments he almost forgot himself and assisted her into the carriage first. His concern quadrupled in an instant. If he was ever to forget himself, and show the least consideration for her true sex, the world he inhabited would be outraged. He didn't care so much for himself. He was Fincham—a matrimonial prize. Shallow society would soon forgive and forget his slight peccadilloes... But the girl...?

No, she would be ruined in the eyes of the world, he reminded himself. And she didn't deserve that, even though she would lend herself to such a disgraceful venture as posing as a page. Furthermore, although she might never be granted entrée into the highest echelons of society, she had been gently reared, that much was crystal clear, and she should not be denied the chance to take her place in the genteel world. Perhaps when he had first embarked on this madcap venture he hadn't considered fully what a responsibility he was taking upon himself. But he realised it now, for he no longer doubted her respectability. Consequently, because he had possibly unwittingly encouraged her, he now felt an obligation to stand if not in place of a guardian, then certainly a protector, until such time as she confided fully her reasons for the charade. Then, once he had discovered why she was so willing to risk her reputation...perhaps even forfeit her rightful place in the world...

Well, he would consider that more fully when the

time came, he decided finally. For now, he would do the honourable thing…at least up to a point.

'Now, child, as this is your first venture into polite society,' he began, then paused as that little head came round and those oh, so revealing eyes, unable to meet his for more than a second or two, lowered. The reluctance to meet his gaze told him much: it wouldn't be her first venture into society; she had socialised with members of the ton before she had ever met him. How interesting, he mused. And, of course, dangerous. It made his task all the more problematic.

For a moment he toyed with the idea of returning to the house and ending the charade there and then by confronting her, but decided against it. She was not dull-witted. Evidently she didn't believe she would be recognised. This time he would trust her judgement, he finally decided.

'As I was saying, as this is perhaps your—er—first venture into society, I wish you to take very great care. Do not speak to anyone unless spoken to first. And in the unlikely event that you are addressed, then you are to say only that you are Fincham's page. Most important of all, do not draw attention to yourself by staring at your betters, otherwise I might feel obliged to send you to await me below stairs.'

She regarded him in silence for a moment, a touch of concern easily discernible in her expression. 'But I may speak with you, sir, if I am…troubled…about something?'

He regarded her intently for a moment. 'You may always approach me, child, no matter where, no matter when, if there is something of importance you wish to discuss with me.'

This seemed to reassure her, for she smiled brightly, almost trustingly across at him. 'You have yet to inform me where we are bound, my lord,' she reminded him, as though she had every right to know.

Retribution would undoubtedly have been swift had his punctilious major-domo overheard an underling commit such a solecism. Or perhaps not where this page was concerned, he corrected silently. Evidently Brindle had obeyed his orders to the letter, with the result that the most recent addition to the staff had yet to learn her place in the Fincham household. Far from annoyed, it rather amused his lordship to have his girl-page so far forget herself on occasions as to treat him as an equal.

'How very remiss of me, Georgie!' he declared, with only the faintest betraying twitch at one corner of his mouth. 'We are bound for the home of the Duke and Duchess of Merton. It is a monstrous pile, so stay close. You might so easily get lost.'

When at last they had arrived at the impressive mansion, his lordship was pleased to note that his advice had been heeded. With the exception of handing their outer garments to a waiting flunkey, she remained dutifully at his heels throughout the time they queued on the impressive staircase, waiting in line to be greeted by the host and hostess. Evidently his major-domo had succeeded during recent days in instilling at least the rudimentary conduct of a page into her. Even so, she did not escape the attention of the eagle-eyed duchess.

'What new affectation is this, Fincham? Never before have I known you to have a page in tow.'

'A whim, your Grace. Merely a whim. I succumbed to the most wicked desire to ruffle Sir Willoughby's feathers. You know how he so hates to be outdone by anyone.'

'Wicked boy!' She tapped him flirtatiously on the chest with her fan. 'I do not doubt you will succeed. A most engaging child you have there. I should be

interested to know where you found him. You, however, shall find Sir Willoughby in the card room.'

Instructing his page to follow with a flick of
one finger, Lord Fincham entered the opulently
decorated ballroom. Huge vases of flowers, supported on marble pedestals, were positioned at frequent intervals down the full length of the long
room. Swathes of silk in peach and cream were
artistically draped across the walls, and gracefully
arching potted palms decorated each and every
alcove. It was a sight to take any inexperienced
girl's breath away, and his newly acquired obligation
proved no exception. Although she refrained from
gaping outright, there was a look of wonder in those
magnificent eyes of hers that could so easily betray
her true sex to any discerning soul. He decided to
veer on the side of caution.

'Await me over there, Georgie, in that unoccupied
alcove. And, remember, do not stare!'

As his hopes were not high at his orders being
carried out to the letter, he was neither annoyed nor
dismayed to discover on several occasions, when he
chanced to glance across at that particular niche, a
certain blue-eyed gaze considering quite a number
of different guests, and by the looks flitting over that

expressive countenance a fair few of those present did not meet with approval.

After doing his duty by standing up with the daughter of the house in whose honour the ball had been arranged, the Viscount wandered across to that certain alcove. 'I should be interested to hear your opinions, dear child, but I rather fancy you had best express them in private, so for the time being you may accompany me into the card room.'

His lordship quickly spotted the worthy he was most desirous to see, and wandered across to the table in one corner, where two gentlemen sat. One was dressed in formal evening garb, whilst the other, in stark contrast, was clad in the height of fashion that had prevailed during the last decades of the previous century.

The bewigged gentleman in the heavily embroidered gold-coloured coat caught sight of him first, and waved one slender white hand in an airy gesture of welcome. 'Fincham, old chap! Will you not join us?'

'Your arrival is timely,' the other said, rising from his chair. 'You may take my place and keep our friend Sir Willoughby company, whilst I do my duty in the ballroom.'

'Poor Gyles. He must keep on the right side of his

brother. If Merton was ever to cut his allowance, he would find it hard, with all his extravagancies, to keep his head above water.' After sweeping the pile of coins before him to one side of the table, Sir Willoughby reached for the cards. 'What is your pleasure—piquet or French ruff?'

'Either will suffice,' the Viscount replied equably. 'I do not intend to remain for too much longer. I have a further engagement this evening.'

Sir Willoughby's painted lips curled in a knowing smile. 'With the divine Caro, I do not doubt.'

When his lordship offered no response, the baronet raised his eyes and, much to his lordship's silent amusement, suddenly felt for his quizzing-glass in order to study more closely the slender form, clad in severest black velvet, standing dutifully behind the Viscount's chair.

'Good gad! That is never your page, Fincham, surely?'

'Loathe though I am to disabuse you, Trent, but it is, indeed, my page.'

The baronet then transferred his gaze to the slender golden-haired youth standing dutifully a couple of feet behind his own chair. 'You wretch, Fincham! You've acquired him on purpose! I do believe he's prettier than my own! Such divine eyes!' He appeared genuinely distressed. 'You know I cannot abide others possessing prettier things than my own. You must sell him to me at once. At once, do you hear! How much do you want for him? Name your price!'

'Now that's an interesting proposition.' Lord Fincham beckoned with one finger. 'How much are you worth, Georgie?'

When blue eyes regarded him in a mixture of outrage and disgust, he came perilously close to dissolving into laughter, but was spared any further attacks on his powers of self-control by the arrival of the hostess.

Fincham rose at once to his feet. 'Your arrival is most timely, your Grace. Sir Willoughby here has lost complete interest in our game. Perhaps you could provide him with another opponent more worthy of his skill?'

'I very much doubt that, Fincham,' she responded. 'Your reputation is widely known. There are few here tonight who would pit their skill against one of the favoured five.' Her smile faded slightly. 'Or perhaps it would be more accurate now to say…the favoured four.'

His lordship didn't attempt to respond to this. After exchanging a few other brief pleasantries with their hostess, he turned to leave and caught an almost frozen look on the face of his page. So deeply entrenched in her own private world did she appear to be that it took two attempts before he could gain her attention and instruct her to follow him from the room.

Putting her sudden disinclination to talk down to the lateness of the hour, and fatigue, he didn't attempt to make conversation until he had taken leave of the host, and had led the way outside to where his carriage stood awaiting him.

'Get in, Georgie,' he ordered, so far forgetting himself as to open the door for her. 'I shall not be returning to Berkeley Square with you.' He then turned to his head groom, perched high on the box. 'I entrust it to you to take care of my page, Perkins. I shall make my own way home in the morning.' And with that he sauntered off down the road, leaving both his servants to stare after him.

'But why isn't he coming with us? Where's he going, do you suppose?' a bewildered little voice enquired.

The head groom looked down, askance, at the slight figure by the roadside. 'Cor blimey, lad. Green by name and green by nature, that's you! He's going to pay a visit to his mistress, o' course! He won't be getting much sleep tonight, if I knows anything. But I needs mine, so climb aboard and let's get going!'

The instruction was obeyed, but a moment later the carriage door was slammed shut with considerable violence.

# Chapter Three

The following morning Brindle located his quarry with no difficulty whatsoever. Seated at the kitchen table, the page was lending Cook a helping hand as usual, although for some reason seeming less sociable than usual. He didn't perceive anything untoward in this slightly subdued state. The child had not gone to bed until the early hours, and was no doubt feeling slightly out of spirits through lack of sleep.

'His lordship has returned to the house, Mrs Willard, and requires breakfast as soon as maybe. He will partake of it in the breakfast parlour and desires you, George, to serve him.'

As this was an undoubted honour bestowed upon one so young and inexperienced, the response was not quite what the butler might have expected.

'Oh, he does, does he!' Looking decidedly mutinous, the page rose abruptly from the chair, very nearly toppling it over in the process. 'Well, he can damn well serve it himself, because I'm going out! Come, Ronan!'

It would have been difficult to say which member of the staff present was most shocked by the outburst. Both the scullery maid and the boots stared open-mouthed as the door leading to the mews was slammed shut by the clearly disgruntled young servant. Even Mrs Willard appeared taken aback by the outburst.

'Well, upon my soul! There's heat for you, Mr Brindle!' Cook declared, when she'd recovered from the shock. 'Have you ever heard the like before? Anyone might suppose the boy doesn't know his place.'

'And there you have hit upon it exactly, Mrs Willard, because I do not believe he does know his place!' Napes announced, having entered the kitchen in time to witness the shocking outburst. 'And he should be made to learn it! It's no good, Mr Brindle,' he continued. 'I know you look kindly upon the boy, and have from the first, but behaviour of that sort cannot go unpunished. His lordship should be told about this appalling breach of conduct.'

'But not by you, Mr Napes,' the butler countered.

'Kindly remember I am in charge here; I shall decide how best to deal with the matter.'

In truth, the highly skilled and diligent major-domo was in something of a quandary. He was fully aware that it was essential to maintain discipline and standards below stairs at all times, otherwise his authority would quickly be called into question. Yet, at the same time, the valet had been so right: he had developed a genuine fondness for his latest protégé.

Only the day before the boy had joined him at the table, without being instructed to do so, and had helped polish the silver. He had performed the task well. But, then, everything the child attempted he did well, Brindle reminded himself. The page's culinary skills were quite remarkable in one so young. Even Cook had said he would make a fine chef if he were ever to apply himself. From the first he had proved himself to be willing and able, and so cheerful for the most part. Yet, today, for some reason…

Undecided how best to deal with the matter, Brindle gave instructions for the selection of break-fast dishes, once prepared, to be conveyed to the small back parlour, and was in the act of arranging them carefully on the side table himself when his lordship entered.

'Where's Georgie? Not still abed, I trust?'

After signalling the footman and parlour maid to leave the room, Brindle poured his lordship coffee. 'No, sir. But he hasn't—er—returned to the house yet. He's taken the dog for his customary morning walk.'

'I see. In that case tell him I wish to see him in the library, when he does return.'

A moment's silence followed, then, 'I'll endeavour to do my poor best, my lord.'

It was over an hour later when the errant page finally put in an appearance. One glance at those delicate features, set in a mutinous glower, was enough to convince the Viscount that all was far from well, and that was even before he received a terse verbal confirmation.

'Well, you wanted to see me, so here I am!'

After very slowly returning his quill to the standish, his lordship gave his full attention to the slender figure still clasping the handle of the door. Naturally enough he was not accustomed to being addressed in such a manner, most especially by a member of his own household; and although it would be true to say he didn't seem able to bring himself to look upon the girl as a servant, he felt it was incumbent upon him to attempt to maintain the status quo.

'I believe I warned you before that I'm not above taking a birch rod to impertinent children,' he said, oh, so very quietly. 'I shall not remind you of it a third time, Georgie. So, for your own continued comfort, I would suggest you close the door, come over here and tell me what has put your nose out of joint.'

At least part of the advice was heeded. She did, after a moment or two, close the door and slowly approach the desk, but remained stubbornly silent. A less tolerant man might have lost his patience at this point. His lordship, however, out of consideration for her sex, was determined to maintain a calm authority.

'And I'm still awaiting an explanation,' he reminded her gently.

If anything the mutinous expression became more marked before she finally unlocked tightly compressed lips to say, 'The only reason I'm here is because I wish to make it perfectly plain that it wasn't Brindle's fault that I didn't attend you at breakfast. So you mustn't blame him. He passed on your message, but…but I was in a bad mood, and so went out.'

His lordship sighed heavily when she volunteered nothing further. 'We progress, but not very rapidly. Might I be permitted to know why you awoke in such a bad humour? You seemed happy enough last night when I left you.'

When she lowered her eyes and stared steadfastly down somewhere in the region of the standish on his desk, he began to fear he'd learn little else without resorting to coercion. 'Did something occur on the homeward journey to upset you?' he asked, grasping at straws. Then a clear memory returned, and he recalled she had seemed rather subdued, after his meeting with a decidedly flamboyant baronet. 'It wasn't Sir Willoughby Trent's nonsensical suggestion about selling you to him that upset you, was it?'

It took a few moments but eventually blue eyes did meet his above the desk for a few brief moments. 'Well, it wasn't very nice, was it?'

'No, it wasn't very nice,' he agreed, 'besides being totally ludicrous. I do not own you, Georgie, you are not my slave. You are free to leave my employ whenever you wish.'

A further moment's silence, then, 'Well, that's all

right, then. We need not dwell on the matter any more.'

Although her eyes had once again met his fleetingly as she had said this, it had offered opportunity enough to glimpse an almost calculating look lurking in those violet depths that had given him every reason to suppose the artful little madam had made use of his suggestion about Sir Willoughby's remarks in order to conceal the source of her true ill humour. He decided, however, not to persevere, and with a complete change of subject asked if she could ride.

She didn't attempt to hide her surprise. 'Well, of course I can ride!'

'In that case you may send word to the stables to have my bay and the chestnut saddled and awaiting us in the Square in fifteen minutes.'

'Can you make it twenty, my lord?' she asked, pausing at the door. 'I must seek out Brindle and apologise to him for my behaviour earlier.'

'Do not consider me for a moment, child,' he responded with gentle irony. 'I shall quite naturally await your convenience.'

It was only by dint of tapping into those deep reserves of self-control that prevented his lordship from bursting into laughter when, half an hour later, they left the house together in order to set off for their ride. She took one look at the chestnut gelding, held securely in the groom's hand, and her jaw dropped perceptibly as she muttered loud enough for him to hear,

'Oh, my, I never thought of that!'

He realised at once that it wasn't so much the horse as the saddle that had brought about mild consternation on her part. Unfortunately, unless he wished to give rise to a deal of gossip and speculation about her, which he had done his utmost to avoid thus far, he could hardly startle the groom by demanding a side-saddle be put on the chestnut. Sensible girl that she was, she quickly realised this herself, and mounted the gelding without further ado and, more importantly, without requesting assistance.

By the time they had ridden out of the Square, Lord Fincham was convinced she was well on the way to mastering the foreign saddle. By the time they had reached Hyde Park, he was satisfied she was an extremely competent horsewoman, possessed of a fine seat and a gentle pair of hands. All the same, he veered on the side of caution and decided to keep to the less crowded areas of the park so that she might enjoy the exercise without having to concentrate on avoiding other riders and the numerous open carriages that filed into the park at, this, the most fashionable hour to be seen abroad. Besides which, he thought it was time to discover a little more about her if he could.

He began with what he considered a fairly safe gambit, and one that wasn't likely to arouse suspicion. 'You ride very well, Georgie, my boy. Who taught you?'

'My godfather, sir,' she answered promptly enough. Then, smiling faintly, 'He was lucky enough to keep a horse or two.'

'Is that so?' He considered her for a moment in silence. 'Forgive me if I am in error, Georgie, but I gained the impression from something you said that there was no one responsible for you.'

'No, you are not wrong, my lord.' She never attempted to look at him, but continued to stare straight ahead between the chestnut's ears. 'My godfather died earlier this year.'

He detected a distinct catch in her voice as she said this, and so decided not to dwell on a subject that had clearly evoked painful memories. None the less, what he had discovered about her thus far, and her general behaviour, only went to confirm what he had suspected from the first.

'Would I be correct in thinking you were never in service before joining my household, child?'

A moment's silence, then, 'You would, my lord. But neither have I lived the life of the privileged few. As I told you, for many years my mother was a cook-housekeeper. I was given an assortment of tasks to do round the vicarage. I was not encouraged to be idle. And my godfather, who resided not too far distant, kept many animals,' she added, as they returned to one of the main tracks. 'He especially liked pigs—restful creatures, he called them. I spent a great deal of time with him…and the pigs.'

His lordship was positive she was telling the truth, as far as it went. Yet, it didn't go anywhere near far enough. There was something fundamental she was keeping to herself. Unfortunately he was denied the opportunity to probe further by the sudden appearance of an open carriage. To have attempted to avoid the encounter by turning his mount in another direction would have been to offer the cut direct, and he had no intention of doing so to the lady whose generous hospitality he had enjoyed the previous evening.

'Great heavens, Fincham!' the Duchess of Merton exclaimed, as her open carriage drew to a halt.

'Twice in as many days! I'm astonished! You usually avoid parading with the fashionable as a rule.'

'Not always, your Grace. Furthermore, I've never attempted to avoid you.'

This clearly pleased her. 'Oh, you wicked creature! If only I were ten years younger! You see, Lavinia,' she added, turning to the vapid young lady beside her, 'you should always heed your mama's advice. I have warned you to avoid such notorious flirts.'

'Unjust, your Grace!' his lordship protested, rising to the occasion by appearing affronted. 'It can never be said of Fincham that he flirted with innocence.'

She favoured him with an arch look. 'Well, yes, that's true enough, I suppose,' she acknowledged, before stretching forwards to tap the coachman on the shoulder with her parasol.

As soon as the carriage had moved away, the Viscount beckoned Georgie to ride alongside again. 'You see now, child, why I avoid this place as a rule, at least at this hour of the day. You are obliged to exchange pleasantries with those you least wish to meet.'

At this admission questioning eyes scrutinised his profile. 'But I thought you liked the duchess, my lord. You seemed very friendly towards her last night.'

'It would be the height of bad taste to ignore one's hostess, my dear child. Furthermore, I cannot help but feel a grudging respect for her. Merton is not an easy man, and certainly not one whose company I would seek too often, either.'

There was a hint of speculation in the eyes that remained glued to his lordship's physiognomy. 'You prefer his brother, perhaps—Lord Rupert Gyles?'

He considered for a moment. 'Yes, I suppose I do, even though he can be quite feckless on occasions. However, unlike me, he is generally a very sociable, easy-going soul.'

'But last night, sir, you seemed very sociable, most especially when you were with Sir Willoughby Trent, and the duchess,' his companion reminded him, turning to stare straight ahead again, 'though I didn't perfectly understand what you were talking about. It puzzled me… Something the duchess said puzzled me.'

'Indeed? And what was it that bewildered you so much?' his lordship asked, in a mood to be indulgent.

'She said something about…"the favoured five".' A troubled frown marred the perfection of a fine young forehead. 'But there were dozens and dozens present last night who have been blessed to live a life of luxury. Which five was she referring to in particular?'

'Ah!' Enlightenment dawned swiftly enough, but the Viscount dismissed the topic with a wave of one shapely hand. 'It is nothing, child, a mere bagatelle.'

'Oh, do tell, my lord! It's so intriguing!'

'It would seem, Georgie, my lad, you can be tiresomely persistent when the mood takes you.' Although he sighed, he was once again inclined to be indulgent. 'Very well. A few high-ranking society hostesses, her Grace the Duchess of Merton included, coined the name for a small group of gentlemen whom Lady Luck seemed to favour at the gaming tables. They have earned the reputation for playing for high stakes. It is perhaps fortunate, therefore, that they win rather more than they lose, as a rule. As I said, child, it is a piece of nonsense.'

'But you haven't told me who these gentlemen are, my lord,' Georgie reminded him, clearly eager to learn more.

'Your curiosity is insatiable!' he scolded, but then immediately afterwards relented when he received a look of wounded pride. 'Oh, very well. You met two of the group last night—Sir Willoughby and the duchess's own brother-in-law, Lord Rupert Gyles. Lord Chard, who wasn't present last night, is a further member, and one of the group died earlier this year.'

'And who was that, my lord?' Georgie asked quietly, while all the time keeping her gaze averted.

'The seventh Earl of Grenville. Apparently he was attacked by a band of highway robbers while returning home to his estate in Gloucestershire.'

'That is four, my lord,' she reminded him, when he fell into a brown study. 'Who is the fifth member?'

All at once there was a suspicion of smugness in the Viscount's expression. 'Why, you are in his employ!'

Young eyes were instantly turned in his direction, but almost immediately afterwards lowered before the Viscount had a chance to interpret what was revealed in those strikingly coloured depths for a few brief moments.

That day set the pattern for the following week. Every afternoon his lordship set out for a ride with his striking page. This in itself would not have given rise to comment had not his lordship allowed his young servant to ride beside him, and engaged him in conversation for the most part.

He remained at home for most of the evenings, too, which was most unusual. Ensconced in his library, with only his page to bear him company, he whiled away many happy hours enjoying games of chess with his increasingly endearing companion. Only after his most favoured of servants had retired for the night did he venture forth, sometimes to his club, sometimes to the more intimate surroundings of his mistress's boudoir.

Then, one evening at the beginning of the following week, Lord Fincham broke with routine and requested his page to accompany him out. Forgoing the carriage, he decided to walk the short distance to where a long-awaited party was being held. Unfortunately the gathering proved a dull affair, and his lordship soon tired of the entertainment on offer. Acting on impulse, he decided to go in search of more genial company, and amusement more fitting his mood.

Consequently, on leaving the party, he hailed a hackney carriage to convey him to a discreet house situated in a much less fashionable area of town, where he knew games for high stakes took place most evenings. He was fortunate enough to discover those he sought, all seated at a table in one of the upstairs rooms, and didn't hesitate to accept the invitation to join them.

As he took his seat he noticed the eyes of the worthy seated opposite glance beyond his right shoulder to the being standing dutifully behind his lordship's chair. Although there was a touch of envy, and perhaps a hint of resentment too, in Sir Willoughby's expression, he made no comment and quickly returned his attention to the cards in his hand.

The man on the Viscount's left, however, betrayed no such reticence, and announced, 'Naturally, I'd heard you'd acquired a page, Fincham. Until now I couldn't quite bring myself to believe it. In all the years we've been acquainted I've never known you succumb to whims and fancies.'

'And he has not this time, Chard,' Sir Willoughby assured him, before the Viscount could respond. 'He acquired the boy merely to vex me, unless I much mistake the matter.'

'And by your peevish tone, Trent, I would suggest he has succeeded in his objective remarkably well,' Lord Rupert Gyles put in, shoulders shaking in quiet amusement. 'But what on earth possessed you to drag him with you to this place, Finch? There are persons enough to fetch wine should you require it, surely?'

This was true enough. Although the owner of the discreet establishment did employ several females to entice customers to part with their money at the various gaming tables, besides encouraging them to drink their fill from his well-stocked cellar, he did attempt to run a respectable house. His lordship wasn't so naïve as to suppose more intimate relationships did not take place between certain regular patrons and the immodestly attired young women, but the liaisons were never conducted openly.

All the same, he did wonder what Georgie made of the various young women clad in low-cut diaphanous gowns, which left absolutely nothing to the imagination. He took his eyes off the cards in his hand in order to glance up at her, only to discover her surprisingly enough staring so fixedly at Lord Chard that it was almost as if she were attempting to etch each and every line of his harsh-featured face into her memory.

Her regard, as she well knew, went far beyond what was pleasing. More disturbing, still, was the possible reaction of Chard himself should he happen to realise he was receiving such close scrutiny. He was no fool. He might so easily pierce her disguise if she gained his full attention for any length of time. This hadn't occurred thus far. Apart from that first cursory glance, Chard had betrayed no interest in the page whatsoever. Lord Fincham decided it would be best if it remained that way.

'Fetch me a bottle and a glass, Georgie,' he said, after gaining her attention by raising a finger, 'and then go downstairs and await me in the vestibule.'

It was quite some time later before his lordship, sated with gaming, went in search of her. He found her easily enough in the vestibule where he had sent her, but not asleep, as expected, in one of the comfortable chairs. Surprisingly wide-eyed and alert, she was in deep conversation with one of the young flunkies engaged to man the front entrance, and deny admittance to any undesirables.

As he led the way out into the early morning air, his lordship heard a distant church clock chime the hour, and experienced yet another of those increasingly regular pangs of conscience where the being beside him was concerned. There wasn't a hackney carriage to be seen, so there was nothing for it but to walk at least part of the way home.

'You should have been in bed hours ago, Georgie. It was extremely remiss of me to drag you out tonight, most especially to that establishment,' he announced as they set off down the street, heading for the more affluent part of town.

'Oh, but I enjoyed it, my lord. For me it was an adventure. I've never been to such a place before.'

He couldn't help smiling at this. 'No, I don't suppose for a moment you have. None the less, I shouldn't have taken you there.' He cast her a sideways glance. 'What did you make of it, I wonder?'

She shrugged, appearing remarkably unconcerned. 'The females are little more than painted doxies, engaged to persuade gentlemen to part with their blunt, I shouldn't wonder. The doormen were characters, though, rather rough and ready, and certainly not to be trusted. But the one you saw me conversing with was rather interesting. His name's George, as it happens. He seems to know everyone. Addressed all the visitors by name. And knew a deal about them, too.'

Discovering this did precious little to ease his conscience. He couldn't help wondering what sordid facts she'd discovered about his fellow gamesters, not to mention himself! 'Dare I ask what he disclosed about me?'

'Nothing that I hadn't discovered for myself already.' She cast him one of those wickedly provocative smiles that he was finding increasingly endearing. 'Said you were a downy one, awake on every suit.'

The instant he learned this, his lordship felt it might almost have been a prophecy. He heard a church clock chime the quarter, and detected something else, too—footsteps behind, closing fast. Crossing the street, he glanced over his shoulder and saw two persons lurking in the shadows, and a possible third on the other side of the road.

'Georgie, perchance, have you any money about your person?'

'Yes, my lord, a few coins.'

'Enough to hire a carriage?'

'I should imagine so.' The look he received was unmistakably one of surprise. 'Why, you didn't lose all your money, did you, at the gaming tables?'

Concerned though he was, he couldn't resist smiling at this. 'What an alarming thought! But, no, child, my reputation remains untarnished, at least where indulging in games of chance is concerned.'

He was suddenly serious. 'Now, listen carefully. A little way ahead is a side alley. When we reach it I want you to run down there and stop for nothing and nobody until you come to the wider thoroughfare at the far end. With luck you should locate a hackney carriage without too much difficulty. Return to Berkeley Square and await me there. No questions, Georgie!' he added, when she opened her mouth to speak, and then quite literally thrust her on her way as they reached the alley.

Almost immediately afterwards he detected the sound of heavy running footsteps and swung round. Whipping aside his cloak, he revealed a sturdy silver-handled walking stick, which he wielded to great effect, rendering the first assailant unconscious with a well-aimed blow to the temple. Unfortunately the footpad's two accomplices bore down upon him simultaneously, one successfully knocking the trusty weapon from his hand, while the other grasped him from behind, holding fast his arms. The second blow directed at his solar plexus had him momentarily gasping for breath. He then attempted to brace himself for the next onslaught. One moment the burly individual standing in front of him was balling his huge boulder of a fist; the next he was, amazingly enough, toppling to the ground, like some sturdy felled oak.

Out of the corner of his eye, his lordship glimpsed his gallant rescuer, silver-handled walking stick still clasped in one slender hand, and cursed under his breath, while successfully freeing himself from the third assailant's grasp. Drawing back his arm, he accidentally made contact with a high cheekbone with his elbow. An indignant squeal quickly followed before his lordship floored the last of the would-be robbers with a powerful blow to the jaw.

With one sweep of his arm, the Viscount grasped a slender wrist and assisted Georgie to her feet, not knowing whether to feel angry or grateful. 'Are you badly hurt, child?' he demanded, attempting to study her in the gloom.

'I do not think so, my lord, just slightly bruised.'

'In that case, remind me to beat you when we get home for disobeying my orders!'

He received a gurgle of mirth in response.

# *Chapter Four*

In view of the fact that he and Georgie had reached their respective bedchambers only just after dawn had broken, the Viscount had left strict instructions that his page was not to be disturbed until he had had sufficient sleep. He himself was denied that pleasure by the arrival the following morning of an unexpected visitor. Ordinarily none of the servants would have entered his bedchamber until he rang for attendance. Brindle, however, was well aware that this particular caller was always welcome, no matter the time of day, and so had no hesitation in making the visitor's arrival known.

All the same, it was almost an hour later before his lordship made his way down to the breakfast parlour in order to greet his very welcome guest. He was almost sure what had prompted the visit, and so didn't waste time on needless pleasantries. 'Would it be presumptuous of me to offer my heartiest congratulations?'

'Not at all!' Charles Gingham assured him proudly, rising from the chair in order to clasp the Viscount warmly by the hand. 'A boy! My wonderful darling girl has only gone and presented me with a fine son. Hale and hearty, the doctor assures me. We've named him after you. I hope you don't object? And we very much desire you to be his godfather.'

'I would have been most offended had you considered another,' his lordship admitted suavely. 'Don't let me interrupt your breakfast, though, Charles. I see my servants have catered for your needs,' he added, after considering the huge quantity piled high on his friend's plate. 'Your second today, no doubt. But, then, you've always boasted a healthy appetite.'

'Let me tell you I was up at five, unlike you, you slug-a-bed!' Charles defended, brandishing his fork like a sabre. 'Why, it's almost midday! Disgraceful!'

His lordship cast a jaundiced eye in the general direction of the mantel-clock. 'Dear God, so early!' he groaned. 'I shall take leave to remind you that one does not keep country hours whilst residing in town. Furthermore, I dare swear I didn't reach the comfort of my bed much before you deserted yours this morning.'

After instructing the footman to serve coffee and supply him with ham and eggs, his lordship gestured for the servant to leave. 'So how long do you propose inflicting your company upon me?'

Charles Gingham frankly laughed, not in the least offended. In fact, he had known the Viscount long enough to be sure that the disgruntled tone of one being imposed upon was a complete sham and that his lifelong friend was in a rare good humour. Which was surprising considering his lordship had had so little sleep.

'Only until tomorrow, old friend. I intend to place an advertisement about our son's birth in various journals, and I'll let a few other friends know personally. But I don't wish to be away from home for too long, though I expect Louise will be glad of the break. She's complaining that I fuss about her and little Benedict like a mother hen.'

When the Viscount made no comment, Charles's thoughts turned from his own domestic bliss to his friend's well-being. 'I must say I was half-expecting to discover the knocker had been removed from the door and that you'd returned to the country. When we met up a couple of weeks ago you gave the impression of being heartily bored with town life.'

'Did I…?' His lordship was nonplussed for a moment, then shrugged. 'No, I'm not bored, Charles. Quite the contrary, in fact! Life has suddenly acquired a new and rather fascinating dimension.'

No sooner had he volunteered this information than the parlour door was thrown wide, and Charles turned to see a young servant come striding, quite unbidden, into the room. 'Do you wish me to accompany you out for a ride later—? Oh, I do beg your pardon, my lord! Brindle quite failed to inform me we had a visitor!'

'How very remiss of him!' his lordship responded with gentle mockery, while smiling faintly at the look of bewilderment on his friend's face. 'No matter, child, come forwards. You remember Mr Gingham, I trust?'

It surprised his lordship not at all when Georgie came forward to study his friend's physiognomy quite brazenly, though it clearly wasn't what Charles was accustomed to. His jaw dropped perceptively when those striking orbs scrutinised his features for a full half-minute.

'Oh, yes, now I remember you, sir!'

'Er—do you, my boy?' Charles asked faintly, much to Lord Fincham's further amusement

'Why, yes! You were with us at Deerhampton that day.'

'Was I…? Yes, I suppose I was,' Charles returned, evidently still unable to recall precisely where he had encountered the singular young person before. 'Er—you appear to have the makings of a black eye, young fellow,' he added, having returned the compliment by scrutinising the delicately featured face and clearly feeling some further comment was expected of him.

'I know I have!' was the proud response. 'His lordship gave it to me.'

This was almost too much for the Viscount's self control. 'Go away, you abominable brat!' he managed with only the faintest trace of a betraying tremor in his voice. 'And, no, I do not require you to accompany me out today, most especially as you're sporting that injury. I'm not having the polite world believing I'm some kind of tyrannical monster. What's more, you are not to venture forth again yourself until the bruise has faded,' he added above that infectious gurgle of mirth that never failed to win an answering smile from him nowadays.

'I'm not ashamed of it,' he was promptly assured.

'I look upon it as a kind of trophy. I've never had one before, you see?'

'Which only goes to prove that those most closely associated with you in the past must have shown praiseworthy forbearance!' his lordship parried, which resulted in a further gurgle of that infectious laughter. 'You may bear me company this evening. I shall not be going out. We shall repair to the library and finish that game of chess we began the other evening.'

Still showing visible signs of complete bewilderment, Charles stared fixedly across the table. 'Who the deuce was that?' he demanded to know the instant he and the Viscount were once again enjoying privacy.

His lordship raised his black brows in mock surprise. 'Why, my page, Charles. Who did you suppose it was?'

'Don't try to flummery me, Finch! I've known you too long. Since when have you ever required the services of a page?'

'It would be more accurate to say I acquired one rather than required one. Master Georgie Green has been with me since the day you and I attended that prize fight at Deerhampton.' He smiled softly as a fond memory returned. 'After all, it was the least I could do after the child had saved me from possible injury.'

'Well, I suppose that's true enough, though I doubt you'd have sustained more than an odd bruise or two, if that,' Charles responded, having at last re-called precisely where he had seen the young person before. 'I must say, though, I'm most surprised at you, of all people, tolerating such familiarity that borders on impertinence, most especially in a ser-vant. Clearly the boy doesn't know his place. I can almost appreciate why you inflicted the black eye, though I don't usually hold with maltreating flunkies.'

At this the Viscount threw back his head and laughed heartily, something his friend had not wit-nessed him do in many a long year. 'I would strongly advise you not to pay heed to everything that little demon tells you.'

'Do you mean he deliberately lies?'

'No, I would say, rather, that on occasions Georgie can be somewhat sparing with the truth. I did, indeed, inflict the injury, though it was purely an accident. Against my expressed wishes, the child returned to help me fend off three footpads.'

Betraying a glint of emotion in his dark eyes that was impossible for his friend to define, his lordship fixed his gaze on the silver coffee pot that held pride of place in the centre of the table. 'At Deerhampton I might, indeed, have sustained only minor injuries— last night was vastly different. Had it not been for my page's courageous intervention, I might not now be sitting here, having only sustained a minor abrasion or two. It is little wonder, therefore, that I have grown inordinately…fond of that child.'

Suddenly realising he was being observed most keenly, his lordship rose to his feet. 'And now, if you have finished your repast, let us depart the house and announce the arrival of your own to the world at large!'

Although he refrained from alluding to the subject again, his lordship's unusual attitude towards one particular servant remained in Mr Gingham's thoughts. He glimpsed the page again on two occasions only throughout the day. All the same, something about the youth, and he knew not what, struck him as odd. It was not until that evening, however, when he returned to the house, after visiting one or two other friends in the capital, that the truth finally dawned on him.

Entering the library unannounced, he discovered the Viscount and his highly favoured young servant seated on opposite sides of the hearth, both engrossed in a game of chess. Consequently he was given a few precious moments in which to study the intimate little tableau without his presence being detected. Not taking his eyes away for a second, he studied the way the page reached for the glass of wine at his elbow and took the most delicate of sips, and the way slender, tapering fingers moved a chess piece across the board with infinite care. There was only one conclusion he could draw.

'Why, if it isn't Mr Gingham!' Georgie announced, catching sight of him at last. 'We didn't expect you back so soon, did we, my lord?'

'Indeed not, child,' the Viscount agreed affably, not taking his eyes off the chess board. 'Draw up a chair, old fellow. I hope you don't object to us playing a while longer. The game is at a most interesting stage, you see.'

Helping himself to wine, Charles took a chair a little away from the players. 'Do not consider me for a moment, Finch. I shall be quite content viewing proceedings from here.'

Try though he might to calculate the state of play, he seemed unable to take his eyes off his lordship's worthy opponent for very long, and the more he studied each and every movement of that slender, lithe young body, the more convinced he became that his startlingly disturbing suspicion was correct. He chanced to glance in the Viscount's direction at one point, and caught him staring directly back at him, the most enigmatic of smiles hovering about those finely chiselled lips.

The instant the mantel-clock announced the hour of eleven, his lordship leaned back in his chair. 'Child, it is late, and time you were abed. I shall concede defeat. Well played!'

'Oh, no, sir! That wouldn't be fair. I have not beaten you. I shall agree to a draw.' The smile that accompanied this contrasting decision was so enchantingly lovely it almost took Charles's breath away.

His lordship seemed quite impervious, however, as he said, 'Very well, stalemate it is. Be sure I shall issue a further challenge in the near future. Goodnight, Georgie.'

As soon as the door had closed behind the servant Charles sat himself in the recently vacated chair opposite his lordship. He didn't attempt to speak. More importantly, neither did his lordship. As the silence lengthened between them, Charles couldn't resist looking across at the Viscount and discovered him with that same inscrutable smile playing about his mouth, while all the time staring fixedly down at the empty hearth. He could contain himself no longer.

'Confound it, Finch! What game are you playing?'

Those mobile black brows rose in exaggerated surprise. 'Why, my dear fellow! What's amiss? You know full well the game ended in a draw, a mutually satisfying result.'

'Don't you try prevarication with me, Finch! We've known each other too long,' Charles countered, refusing to be diverted from the seriousness of the issue. 'That page of yours is…is a confounded girl! Deny it if you dare!'

When his lordship made no attempt to do so, and continued to smile in that same infuriating way down at the hearth, Charles began to feel increasingly annoyed. 'Damn it, man! It's no laughing matter. What the deuce are you about? If you're not concerned about the chit's reputation, then think of your own. You risk being shunned by society, or at the very least made the butt of most every vulgarian's ill humour.'

'Neither of which would concern me overmuch,' his lordship assured him, his expression suddenly serious. 'But the girl's reputation is a different matter entirely. And that is why I have decided to remove to Fincham Park at the end of the week. Increasingly I have begun to believe it is my duty to protect her and I see no other way.'

Charles was at a loss to understand, and it was quite evident in his voice as he said, 'But why should you want to, Finch? After all, a filly that would lend herself to such a start must surely be—' He checked at the dangerous expression that suddenly flickered over the Viscount's ruggedly masculine features, making them appear far harsher than usual. 'Well, I suppose you've experience enough to be able to judge her character,' he finally conceded

'Indeed, I have,' his lordship agreed softly. 'Experience enough to be absolutely certain that child is no wanton.' His features were softened by the warmth of an unexpected smile. 'Nor, which I find faintly dispiriting, has she attempted to cast out so much as a lure in my direction. She treats me like some—dare I say it?—trustworthy uncle. Hardly flattering, you must agree, to a gentleman of my reputation where the fair sex is concerned!'

Charles regarded his friend in silence for a moment, before asking the most obvious question. 'Would you want it any other way?'

Rising to his feet, his lordship went across the

room to replenish their glasses. 'Well, let us be frank. Dressed appropriately she would make a damnably lovely young woman. But, no, strange though it might seem, I rather enjoy the company of my unconventional page. She's so refreshingly natural and uncomplicated in so many ways. She tells me precisely what she thinks about most things. And I truly believe, with a few exceptions only, she has not lied to me. For my part, I am enjoying the novelty of it all… But I'm sensible enough to know, for several reasons, this relationship between us cannot possibly continue indefinitely.'

Charles waited for the Viscount to make himself comfortable in the chair opposite before satisfying his curiosity over something. 'Have you always known her true sex?'

'I was suspicious from the first,' he confided, smiling reminiscently. 'But I swiftly became convinced of the fact when I chanced to pass her on the road that day and conveyed her to London. What she intended to do upon reaching the capital, I have no notion. I truly believe it was I who first put the nonsensical notion of becoming a page into her head.' He shrugged. 'I suppose I felt obliged to offer her the protection of my home after such foolishness on my part.'

'And now?' Charles asked, when the Viscount fell silent, merely staring down into his glass.

'Now, more than anything, I want her to confide in me fully so that I might aid her if I can. Believe me, she is no light-minded schoolgirl indulging in some lark, of that I'm absolutely certain. No, there is some very real purpose in this masquerade of hers. I believe, too, that she is older than I first supposed, perhaps as much as one-and-twenty, though she appears much younger.'

He paused for a moment to sample his wine. 'She is both a charming and intelligent young woman, Charles. She must appreciate herself that she cannot possibly continue with the deception indefinitely. Nature alone will decree that. If she were to keep to her room for a few days each month, the servants would certainly become suspicious. But I hope she might avoid that embarrassment by confiding in me long before then. If, however, I find that I can no longer trust myself to treat her like the innocent I know her to be, then I shall enlist the aid of my sister-in-law.' He couldn't resist a further smile as he said this. 'Eleanor, quite naturally, will be shocked. But she has a fondness for me and a good heart. She will take the girl in, if I ask it of her.'

Charles, a look of admiration in his eyes, gazed

across at his friend. 'What you're doing is damnably good, Finch.'

The Viscount dismissed this with a wave of one hand. 'Nonsense! I'm merely preventing myself from becoming bored. Playing the protector will amuse me for a while longer, but eventually I shall grow weary of it. Then I shall find a new distraction.'

'I wonder if you shall,' Charles returned softly. 'I wonder if you really appreciate fully yourself just why you're so determined to help this girl.'

'Oh, that's far too deep for me, dear boy,' the Viscount responded with yet a further dismissive wave of his hand.

The following day, after seeing his friend safely on his way, the Viscount sent for his page. She came tripping lightly into the library a few minutes later, Ronan, tail wagging merrily, at her heels, just as though they had been lifelong companions. Undeniably there was an elfin quality about Georgie at times that certainly made her appear far younger than her years, he decided, setting aside his papers so that he might favour her with his full attention. Clearly the outrageous little baggage enjoyed the freedom her boy's raiment afforded her. And it was true to say that for the most part she did make a passable lad, he mused. At least the servants hadn't rumbled her secret as yet. Perhaps it was only with him that she ever allowed her guard to drop.

He smiled at this very satisfying thought as he beckoned her over to the desk. 'Now, Georgie, I have instructed Brindle to make ready for our removal to Fincham Park early on Friday morning, so I expect you to make ready also.'

The initial response was not what he might have expected, or hoped. That wonderful smile disappeared in an instant, and there was a definite troubled look dulling the normal healthy sparkle in her eyes.

'What's amiss, child? Do you not wish to accompany me into the country?'

'I-I hadn't considered it, sir,' she responded, staring meditatively down at the desk. 'I suppose I thought you'd be staying in town until the Season had drawn to a close.'

'I have been known to do so,' he admitted. 'But this year I wish to leave early. I believe the country air will do us both good, enable us to relax a little more together.' No response was forthcoming. 'Is there a particular reason why you wish to remain in town?'

She appeared to consider for a moment or two,

then, 'No, now you come to mention it, I don't suppose there is, really. But—but, might I borrow pen and paper to make a list of some—er—necessities I must purchase and take with me, my lord?'

'Be my guest,' he invited, obligingly rising to his feet so that she might make use of his chair. 'It just so happens I must needs consult one of my ledgers.'

He left her to seat herself while he wandered across the room to extract the leather-bound tome he required from one of the shelves. He then made himself comfortable in a chair by the hearth so that she might enjoy privacy. He was fairly certain, as he surreptitiously studied that slender white hand moving back and forth across the page, that it was not a list she was composing, but a letter. Naturally he was curious to discover to whom she was writing, but resisted the temptation to pry, and merely said, 'Was it the good vicar who taught you to write?'

There was a suspicion of a twitch at the corner of her mouth. 'And my mother. She was not an illiterate, my lord.'

'I never for a moment supposed she was,' he assured her, and then remained silent so that she might finish the missive in peace.

The instant she had sanded down the letter, she left

him alone, and he wandered across to the window. As expected, within minutes he saw her leave the house, Ronan, again, at her heels, their destination a complete mystery. Of one thing he was convinced—she was letting someone know where she was bound…

Therefore she was not totally alone in the world. Someone, somewhere, was concerned about her.

Although the journey was completed in a day, the afternoon was well advanced before the small cavalcade passed between the impressive wrought-iron gates of Fincham Park's northern entrance.

The Viscount had allowed Georgie to spend part of the journey perched up on the box with the head groom, but had insisted she sit inside the well-sprung travelling carriage with him for the last stage. He had wanted to see the expression on those lovely features when she caught her first glimpse of the ancestral home of which he was secretly so very proud, and she didn't disappoint him. Perfectly shaped lips parted and eyes widened in wonder as the carriage journeyed along the sweep of the drive and the mansion at last came into view.

The original part of the house had been constructed in the early sixteen hundreds. Although extensive alterations and additions made during the first half of the previous century by both his lordship's grandfather and great-grandfather had resulted in the mansion more than doubling in size, the architectural splendour of the original building had been maintained.

'You approve my ancestral home, child?' he re-marked, as the carriage drew to a halt before the impressive front entrance.

'Oh, it is truly splendid, sir!' she enthused, much to his satisfaction. 'So fine and well proportioned,' she added, alighting before him.

'Ah! So you are something of an expert when it comes to the finer points of good architecture,' he teased gently, but she didn't appear offended.

'Not at all, my lord,' she returned. 'I just know what I find aesthetically pleasing.'

'Well said, child!' he approved. 'I sincerely trust you will find the interior equally to your taste,' and so saying he led the way into the wood-panelled hall, where he discovered his trusty major-domo hovering in the shadows.

As was the custom, the butler had left London three days before in order to ensure all was in readi-ness at the ancestral home of the Finchams for the arrival of its master. From what his lordship could see his diligent head servant had not failed in his duties yet again.

'Our rooms are ready, I trust?' he remarked, after handing the butler his outdoor garments and receiving a bow in confirmation. 'Then be good enough to show Master Green his bedchamber. When you're settled into your new quarters, Georgie, you may join me in the library. And if I am feeling particularly well disposed towards you, you might even persuade me to take you on a guided tour of my home. We shall see.' With that he wandered across the hall to his sanctum, smiling to himself.

He could not help wondering what Georgie herself thought of the preferential treatment she had received since entering his employ. She was far too astute not to have long since appreciated that she was not looked upon as a mere servant. Perhaps she believed she was just her eccentric master's pampered pet, or maybe she supposed it was reward for her acts of courage on those two occasions when she had come to his aid. Who could say? What his servants thought of his behaviour towards Master Green was quite another matter, however.

After closing his library door, the Viscount poured himself a glass of wine before settling himself in his favourite winged-chair by the hearth. He considered it safe to assume that Georgie was more conscious of the role she was assuming when in the company of the servants. Even so, there must have been a deal of speculation about his own treatment of his page. It was quite possible that several below stairs had suspected Georgie might be the fruit of their master's own loins, or maybe even the illegitimate offspring of a close friend of his lordship. They could speculate all they wished, as far as he was concerned, so long as her true sex was not discovered.

It was just as this very troubling possibility yet again crossed his mind that the object of his concerns sauntered brazenly into the room, after the lightest of taps on the door, and appearing as though she'd not a care in the world. Really, he ought to reprimand her for such forwardness! But how could he when he had actively encouraged her to take such liberties with him? Furthermore, her behaviour was so natural where he was concerned that it seemed almost safe to assume that, at some stage in her life, some person of high standing, somewhere, had allowed her equal freedoms, and to behave in a most casual way, because it was patently second nature for her to do so... It was all so damnably intriguing!

\* \* \*

A short time later his lordship was fulfilling his promise and showing Georgie round his country home. After exploring each and every ground-floor room, Lord Fincham led the way up the ornately carved Jacobean staircase to the upper floor, where a long and well-lit picture gallery granted access to both east and west wings. It was here that Georgie betrayed most interest, studying each portrait of his lordship's ancestors in turn, before pausing before one of the present holder of the title, painted only a few months after he had attained the viscountcy.

'You do not approve, child,' he remarked, observing the slight frown. 'It is considered a fine painting by most.'

'I'm sure it is, sir. Just as I'm certain the artist is extremely skilful. It's a pity, though, he captured you in such a bad humour.' She turned her head on one side as she continued to study the likeness. 'You do have a way of looking down your long nose that way, it's true—most especially when in a haughty frame of mind. More often than not, though, there's a glint in your eyes that proves you're not really in a bad mood. I've witnessed it often when you've been speaking with me,' she continued ingenuously. 'But it's lacking in this picture. Of course, you were still mourning the loss of your brother. But it isn't so much sadness I see in your eyes as anger…or bitterness, maybe. No, you were definitely not yourself.'

Dear God, he reflected, how right she was! He'd never considered it before, but he was now seeing the painting through new eyes. In the months after his return from France he'd been both angry and resentful at the way Charlotte Vane had behaved towards him. He'd hardened his heart, and with very few exceptions had allowed no females to get close to him, most especially those with whom he had since enjoyed more intimate relations. Over the years he had thought less and less of the woman who had destroyed his youthful romantic notions in that single act of treachery. In recent weeks he'd recalled her to mind not at all. Was this simply because she had not put in an appearance in town throughout the entire Season…or for a different reason entirely?

He raised his eyes from that imaginary spot on the wooden floor to discover a violet pair regarding him with keen interest and smiled. 'You are right, child. This is not a particularly good likeness. It is high time I commissioned another—one that captures the true character of this handsome, debonair aristocrat. What say you?'

There was no mistaking the glinting mischief now dancing in her eyes. 'It all depends whether you want the artist to paint an honest representation, or merely pander to your ego.'

He adopted the haughty pose of his likeness on the wall before them. 'Do I infer correctly from that, that you do not consider me an Adonis, child?'

'Since you ask…no, not particularly,' she returned, at her most candid. 'You have strong, regular features, a face of character not masculine beauty. That said, I do not consider you ill looking—far from it, in fact.'

Ignoring his twitching smile, she considered him for a moment. 'I think, though, if you are seriously considering sitting again for a new portrait, you should adopt the new mode of attire advocated by Brummell. I saw him first at the Duke and Duchess of Merton's ball, remember? I didn't know who he was then, of course. It was only later I discovered his identity, when we visited that gaming house, and he happened to put in an appearance shortly before we left. But I did think his attire most becoming. Like yourself, my lord, he's a most striking gentleman. It's just a pity that most of those who are now attempting to ape him fall far short of his high standards.'

'And you would expect me to become one of their number?' He paused to remove a speck of fluff from his heavily embroidered dark blue coat. 'I think not.'

'Ah, but you see, my lord, you would maintain your own distinctive style,' she argued, clearly not ready to admit defeat quite yet, 'even if you were ever to adhere to the Beau's strict rules governing male attire.'

'Now, there's a thought!' he remarked, no longer prepared to dismiss the suggestion out of hand. 'It might be amusing, at that, to offer the young dandy some serious competition. I shall consider it. And now, if you're ready, we shall repair to the west wing, where you may cast your eyes over my private apartments.' He slanted a half-mocking glance down at her, which contained an element of a challenging gleam. 'Unless, of course, you'd rather not?'

'Why should I not wish to, sir?' She appeared genuinely nonplussed. 'You've never given me reason to mistrust you. In truth, I cannot think of anyone I trust more.'

He was all at once serious. 'In that case, I earnestly hope, my child, that I never give you any reason to alter your high opinion of me.'

# Chapter Five

**W**hat his lordship had expected to happen sooner rather than later occurred the following day. Brindle informed him, shortly after breakfast, that Georgie had complained of feeling not quite the thing and had remained in bed, having succumbed to a suspected chill. His lordship didn't hesitate to endorse this course of action, suggesting also that it would be best for all concerned if the child was allowed time to recover in the privacy of his own room. Furthermore, Georgie was not to be disturbed, except on those occasions when meals were taken up to him. After all, it wouldn't do for the rest of the staff to contract the malady, he had added artfully.

Feeling he had done all he could to ensure Georgie had as much privacy as possible, his lordship took himself off to the library in order to deal with urgent estate matters. Unfortunately it swiftly became clear that he just wasn't in the mood to concentrate.

Rising from his desk, he went to stand before the window and stared out across the acreage of majestic parkland that surrounded the house. Usually the sight never failed to stir him; today he was hardly conscious of its natural beauty. His mind was fixed on that being alone in one of the smaller and much less impressive bedchambers in the east wing.

He supposed it ought to have offered him immense satisfaction to have had this further proof that his judgement was sound: Georgie had not run away from home because of a foolish indiscretion and was not carrying another man's child; she was indeed the innocent he had always believed her to be. Strangely, though, it brought scant consolation. If anything her having to endure the monthly curse only went to substantiate his belief that their somewhat unorthodox situation couldn't possibly continue for very much longer.

With a feeling of deep regret, he returned to his desk and, before he could experience second thoughts, penned a missive to his sister-in-law, requesting she call upon him at her earliest convenience. The servant despatched to deliver the letter by hand duly returned with a reply. It was from Lady Eleanor Fincham's housekeeper, who had written to inform his lordship that she expected her mistress to be away from home until the following week. The Viscount didn't know whether to feel relieved or disappointed. At least, though, he had been granted a little more time to enjoy the companionship of his unique page.

Once Georgie had emerged from her bedchamber, after the customary number of days, he wasted not a precious moment of the limited time left to him to enjoy the singular and poignant relationship he had experienced with this very special young person. Had he considered her a typical member of her sex, it might have occurred to him to suggest a visit to the local town, where they might explore the more fashionable shops that had sprung up in recent years in the thriving community; since she was a most unconventional member of the weaker sex, he suggested, instead, a visit to the trout stream so that they might enjoy a morning's pleasant relaxation, a suggestion she heartily embraced.

It quickly became apparent that she was no novice with a rod. Half-a-dozen fine specimens were soon safely contained in the fishing basket and two more rapidly followed. Well satisfied with the bumper catch, his lordship set rod aside and lay down on the grass, happy to relax in the pleasant warmth of the early June sunshine.

'It goes without saying, Georgie,' he remarked, opening one eye to see her deposit yet another meaty specimen in the basket, 'that you have enjoyed this pastime on many occasions before. I trust you were not indulging in any unlawful practices?'

She chuckled at this. 'Assuredly not! I had my godfather's full permission. In fact, on numerous occasions he came with me.'

Indeed, he mused. Then it was perhaps safe to assume this godfather of hers had been a man of property—interesting, but not wholly surprising.

Before he could enquire further into the identity of this unknown worthy who had evidently been a real and, he very much suspected, beneficial influence in her life, she touched upon his own skills with a rod. 'I expect you spent much time here in your youth with your elder brother.'

'We did sometimes fish together,' he acknowledged. 'More often than not, though, I used to come down here with Charles Gingham. He was a frequent visitor to the house back then, in the heady days of our youth.'

Evidently she had detected the hint of melancholy in his voice, for she regarded him keenly. 'But he doesn't visit so often now, and quite naturally you are sad about that. But then, he wouldn't, of course. He's married, and has other responsibilities.' She continued to regard him in a thoughtful way. 'I believe I'm correct in saying he married a Frenchwoman, a girl you saved on the occasion you both went over to France to rescue Mr Gingham's cousin?'

He slanted a look of reproach in her direction. 'I very much fear, Georgie, my boy, that you are guilty of the sin of listening to servants' gossip. You should be ashamed of yourself!'

Clearly unrepentant, she gurgled with mirth, and then, abandoning further attempts to catch more fish, sat companionably beside him on the bank. 'You forget, my lord, I am a servant. It's only natural, therefore, that I should enjoy the society prevailing below stairs.'

'You may well do so, child,' he returned abruptly, 'at least the novelty of it. But you'll never be one of their number.'

Again she glanced at him sharply, only this time there was an element of wariness in her regard, before she hurriedly returned to the subject of his jaunt across the Channel, requesting a more detailed account.

As always with her he was of a mind to be

indulgent, even though he did sigh. 'There's very little to tell, Georgie. Many years ago, long before you were born, one of Charles's aunts married a Frenchman. After the Terror had begun, news reached Charles that the family was in trouble. By the time we arrived in France both his aunt and the Frenchman she had married had been executed. However, their only son, Henri Durand, was being held, awaiting trial—ha, if you can call it that!—in a town some thirty miles west of Paris. The prison there was little more than a moderately fortified house. Adopting various stratagems, and with the help of a few sympathetic local peasants, we managed to break in. There were only two prisoners being held at the time in the cellars: Henri and a young girl, Louise Charvet, who was little more than a child.

'Her parents had not been aristocrats, merely wealthy. But that was sufficient inducement for corrupt local officials to trump up charges against them, and claim all property and possessions for the state. Louise's father, having guessed what was coming, had the foresight to bury the family jewels, together with a considerable amount of gold coinage, in a chest in the garden, where he hoped to retrieve it once he had completed arrangements to get his family safely across to England. Unfortunately they were all taken into custody before he could effect the escape.

'Charvet had had the foresight to tell his wife and children where he had hidden the loot, and Charles, under cover of darkness, spirited Louise back to her home in order to retrieve the family coffers. Meanwhile, I accompanied Henri to a certain French village on the coast and arranged for a fishing vessel to take us back across the Channel. Charles and Louise arrived two days later, and we all returned to England without having to contend with further difficulties, except perhaps a touch of seasickness.' He shuddered at the memory. 'It was a rough crossing, as I recall.'

Anyone listening to the recital might have been forgiven for supposing Lord Fincham had been recounting nothing of more moment than a pleasant Sunday afternoon jaunt in a park, so deliberately matter of fact had he sounded about it all. Consequently, it came as no very real surprise, when he happened to glance up in a certain someone's direction, to find himself being regarded with no little amusement.

'It is little wonder you didn't plan a return visit, my lord. It sounds as though you had a devilish dull time of it all!' Finely arching black brows adopted a decidedly mocking slant. 'As I'm fairly certain you'll not satisfy my curiosity by relating a more detailed account of what took place, would you at least satisfy my curiosity over what became of Henri…? Louise, I know, married your friend.'

'But not immediately,' he willingly revealed. 'As I mentioned, when rescued she'd just turned sixteen, could only just make herself understood in English and had no family connections living in this country, not even distant ones. So Charles took it upon himself to place her in the care of his mother, who still resides with him, as it happens.

'If my memory serves me correctly,' he continued, after taking a moment to gather his thoughts, 'Charles came into a sizeable property around that time, left to him by his uncle on his father's side. As Charles much prefers life in the country, he sold the London home his late father had acquired years before, and removed, with his mother, to the property a few miles south of Deerhampton. So it was quite in order for him to install little Louise in his newly acquired home.'

He smiled reminiscently. 'I think it would be true to say that thoughts of romance didn't enter either of their heads, at least not at the beginning. Indeed, at first Louise looked upon him as an indulgent older brother. Sadly, she lost both of hers to Madame Guillotine. Young girls grow up quite quickly, however, and not too many years had passed before Louise viewed Charles quite differently.'

Again his lordship smiled. 'Certainly I gained the distinct impression as the years went by that the relationship between the pair was changing. But, unlike me, Charles is a very noble fellow. Instead of whisking his beloved down the aisle without further ado, he proposed a Season in town so that she might experience the company of other young men. Being something of an expert where precious gems are concerned, he had persuaded her to retain certain items of jewellery they'd brought over from France, and sell other pieces, so that she might invest the money in order to offer a prospective husband a reasonable dowry. She'd been more than happy to allow him to deal with money matters. But being a sensible young Frenchwoman she had no intention of wasting any of his on the needless expense of a Season, when she had already decided upon the gentleman she wished to wed. Charles's mother, of course, was delighted. She'd come to look upon Louise as the daughter she had never been blessed with. So as you can imagine, my dear Georgie, with the new arrival, it is undoubtedly an extremely happy household indeed!'

Typically female, she appeared very well pleased to learn this, then asked, 'And what of Cousin Henri…? What became of him?'

'Ah! That, my dear, is not such an edifying tale. He, sadly, turned out to be something of a wastrel. He hoped Charles would support him so that he might continue to live as he had in France. He soon realised his mistake. Charles did indeed support Henri financially for very many months in the hope that his cousin might find some useful occupation. Sadly, it was not to be, and so Charles withdrew his support. Although I have had no contact with him for several years, I believe Henri is still accepted on the very fringes of society. Just how he's managed to support himself down the years, I have no notion, but I'd wager whatever he's been doing could not withstand close scrutiny.'

'Well, at least life improved for one of the exiles,' Georgie remarked, before a sound caught her attention and she turned to see a carriage making its way along the drive. 'You appear to have a visitor, my lord.'

The Viscount half-expected it to be his sister-in-law paying the call in response to his letter, and didn't know whether to feel relieved or disappointed when he recognised the conveyance as that belonging to his nearest neighbour.

'Now, what the deuce can he want, I wonder?' his lordship muttered testily, experiencing a touch of irritation as he got to his feet. He'd enjoyed an extremely relaxing morning, and was loath to bring it to an end. 'Unless I'm much mistaken, child, that's Squire Wyndham. I'd best see what he wants, if only to maintain cordial relations.'

After collecting the rods himself, his lordship automatically grasped one handle of the basket so that they might carry it back to the house together. It never occurred to him for a moment to consider that his actions might be viewed as rather odd in some quarters. Certainly the young footman, despatched hotfoot from the house to inform Lord Fincham there was a visitor awaiting him, betrayed no surprise whatsoever as he relieved his master of his share of the burden. It was only after his lordship had entered the front parlour that he was made aware of his slight solecism.

'Do you know, Fincham, it's rather bad form to employ servants, then do the bally work yourself! Gives the lazy blighters ideas above their station, don't you know?'

His lordship paused in the act of filling two glasses. Clearly his return to the house had been viewed from the window. It was on the tip of his tongue to tell the squire to mind his own business, but then he thought better of it. Sir Frederick could be a bluff, self-opinionated so-and-so on occasions, but there was no real malice in him. Relations between them had always been cordial enough, and Lord Fincham preferred to keep it that way.

'We enjoyed an exceptionally profitable morning down at the trout stream. Consequently the basket was heavy. I hope I never become too high in the instep to carry my own rod, and lend a helping hand when needed… And to what do I owe the pleasure of this visit, Wyndham?' he added, after handing the squire his wine.

'Oh, nothing in particular, m'boy. Heard you were back and thought to pop across to see how you're faring. Haven't seen much of you at all this year.' He took a moment to sample his wine. 'Thought to kill two birds with one stone, so to speak. It was my little Mary's birthday last week and I bought her a dapple-grey mare. She wanted to try it out, so I said she might ride over this way. Hope you don't object? Said they might skirt the home wood and meet me here. Her elder sister's with her, and

*Miss in a Man's World*

our groom, of course. Didn't want her about on the roads until she'd got the measure of her new mount. She lacks her sister's confidence in the saddle.'

'Of course I don't object,' his lordship didn't hesitate to assure his visitor. He then wandered across to the window himself in time to catch sight of Georgie, yet again, heading out across the park in the general direction of the home wood, the ever-faithful Ronan at her heels this time.

As there was no possibility, of course, of his accompanying her, he set himself the task of entertaining his visitor and joined him by the hearth. Sir Frederick was always a mine of local gossip. Not much went on in the locale that he didn't get to hear about eventually, and so his lordship was soon being kept abreast of events.

'And your sister-in-law's away at the moment, so I've heard, Fincham?'

He confirmed it with a nod of his head. 'Been staying with her mother for a few weeks, so I understand. I'm reliably informed she should be returning any day now.'

'Well, I hope to God she ain't carrying a load of jewels with her,' the squire responded gruffly. 'Seen the paper today, Fincham…? Only another robbery taken place on the King's highway. Some famous pearls were taken this time. That's the third this year, that I know of! It's high time something was done about all these robberies. It's getting so it ain't safe to travel any great distance any longer!'

'Whose pearls, I wonder?' his lordship murmured, moderately interested. 'I was up and about rather early this morning, so haven't had a chance to glance at the journal. Was anybody hurt, do you know?'

Sir Frederick shook his head. 'Not that I know of, no.'

'Then whoever it was fared rather better than poor Grenville earlier in the year. He lost his life, you may recall.'

'Yes, a bad business, a very bad business. Didn't know him personally. Don't spend a lot of time in the capital, as you know. Was he a particular friend of yours, Fincham?'

'I wouldn't go as far as to say that, no. But I certainly knew him well. He was a member of my club, so we bumped into each other from time to time, as you can imagine.' He frowned as a recent memory returned. 'I was reminded of him only the other week. When I first heard about his death I suppose I felt it was damned bad luck to be travelling at the time, but now, after this most recent attack... It certainly makes one wonder. Several people, myself included, knew he would be taking the famous Grenville diamonds back to his country home. He'd brought them to London with him for some reason or other, though I cannot now recall why.'

It was at this point that his lordship detected a raised female voice in the hall, and so wasn't unduly surprised when, a moment later, the squire's elder daughter burst into the room. One glance was sufficient to assure him all was far from well. For once she was not perfectly groomed. Numerous strands of fair hair were hanging wildly down her back, and her face, clearly tear-stained, was streaked with grime. Throwing herself into her father's arms, she began crying anew rather noisily.

'My dear child, whatever's amiss?'

It was only natural that the squire should be concerned. His lordship, on the other hand, was less convinced by the renewed bout of weeping. Perhaps it was his innate scepticism where the fair sex was concerned that was coming into play, for it seemed to him as though the display was rather theatrical.

'It—it was one of Lord Fincham's servants, Papa,' she at last revealed in a pathetically throbbing voice. 'Mary permitted me to ride her new mare, you see, and I was trying to persuade the creature to ford a shallow stream by his lordship's home wood, when this horrid boy appeared from nowhere, and hauled me from the saddle, calling me all sorts of terrible names, and even threatening to use the crop on me. I—I was so frightened.'

With the exception of one stable lad, and two of the head gardener's underlings, only one of his lordship's employees might be described as a boy. Yet, something about the account just didn't ring true. Georgie was quite capable of losing her temper on occasions and wasn't afraid to speak her mind. But going out of her way to interfere in matters that were none of her concern…? No, his lordship decided, she wouldn't do that. Not unless there was a very good reason for her to do so.

'And where, may I ask, was the groom engaged to protect you all this time?' the Viscount enquired, while the squire appeared as if he were attempting to suppress an explosion of wrath.

This point, however, did succeed in capturing his interest. 'Yes, by gad! Where was he, Clarissa? Why didn't he protect you?'

'Well, Papa, he tried his best to do so,' she answered, staring up at him through damp lashes, 'only the boy had a fearsome dog with him that growled so loudly we all thought it might attack.'

'By heavens, Fincham! The whelp deserves a sound thrashing!'

'Ah, but which one?' his lordship returned. 'The boy or the dog? The bond between them has become much stronger than even I had supposed.'

This distinct lack of sympathy for his daughter's recent ordeal, understandably enough, didn't commend itself to the doting parent, whose face turned a more virulent shade of purple.

'Confound it, sir! Do you consider this a matter for levity, for I tell you plainly I do not! Had I been there at the time, I would have taken the skin of the boy's back!'

'Then it is most fortunate for you that you were not there,' his lordship returned in an ominously quiet tone. 'Had you laid so much as a finger on my page, you would have had me to contend with.'

For a few moments it seemed as though the squire was incapable of uttering a coherent word. Then he managed to say in an astonished tone, 'Are you trying to tell me, sir, that you approve your servant's behaviour?'

'Not at all,' the Viscount was swift to assure. 'But neither do I mete out punishment without discovering all the facts. You may be sure I shall not let matters rest and shall question my page at some length. And now, Wyndham, I would suggest you take your daughter home, for she is looking decidedly pale now. I'm sure she will recover her spirits more quickly in her mother's care.'

After ringing for his butler and requesting him to show his visitors out, his lordship awaited the servant's return at the window. From where he stood he could see part of the perimeter to the home wood, but, alas, no sign of Georgie.

'Has my page returned to the house, Brindle, do you happen to know?' he asked, after detecting the click of the door.

'Not to my knowledge, my lord. I haven't seen him since he brought the fish into the house. Might I be permitted to say a very fine catch, sir. Cook is delighted.'

The praise, far from giving his lordship pleasure, gave rise to a pang of sadness, for he knew there would be no further fishing expeditions. The incident in the home wood—and he was sure something must have occurred—had forced him to acknowledge that even here on the estate Georgie's well-being could not be assured. Her disguise, far from protecting her, left her open to a different form of abuse. Sir Frederick might well have vented his spleen in a display of physical violence had he happened along at the time, as might any other over-protective father. Only by confining her to the house could he ever hope to ensure her complete safety, and he could never see her tamely submitting to that kind of treatment for any length of time. Nevertheless, until he could find the courage to confront her, to reveal what he had known from the first, he would need to resort to just such a tactic.

'When he does return, Brindle, you are to order him to his room, where he is to remain until I send for him. Is that clear?'

A moment's silence, then, 'Very good, my lord. The steward is here and is awaiting you in the library.'

'Inform him that I shall join him presently.'

The afternoon was well advanced before his lordship had finished dealing with matters relating to the estate. No sooner had the steward departed than he was informed that Sir Frederick Wyndham had surprisingly made a return call, and had been patiently awaiting his lordship's pleasure in the front parlour. For a second or two it did cross the Viscount's mind to refuse to see him, but then, in an attempt to maintain the cordial relationship, he thought better of it.

Given that the squire had left that morning in high dudgeon, his lordship was rather surprised to see him enter the library appearing somewhat chastened.

'It's no good beating about the bush, Fincham,' he announced, more like his usual bluff self. 'I'm here to apologise on my daughter Clarissa's behalf, and sincerely hope you didn't take my advice where that young servant of yours is concerned. Now, I'm not saying he oughtn't to mind his manners when dealing with his betters…but, well, from what my little Mary tells me, he wasn't as high-handed as my elder daughter would have had us believe. In fact, the young fellow saw Mary safely back home after Clarissa had ridden off, taking the groom with her. So what I say is we should forget about the whole business.'

Leaning back in his chair, his lordship regarded his visitor in amused silence for a moment. 'You have the advantage of me, Wyndham,' he admitted. 'I have yet to question my page about the incident. Before I do so, I am curious to know your younger daughter's version of events.'

The squire once again appeared decidedly ill at ease and began to beat a tattoo on the desk top with his fingertips. His lordship, however, refused to ease his visitor's obvious discomfiture by announcing that no more need be said. Seemingly something in his expression betrayed his determination to have his curiosity satisfied, for eventually Sir Frederick ceased his fidgeting and leaned back in his chair.

'Oh, very well, Fincham. According to what Mary tells me, Clarissa was fretting to ride the new mare. Being a good-natured gel, Mary agreed, and they exchanged mounts. Apparently Clarissa then attempted to ford the stream on the outskirts of the wood, but the mare would have none of it and refused to go into the water. It was at this point Clarissa had recourse to her crop.'

He sighed, clearly not approving his elder daughter's behaviour. 'That mare is a good-natured creature. I chose her myself. But I suppose it was only to be expected that she would take exception to the over-use of a crop and succeeded in unseating Clarissa, which was no mean feat, as she is a competent horsewoman. It was at this point your lad arrived on the scene.'

Again he sighed. 'Apparently it was he who succeeded in calming the mare. Wonderful he was with her, according to Mary. But no sooner had he soothed the creature than Clarissa—confound her!—demanded to remount. Mary refused permission, but

I'm afraid my elder daughter can be headstrong on occasions. Taking Mary's part, the lad intervened again and pushed Clarissa away. She stumbled over a tree root or some such and then ordered my groom to intercede on her behalf.'

'Without much success, I seem to recall,' his lord-ship remarked, smiling faintly. 'My dog Ronan has become inordinately fond of that child, Wyndham. These past weeks they have become inseparable.'

'Ah, well, my lord, only natural—a boy and his dog, eh, what?'

'A boy and his dog,' his lordship repeated. 'Yes, quite! But getting back to the unfortunate incident.' He raised one dark brow in a quizzical arch. 'I assume it was at this juncture that Clarissa, forced to admit defeat, headed here with the groom, leaving Mary with only my ill-mannered servant and a vicious hound to bear her company?'

The inference was clear and the squire had the grace to look a little shamefaced. 'Well, as to that, my lord…Mary assures me the lad behaved with the utmost propriety towards her. He succeeded again in calming the mare and mounting her himself to prove to my daughter that the horse was not in the least ill natured if treated with kindness. He handled the animal beautifully from what Mary tells me. And took to the side-saddle as though born to it!'

His lordship rolled his eyes ceilingwards. 'Believe me, Wyndham, that child has abilities that would astound you!'

'Well, as to that, my lord, I couldn't say. All I do know is the boy was decent enough to help Mary remount, and walked with her all the way back to the house, so that she got her confidence back with the mare. Now, I call that dashed decent of the young fellow! And I shouldn't like the boy to be punished in any way for what took place.'

His lordship, suddenly serious, stared sombrely down at his desk. 'Be assured, Wyndham, I've already decided on what action must be taken with regard to my page. Wielding a birch rod, however, does not enter into it.'

As he spoke his lordship wandered over to the bell pull, and waited for the summons to be answered before bidding his visitor a final farewell. 'When you have shown Sir Frederick out, Brindle,' he said, 'be good enough to instruct Georgie to attend me here in the library.'

Left alone once more, his lordship returned to the desk in order to finish a letter he had begun earlier. He had completed the task and was sealing the missive with a wafer when Brindle finally returned with a letter in his own hand.

'I'm sorry, my lord. Georgie doesn't appear to be anywhere in the house, but the maid did find this on the pillow in the room.'

Reaching out a hand that was surprisingly steady, considering he suddenly viewed the missive as a portent of doom, his lordship saw that the communication was addressed formally to him in stylishly sloping characters. It was with rapidly increasing foreboding that he broke the seal to read:

Sir,

It is with the deepest regret that I must write this, but the time has finally come for me to leave you. I sincerely hope that what occurred earlier in the home wood has not vexed you or caused you embarrassment. What you said to me earlier today is all too true—my nature being what it is, I should never make a respectful servant. My one regret is that I didn't make my farewells in person. Maybe, however, it is better this way.

I shall never forget you, my lord, nor your many kindnesses to me during these past few short weeks. I take with me only what I brought

into your house. And so many precious memories of having known you.

May God keep you safe always,
Georgie

Studying his master closely, Brindle watched an
almost frozen expression grip those strong features,
before the slightly swarthy complexion turned ashen.
He had seen his master suffer adversity in the past—
the return from France, when he had discovered the
girl he had wished to marry had wed another, and
when he had learned of his brother's tragic death a
matter of a few weeks later. But never before could
Brindle recall seeing such a look of desolation in
those dark eyes when his lordship finally raised his
head and stared at the wall opposite.

Yet, within a matter of seconds his expression had
changed, and dark eyes, with a fierce intensity in
their depths, turned to the butler again. 'When did
Georgie return to the house?'

'I'm not altogether sure, my lord. It was during
the time you were with your steward. Maybe one
o'clock, or soon afterwards. The maid took luncheon
up to the room and said the page was engaged in
writing a letter even then. When the servant went

up a short while ago, the tray, empty, was still there, but the…girl was not.'

Consumed with anxiety though he was, his lordship was quick to note what his trusty servant had finally revealed. 'Do the other servants know her true sex?'

'Not to my knowledge, my lord, no. I thought you preferred it remain that way.'

'Thank you, Brindle,' he acknowledged with real gratitude. 'And for the time being, in order to protect her, I should prefer if it continues to remain that way.'

He went over to the window, his stride purposeful. 'Make a thorough search of the house again, from attic to cellar. If she is not found, then send out orders that every able-bodied man on the estate is to begin searching for…for Fincham's page. She may have several hours' start, but there is just the chance that someone, somewhere in the locale, saw her.'

Raising his dark eyes, he scanned the acres of parkland. 'She must be found, Brindle. I shall never rest until I've found her.'

## Chapter Six

'Child, it was madness, unutterable madness!' the Dowager Countess of Grenville declared, clearly agitated. 'When I asked you to look into this matter of my son's death on my behalf, I knew you could be taking grave risks. That is why I wished you to remain as the guest of Lady Pickering for a few weeks in order to minimise the dangers. But when I agreed to grant you free rein in the venture, I never for one moment supposed you would embark on something so outrageous!'

Miss Georgiana Grey, far from chastened by the reproof, smiled fondly at the elderly lady seated on the opposite side of the hearth. She had been travelling for the best part of four days, and by various means, in an attempt to frustrate pursuit. She believed she had succeeded in all her endeavours during the past weeks, and was therefore far too smugly satisfied with the success of the undertaking to be even remotely subdued by the formidable matron's condemnation of her actions.

'Ma'am, if I had gone about things your way and stayed with your friend in London, I would have discovered little or nothing to the purpose. I know what would have happened—I would have been taken to a few discreet parties, where only genteel conversation prevailed. What good would that have done, pray? No, I had, somehow, to gain entrée into a man's world, come face to face with those acquaintances of my godfather's, and venture into those places he frequented. I could never have done so had I stayed with Lady Pickering.'

'But, child, anything might have happened to you.'

At this Georgiana was unable to suppress a tender little smile. 'I'll admit I had no very real idea of what I was going to do when I reached the capital. I thought, perhaps, to rent furnished rooms somewhere for a few weeks in the hope of making the acquaintance of some personable young gentleman about town who was abreast of all the gossip, and who might have taken me under his wing, as it were. It was just a marvellous stroke of good fortune that I crossed Lord Fincham's path that day at Deerhampton.'

'Fortunate…?' The Dowager raised her eyes to-wards the heavens, as though seeking divine guid-ance. 'You place yourself in the power of one of the most notorious rakes in England, and you call it luck!'

Georgiana's amusement at the Dowager's outrage died in an instant, and she stared gravely across at the lady whom she had always held in high regard. 'Ma'am, much of what is said about Viscount Fincham, in my opinion, is conjecture, based on nothing more than scurrilous gossip circulated by those who ought to know better. He keeps a mis-tress, it is true.' She shrugged, attempting to appear indifferent to the fact. 'But then, what wealthy bach-elor does not?'

'That is true enough, I suppose,' the Dowager acknowledged fair-mindedly. 'We must just give thanks to the Good Lord that Fincham never dis-covered your true sex.'

'I rather fancy he did know, ma'am,' Georgiana didn't hesitate to enlighten her. 'In fact, I'm cer-tain of it!'

'Then it's a wonder you retained your virtue that first night under his roof!' the Dowager retorted.

A rather embarrassing memory, quite unbidden, returned to add extra colour to delicate cheeks.

'Apart from—er—just one occasion, he behaved towards me with the utmost propriety, much better than I deserved, considering I attempted to conceal so much from him. He was kindness itself for the most part and treated me like…well, I can only describe it as some troublesome younger sibling.'

The Dowager shook her head, seemingly having difficulty in coming to terms with what she was being told. Then she said, 'But, child, what on earth possessed you to remain under his roof when you discovered he was none other than one of those who could well be responsible for your godfather's death?'

Yes, why had she? Rising to her feet, Georgiana went across to the window, and stared down absently at the traffic making its way along the fashionable Bath Street. Had she even then, after having known him for so short a time, already fallen victim to a sardonic gentleman's irresistible charm? She had finally been obliged to acknowledge her feelings after spending that unforgettable morning with him by the trout stream. Had the truth been known, that was the reason why she had taken darling Ronan out for that last walk. She had been determined to acknowledge both the depth of her feelings and the course of action she must take in order to conceal them.

She couldn't suppress a wry smile. Perhaps it had been Providence that had decreed she should come upon the daughters of Lord Fincham's nearest neighbour that day. At least the incident in the home wood had given her the excuse she needed to flee Fincham Park and its all-too-captivating master. She might not have left that enchanting ancestral mansion heart-whole, but at least she had possessed strength of character enough not to allow that most tender of organs to rule her head. She could only pray that same fortitude would see her through what was likely to be very desolate times ahead.

'Because by that time, in my heart of hearts, ma'am, I knew he could never be involved,' she at last revealed. 'I'm not so foolish as to suppose that one wouldn't glimpse a darker side to his nature if one was ever imprudent enough to cross him. That said, he is an honourable man and one who would never lend himself to such a dastardly venture as committing murder for financial gain.' She shrugged. 'Besides, he has absolutely no reason to do so. He's a wealthy man, remember?'

The Dowager acknowledged this as well. 'But do not forget, child, there is, I believe I'm right in saying, a reckless streak in his nature. I believe also that he too has been known to wager large sums on games of chance. Furthermore, it is common knowledge that he went over to France at the height of the Terror in order to rescue someone or other. Which goes to prove, does it not, that he's quite willing to take grave risks?'

Although she felt obliged to agree with this, Georgiana genuinely believed they should concentrate on the other three, and didn't hesitate to say so. 'What do you know of them, ma'am?'

'Very little, I'm afraid. I know of them, naturally. Sir Willoughby Trent is little more than a middle-aged fribble, who has a penchant for collecting items of great beauty. I believe he did marry some years ago, but I have no knowledge of what became of his wife, or whether or not she is still alive. Lord Rupert Gyles is a renowned gamester and a bachelor, and dependent on his brother, for the most part, for his livelihood. And as for Chard—he married a wealthy cit's daughter some half a dozen or so years ago and is able to maintain a fine country property in Kent. I dare say my good friend Lady Pickering will be able to furnish me with more up-to-date snippets about them all when I remove to the capital in the spring.'

'You've decided on a Season in town, then, ma'am?' Georgiana enquired, thinking a second sojourn in the capital might prove invaluable in discovering more about the three suspects.

'Certainly. I must honour my obligations where my grandchildren are concerned. Richard, thankfully, will remain safely at Eton for a further year, before going on to Oxford. And Sophia, now, is quite looking forward to the prospect of a London Season. These past weeks in Bath have done us both the world of good, even though we have socialised very little. By next April, of course, our year of mourning will be at an end.' Raising her head, she stared fixedly at the slender figure by the window. 'Life goes on Georgiana. I lost a son and you a very loving godfather. But we cannot mourn for ever. My only fear is that Fincham, no fool, will more than likely recognise you.'

'What has that to say to anything, ma'am?' Genuinely bewildered, Georgiana returned to her seat by the hearth. 'Comfortably circumstanced though I am, I couldn't possibly afford to move in his exalted circles. Our paths are never likely to cross again.'

'I'm afraid they are,' the Dowager countered. 'I have not mentioned this before, because I knew you were far too upset by your godfather's tragic death to consider any form of enjoyment. But the fact is, my dear child, he made further provisions for you in his will. He set money aside so that you might enjoy a Season in town, and also provided you with a dowry. It is nothing when compared to Sophia's, of course, but it is not to be sneezed at.'

Dark blue eyes misted over with unshed tears. 'He did that for me?'

'He loved you, child. He could not have loved you more had you been his own flesh and blood.' The Dowager opened her mouth as though to utter something further, and then, seemingly, thought better of it and shook her head gravely, before adding a moment later, 'He wanted you to have the opportunity of meeting some fine young gentleman. It was his dearest wish that you should accompany Sophia for the whole Season. You would disappoint her hugely if you refuse. She looks upon you as a sister, as you well know.'

'Then, of course, I shall be only too happy to bear her company, ma'am,' Georgiana assured her. 'Besides, it will offer me the golden opportunity to find out more about those three suspects.'

'Absolutely not!' The determination in the elderly lady's voice was unmistakable. 'You have done more than enough. I shall pass on what you've discovered to Bow Street.'

'Engaging the services of the Runners at this stage might be a grave mistake,' Georgiana countered, never having been afraid to speak her mind in front of the formidable Dowager. 'After all, the last thing we want is to alert any one of them to the fact that he is a possible suspect. No, I think you should wait until we've managed to uncover more…have definite proof of the identity of the one responsible.'

'If you imagine I shall countenance your further involvement in this matter, after what you have revealed today, you may think again, child! You've already risked your life, not to mention your reputation.'

'I wasn't thinking of involving myself again at this juncture, ma'am. I was thinking, rather, of engaging my darling Digby's help. If I hadn't been such a complete idiot, I would have taken him with me, not left him kicking his heels back home in Gloucestershire. As things turned out he would have been invaluable.'

'Your manservant, child…?' The Dowager was clearly perplexed. 'But what possible use could he have been?'

'He was born and bred in the capital, ma'am,'

Georgiana reminded her. 'He spent the first eighteen years of his life there, striving to keep alive in the most lawless areas of the city. He was conscripted into the army, after being convicted of stealing. It was either that, or Newgate and possibly the hangman's rope.'

'Heavens above!' the Dowager murmured faintly. 'What on earth possessed your late grandfather to employ such a fellow?'

'You know why, ma'am,' Georgiana responded, amused by this show of staunch disapproval, for she well knew that little shocked the Dowager nowadays. 'He was with Papa in America. He took it upon himself to return several of my father's possessions personally. Grandpapa was so moved by the unselfish gesture that he instantly offered him employment at the vicarage. Digby has never been in any trouble since. Besides which, he is touchingly devoted to me.'

'That is true enough,' the Dowager conceded. 'But what on earth do you imagine he could do? He hasn't been back to London in over twenty years.'

'I know that, ma'am. But I'm sure if he did go back it wouldn't take him long to familiarise himself with his old haunts. He might even be lucky enough to meet up with one or two acquaintances of bygone years.'

'Pray continue, child,' her ladyship prompted, when Georgiana, in a brown study, stared silently down at the empty hearth. 'You are beginning to interest me vastly.'

'Whoever stole the Grenville diamonds had to dispose of them somehow. No reputable jeweller in the capital would have touched them. The set was too well known, too easily recognised. Which leaves us with two distinct possibilities—either they were passed on to some disreputable dealer in stolen goods who possibly had the stones made up in a different setting or they were smuggled abroad.'

The Dowager appeared to consider. 'Yes,' she finally agreed, 'I believe you may have hit upon something there, my dear. So what do you propose we should do?'

'Continue to leave the authorities out of it, at least for the time being. When we return to Gloucestershire at the end of the week, I shall take Digby into my confidence. Then, if he thinks he might be of help, we'll dispatch him off to London as soon as maybe.' Georgiana again considered for a moment, before adding, 'Of course, the majority of the ton has left the capital for the country. But I discovered, only a few days ago, that Lady Smethurst's famous pearls were purloined whilst she was travelling the King's highway. Fortunately no one was hurt that time. Evidently, unlike the late Earl, no one travelling in the carriage put up any form of resistance. Perhaps Digby can discover something about the pearls—what may have become of them. He'll need to remain in the capital for some weeks, because I'd rather like him there when the Little Season begins in the autumn, especially if he has managed to uncover something of interest, and the suspects happen to have returned.'

'In that case send him to me and I shall ensure he has sufficient funds before he leaves.' The Dowager leaned back in her chair, at last appearing reasonably well pleased; until, that is, a deep frown added further lines to her forehead. 'That only leaves me with you to consider,' she added, fixing her gaze on the short, silky black locks. 'Your poor hair will have grown, of course, by the spring. But will that be enough?'

'Do not concern yourself, dear ma'am,' Georgiana responded, easily following the Dowager's train of thought. 'By springtime most people will have forgotten that Fincham ever had a page… Only the

Viscount himself might possibly have remembered…
and he, I feel certain, will never betray me.'

'I sincerely hope your evident high opinion of him
is not misplaced, child.'


'Oh, isn't this exciting, Georgie!' Lady Sophia exclaimed, helping to unpack the stack of boxes which
had arrived from various milliners and mantua-
makers that very morning. 'Now we shall both be
dressed in the height of fashion for Lady Pickering's
party tomorrow night, and our very own ball on
Friday.'

'Your ball, Sophie,' Georgiana corrected. 'At
three-and-twenty I'm well past the age for embark-
ing on a come-out. I'm here simply because your
father wished it. I fully intend to sit by the wall with
all the other slowly fading blooms and revel in your
success.'

'Faded bloom, indeed!' Sophia scoffed. 'You'll
never be a wallflower, Georgie. You're far too lovely.
What's more, no one would ever suppose you're that
old. I swear in some lights you look little older than
I do!'

'It's lucky for you, Sophie, that I happen to know
there's not an ounce of spite in you anywhere, otherwise I'd be tempted to box your ears for that

backhanded compliment,' Georgiana declared, half-laughing. 'But seriously,' she added, plumping herself down on to the bed, smile fading, 'I didn't come here with the intention of finding a husband.'

Unbidden, a pair of frighteningly penetrating dark eyes, set in a ruggedly masculine face, appeared in her mind's eye yet again to evoke that painful longing that had rarely left her during many long and lonely months. 'You see, Sophie, I do not believe I shall ever meet anyone to equal the very particular gentleman of my...of my dreams.'

Sophia clapped her hands delightedly, displaying all the enthusiasm of youth. 'Oh, is he some imaginary knight in shining armour—tall and dark and handsome?'

Georgiana considered for a moment 'You're two parts right, at any rate—he's definitely tall and dark. But by no stretch of the imagination would one consider him a Sir Galahad, although one never knows just how he might react in certain situations. He doesn't lack for courage, that's for sure.' She stared for a moment at one ornately carved bedpost. 'So long as he doesn't turn out to be my particular nemesis.'

Sophia, all at once, looked doubtful. 'I shouldn't like to meet anyone like that,' she declared. 'He sounds frightening, not a very personable gentleman at all.'

'Oh, he can be very agreeable when the mood takes him,' Georgiana assured her. Then, noticing she was being regarded with keen interest, hurriedly got to her feet to continue the unpacking.

Sophia, however, was not to be so easily diverted. 'You've met him already!' she divined triumphantly.

Georgiana raised her shoulders, desperately striving to appear nonchalant. 'And where, pray, do you suppose I met my Sir Galahad? Back home you're acquainted with most everyone I know. Do you know of anyone who fits the description? I most certainly do not.'

'True,' Sophia acknowledged, with a speculative glint in her eyes. 'But what about that time last year when you travelled to Bath with Grandmama and me, and then disappeared for those few weeks?'

'You know full well I took the opportunity to stay with my cousin and her family near Oxford. It was just unfortunate I wasn't able to shake off that terrible chill whilst there, and that foolish practitioner insisted I cut my hair.'

Georgiana hated lying to the girl whom she looked upon as a young sister, but felt she had no choice.

Sophia and her younger brother Richard were not privy to all the details surrounding their father's death, and their grandmother wished it to remain that way, at least for the present.

'So I cannot imagine how you suppose I became acquainted with the gentleman of my dreams. I'm not in the habit of receiving members of the opposite sex in my bedchamber. So pray do not attempt to spread such a rumour abroad. I do not wish to become the butt of the gossips' ill humour.'

It was at this point that both young women realised they were no longer alone in the room. Just how long the Dowager had been standing by the door was impossible to judge. All the same, her face wore an extremely thoughtful expression, as though something had displeased her.

'Leave this now, my dears,' she said. 'The maids will finish the unpacking. The dancing master has arrived, Sophia, and awaits you in the ballroom. Georgiana, be good enough to accompany me to my private apartments before joining the lesson. There is something I must discuss with you, child. Unfortunately it can wait no longer.'

More intrigued than anything else, Georgiana obliged her ladyship by accompanying her to her private little sanctum further along the passageway.

That something was troubling the elderly lady deeply was obvious. She knew the Dowager had received a visit from Lady Pickering that morning, and couldn't help wondering whether it was the visitor who had brought some disturbing tidings.

Although they had refrained from accepting any evening engagements thus far, they had been in London nearly a whole month and had been out and about visiting the fashionable shops, and paying morning calls on certain of the Dowager's close friends. A disturbing possibility therefore quickly occurred for the Dowager's present melancholy mood.

'Ma'am, clearly you are troubled over something,' she ventured, when all her ladyship did was to stare down broodingly at the coals burning in the hearth. 'I trust your good friend Lady Pickering was not the bearer of bad news?'

There was no response.

'Have I had the misfortune to have been recognised by someone already?'

The sigh that followed the question was clearly audible. 'If only it were that!'

Very slowly the Dowager raised her head to stare across the hearth. Suddenly she appeared very weary and considerably older than her years. 'Child,' she began softly, 'has it never occurred to you to wonder just why my son loved you as though you were his own daughter, not merely his godchild?'

Georgiana wished with all her heart that she could dismiss it as errant nonsense, but she was too honest a person even to attempt to try. Recollections of half-whispered words, rumours and lingering looks of affection that had faded since her mother's demise some six years before returned with a vengeance.

'I know the late Earl and my mother were once engaged to be married, and that my mother broke off the engagement when your eldest son died and my godfather became heir. She told me once she felt unequal to take on the duties of a countess, and so for the good of all concerned she broke off the engagement to enable my godfather to marry someone more suitable.'

The Dowager gave vent to a mirthless cackle. 'Told you that, did she? Dear Frances, it would seem, remained loyal to me to the end,' the Dowager revealed, an unmistakable catch in her voice.

'Ma'am, I do not perfectly understand what you are trying to tell me.'

'No, child, I know you do not, and it is high time you knew all… It might help you to understand,

and to deal with a certain unfortunate matter that has arisen.'

With the aid of her ebony stick the Dowager rose to her feet and went to stand by the window. 'My son loved you, child, just as he always loved your mother. He never ceased to love her. And it is to my everlasting shame, everlasting self-reproach, that I succeeded in persuading her to break off the engagement so that my son could marry Matilda Castleford, a woman he came to hold in high regard until the day she died, but never truly loved.'

Although she was naturally shocked to learn this, Georgiana was able to say with absolute conviction, 'My mother must have understood your reasons, ma'am, for I never once heard her utter a word against you...not ever.'

'No, dear God, I only wish she had!' Once again there was a betraying tremor in the Dowager's voice. 'I adored your mother,' she admitted, breaking the short silence. 'Frances was a lovely girl. She and William were close as children, and that bond between them was never broken. Your mother was a member of an old and respected family. As you are well aware, your late grandfather was the youngest son of Lord Brent. Consequently, she would have made my younger son a suitable wife. I was guilty of encouraging their close association; until, that is, William's elder brother died so unexpectedly and he became heir. My husband's reckless gaming in later life left the family with a mountain of debts. William had to marry an heiress... And that was the one thing your dear mother was not. She was raised in comfort at the vicarage, not luxury. She had no dowry to speak of.'

Raising her eyes from the imaginary spot on the carpet, the Dowager discovered Georgiana gnawing at her bottom lip, a sure indication that what she had learned had genuinely distressed her. 'My dear, I wish I could have spared you this, but I dare not. And that is why I must ask you yet again—did you never wonder why my son took such a keen interest in you? Why he chose to spend so much time in your company? Why, when your grandfather died, he moved you into one of the houses on the estate and provided you with a suitable companion, so that you might reside there quite independently?'

'Ma'am, I would need to be a halfwit not to know what you're hinting at,' Georgina responded in a calm and dignified manner that concealed quite beautifully her rising anger. 'But even to suggest such a thing is to discredit my mother, who is no longer here to defend her good name, and makes a figure of ridicule of my late father, a brave man who gave his life in the service of his country, not to mention dishonours the memory of your own son.'

'Believe me, the last thing I should wish to do is dishonour anyone, least of all you,' the Dowager quickly admitted. 'I have watched you grow over the years into the image of your lovely mother. You have been blessed to inherit many of her fine qualities. Furthermore, you do not lack for courage or sense. Whether these traits were inherited from the late Colonel George Grey or the late Earl matters little. It is how people have interpreted my son's regard for you. And it is those whom he possibly offended, and who still bear a grudge against him, who are intent on besmirching his memory.'

All Georgiana's anger disappeared in an instant and she felt moved by the Dowager's obvious concern. 'Oh, I think I begin to understand,' she revealed. 'Unless I much mistake the matter, Lady Pickering came here to warn you of a rumour circulating about me being the late Earl's bastard.'

The Dowager didn't attempt to deny it. 'Believe me, child, I would be proud to call you granddaughter, but I truly do not happen to believe we are related by blood. Your mother was the most honourable woman. I sincerely believe she named you after your father, but it doesn't matter what I believe. None the less, I shouldn't want you to be distressed by some wicked gossip's acid tongue, so shall quite understand if you should wish to return to the country.'

Smiling faintly, Georgiana rose to her feet. 'I am my father's daughter and shall not turn tail and run at the first sign of adversity. Rumours cannot harm me, your ladyship. Firstly, because I know they are untrue; and, secondly, because I am not here to find a husband. I am here to discover who killed a man I loved and respected and who stood in place of a father.'

No one could have mistaken the respect shining in the Dowager's eyes. 'There is one other thing you should know, my dear child,' she announced, arresting Georgiana's progress across to the door. 'Apparently, Viscount Fincham has arrived in town and Lady Pickering has every expectation of seeing him at her party tomorrow night.'

Only for a second or two did Georgiana's fingers tremble as she reached for the handle of the door. 'In that case, ma'am, I'd best not tarry in joining Sophia in the ballroom. I must master all the dances, lest he should ask me to stand up with him.'

The instant she had closed the door quietly behind her, Georgiana released her breath in a long sigh. All at once her heart was racing and her palms felt sticky. The day she had longed for and dreaded by turns had at last arrived! With all her heart she longed to set eyes on that unforgettable, sardonic countenance again. Yet she couldn't suppress a frisson of fear at his possible reaction, for she didn't doubt for a moment that he would recognise her.

Georgiana felt as nervous as Sophia as they left the mansion that evening, and travelled the short distance to Lady Pickering's fashionable London residence to enjoy their first social engagement of the Season. No expense had been spared and they were both dressed in those high-waisted gowns that had become so fashionable and were admirably well suited to their trim figures. The Dowager had engaged the services of an experienced abigail whose skill at dressing hair had resulted in Georgiana's glossy black tresses being artistically arranged in a Grecian style, with curling wisps feathering her cheeks. Sophia's fair locks had been arranged in a simpler style that more suited her tender years, as did the pastel shade of her charming gown. Georgiana, being some five years her senior, had been inclined to choose darker shades for most of her dresses and that evening had selected to wear an amber silk creation for her first real venture into London's polite society.

One quick glance around Lady Pickering's elegant drawing room was enough to assure Georgiana that Viscount Fincham was not there. Taller than average height, he always stood out in a crowd. She didn't know whether to feel relieved or disappointed not to find him there, but was hardly given time to consider her contrasting feelings. No sooner had she and Sophia seated themselves against a wall than two personable young gentlemen requested their hands for the first set of country dances taking place in an adjoining salon. Sophia didn't attempt to hide her delight; Georgiana was somewhat less gratified, though she did her utmost to conceal the fact.

The truth of the matter was she had grown accustomed over the years to receiving admiring glances from members of the opposite sex. Times without number she'd heard herself being compared to her mother, and although it had always pleased her to think she had inherited her mother's good looks, she didn't believe she was in the least vain. In fact, she liked to think the opposite was true. Although she was grateful to Mother Nature for favouring her with a better-than-average countenance, she much preferred to be with people who took little notice of her fine looks. Her godfather had been just such a one, and so was her ever-loyal servant, Digby. Then, of course, Lord Fincham had very much fallen into this same category. More often than not he had treated her as though she had been some troublesome urchin. And she had loved the novelty of it all!

Almost at the very moment the memory drifted into her mind, Georgiana felt a strange tremor ripple through her and raised her eyes to discover a tall gentleman standing in the doorway leading to the larger salon, staring casually about the room through his quizzing-glass. Dressed in the impeccable style advocated by George Brummell himself, and with black hair cropped short and artistically arranged in the windswept look, he seemed to make nearly all the other gentlemen present appear slightly ill groomed in comparison.

So striking was the change in appearance that Georgiana didn't immediately appreciate precisely who it was. It was only when stark recognition on his own part replaced affectation, and the quizzing-glass fell from his fingers, and those unforgettable dark eyes stared fixedly in her direction, did she know for sure. Then she very nearly forgot the movements of the dance, and almost disgraced herself by missing a step, when his heavy lids lowered and a look of such contempt took possession of those rugged features, a moment before he swung round on his heels and walked away.

Resisting the temptation to follow, Georgiana somehow managed to complete the dance, before rushing back into the drawing room, only to find it devoid of the one person she most wished to see.

'Well, upon my word!' Lady Pickering declared, plumping herself down beside her friend the Dowager, just as Georgiana had returned to her ladyship's side. 'Although I'd heard rumours that Viscount Fincham's behaviour had become increasingly eccentric of late, I couldn't quite bring myself to believe it. His manners have always been impeccable and his address second to none. Yet, this evening he arrives here graciously suggesting he's looking forward to enjoying this, his first engagement of the Season, and then five minutes later is taking his leave in the most brusque manner possible, declaring he's recalled an urgent appointment he simply must keep.'

'How very fortunate that he did recall the appointment,' the Dowager opined, when her friend had hurriedly departed to greet some late arrivals. 'I didn't even know he was here.'

'Oh, he was here right enough, ma'am.' Georgiana assured her softly. 'And I strongly suspect he left because he recognised me.' She took a moment to contemplate the delicately painted figures on her fan. 'It would seem my worse fears have been realised  My Sir Galahad has become my nemesis. Now it only remains to be seen just how he will extract retribution.'

# Chapter Seven

'Well, Miss Georgie, there's little more we can do now, 'cept wait and see what 'appens. It was the greatest bit of good fortune I came across Jem Fisher. As I said months back, after I'd managed to track 'im down after all these years, 'e ain't no saint, but 'e ain't no out-and-out rogue neither. Jem and 'is sons will keep their eyes and ears open. Not much goes on in that part of town that they don't get to know about sooner or later.'

Although at this time of day the park was virtually deserted, Georgiana remained well clear of the more popular paths in order to enjoy complete privacy with her loyal servant of long standing.

'You've done well, Digby. At last we can attempt to follow the movements of each of the three suspects. What else was your good friend Master Fisher able to tell you yesterday?'

'As you can imagine, miss, not much 'as been

going on since the autumn. But 'e seems sure them there pearls, stolen last summer, didn't pass through the 'ands of the usual receivers, thems that deals in precious stones. 'E's 'eard of some Frenchie taking gems out of the country. What's more 'e's almost sure, now, stolen goods 'ave been passed on at some gaming 'ouse.'

When Digby went on to divulge the establishment's precise location, Georgiana almost stopped dead in her tracks. 'Good Lord! What a coincidence! I visited that very place myself once.'

Digby appeared anything but pleased to learn this. 'Lord, Miss Georgie! You'll be the death o' me, so you will! A lady like yourself in a place like that—it don't bear thinking on.'

'I told you I was in disguise,' she reminded him, completely unabashed by this, a further show of disapproval at her escapade of the previous year. 'Besides which, Lord Fincham was with me, so I was perfectly safe. In fact, it was on that occasion we were set upon by footpads.'

'Don't tell me n'more, miss, m'poor ticker won't stand it!' Digby implored.

He was the only other person in whom Georgiana had confided. It went without saying that, because he had designated himself the role of her protector down the years, he, like the Dowager Countess, hadn't been at all happy about her adventures last summer. Thankfully his staunch disapproval hadn't deterred him from assisting in her endeavours, and his visit to the metropolis the previous autumn was now beginning to show results.

'So, how is the booty getting into the hands of this Frenchman, do you suppose? Is he a regular visitor to the gaming house?'

'Jem Fisher don't seem to think so, no. Reckons 'tis one of the flunkies by name of Arthur Tate that works there that passes on the jewels to this 'ere Frenchie. Easiest thing in the world, miss, for one of the visitors to 'and over his coat, like, and for Tate to remove whatever's in the pocket. Seemingly on two or three occasions during the past eighteen months or so Tate's been spreading his blunt about quite freely.'

'His share of the ill-gotten gains, no doubt.' Georgiana nodded. 'Yes, it would seem Master Tate requires watching also.'

'Don't you trouble, miss. 'Tis all taken care of. As soon as there's another robbery, they'll be someone watching 'im closely too.'

'Although it's a terrible thing, sadly, that's what we must wait for,' Georgiana agreed, a moment before she detected some loud and excited barking and turned to discover a crossbred pointer emerging from a clump of bushes, before gambolling across the grass towards her.

Not considering her attire for a second, she uttered a spontaneous squeal of recognition and dropped to her knees. Digby, who had raised his walking-stick in order to ward off the four-legged interloper, instinctively lowered it again, as the dog, tail wagging furiously, bounded into Miss Grey's welcoming arms.

It took Georgiana a few moments to calm Ronan's enthusiasm sufficiently for her to rise to her feet. It was only then that she caught sight of the tall, impeccably attired figure of none other than Ronan's master striding down the path towards her, when it was far too late to attempt to avoid the encounter. Her spirits plummeted in an instant. One glance at that forbidding countenance was sufficient to warn her he was anything but pleased by her unexpected presence in the park at this early hour.

Calling Ronan to heel sharply, he at least paid her the common courtesy of doffing his hat as he approached. 'My apologies, ma'am, for my dog's conduct. He isn't a pure-bred specimen and, as such, behaves abominably on occasions. Breeding always will out, will it not?' And with that verbal slap in the face he walked on, without so much as a backward glance.

'Mistress, that were never...?'

'I'm afraid so, Digby. That is none other than Viscount Fincham, the gentleman who, believe it or not, took such great care of me during my time in London last year.'

Swinging round, Georgiana headed back along the path, making a beeline for the nearest park exit in order to prevent a further encounter with the Viscount. She felt both angry and hurt by his attitude, and so frustrated because she couldn't explain her past behaviour; not that she supposed for a moment he would offer an opportunity for her to do so in his present frame of mind.

'I can only imagine, Digby, that he supposes I was making a May-game of him. Naturally he's experiencing a degree of hurt pride, and intends to make me suffer in return.'

The servant looked at her closely, easily detecting the sadness she made no attempt to disguise. 'Well, mistress, at least he's not tried to ruin your reputation by revealing what he knows about you.'

'I never for a moment supposed he'd do that,' she returned. 'I could almost wish he would, though.

Anything would be better than the icy-cool disdain he seems intent on showing me now. I don't know how much of it I can take. I'm only flesh and blood, after all, and if he pushes me too far…'

Although it was impossible to forget the chance encounter with the Viscount, thankfully it didn't remain long in the forefront of her mind after Georgiana had returned to the house. No sooner had she stepped into the hall than she was informed the Dowager wished to see her.

Only taking the time to change out of her slightly soiled walking dress, she went along to her ladyship's private apartments, where the latest edition of the Morning Post was thrust before her and a thin, arthritic finger was indicating the relevant column.

'What we've been waiting for has happened at last!' her ladyship declared almost triumphantly. 'Lady Chalmondley, it would appear, has been relieved of her emeralds whilst travelling from her home in Kent. Worth a king's ransom, according to the article, there.'

'Kent…?' Georgiana echoed, after reading the piece for herself. 'Doesn't one of our suspects hail from that part of the country, ma'am?'

'Yes, Chard. But he's hardly likely to commit an offence so close to home, surely?'

Georgiana wasn't so sure. 'I doubt very much he's involved in the robberies himself. Digby informs me Chard arrived in town early, in the middle of March, and this robbery, according to the paper, took place last week. Of course, that doesn't mean he doesn't organise the thefts and arrange the disposal of the jewels, once purloined. Furthermore, if he just happens to be well acquainted with Lady Chalmondley, he would perhaps have known of her intention to travel with the emeralds, and maybe even when she intended to make the trip.'

She went across to the door, taking the newspaper with her. 'I'd best let Digby know about this right away. Perhaps we'll see some action now.'

'Before you go, dear,' the Dowager said, delaying Georgiana's departure from the room, 'are you sure you wish to forgo the party this evening? Sophia is keen to go and Lady Pickering has very kindly agreed to chaperon her in my stead. She'd be only too delighted to take care of you also.'

'Ah, but could she protect me from Fincham's icy-cool disdain, if he should happen to attend?' She smiled in spite of the fact that the attitude he seemed intent on adopting towards her couldn't possibly have distressed her more. 'No, ma'am, I should much rather bear you company here this evening and build up some impenetrable defences before Friday, lest he should take it into his head to extract further revenge and attend Sophia's ball.'

The Dowager's dark eyes narrowed, much as Viscount Fincham's tended to do on occasions. 'I sincerely trust, Georgiana, that you have not foolishly developed a tendre for that particular gentleman.'

'Yes, folly indeed, ma'am,' she was obliged to acknowledge, 'especially after our brief encounter in the park earlier today, when he made his own opinion of me perfectly plain. From what little he did say, I gained the distinct impression the rumour concerning me must have reached his ears. Foolishly, perhaps, my high opinion of him remains unchanged.'

Although she tried desperately to get her feelings well under control during the next couple of days, Georgiana fervently hoped, as she stood dutifully beside the Dowager Countess on Friday evening, greeting the guests, that the Viscount wouldn't put in an appearance, especially as he had failed to respond to the invitation sent the month before.

After spending over an hour greeting the cream

of society, she left her ladyship to welcome any late arrivals, and sought out Lady Pickering, firmly believing her prayers had been answered.

'Ah, my dear Georgiana! Yes, come and sit beside me for a while. You deserve a rest. You have been supporting my dear friend quite wonderfully well. How is the dear Dowager bearing up?'

'She's a little tired, ma'am, but determined to do her duty by doing everything within her power to ensure Sophie's come out is a success.'

'And yours, too, my dear.'

'I'm here merely because my godfather wished it,' Georgiana assured her. 'I have no expectation of making a suitable match. And, in truth, I have no real desire to do so. Which, in the circumstances,' she added, recalling clearly the insult she had received in the park earlier that week, 'is perhaps just as well.'

'My dear girl, you must not take any notice of any silly, spiteful rumours circulating. It will not be too long before something else reaches the tattle-mongers' ears, and the piece of nonsense concerning you is forgotten,' Lady Pickering assured her, having considered what might be behind her young companion's negative attitude to marriage.

Georgiana chose not to enlighten her that it was

only one gentleman's good opinion that really mattered to her. Instead, she decided to take full advantage of this little tête-à-tête with one of society's recognised leading hostesses by attempting to discover more about one guest in particular. So as not to arouse any suspicion, she began by enquiring about suitable candidates for Sophia's hand, before finally drawing attention to that certain gentleman who had, thankfully, quite failed to recognise her when she had greeted him earlier and who was of most interest to her.

'I hardly think Lord Rupert Gyles could be considered a suitable candidate for Sophia's hand, my dear,' she said, after the gentleman in question had been pointed out. 'He's a little too old for one thing. Definitely the wrong side of five-and-thirty. Besides, there's no reason why Sophia must choose a husband from this year's crop. She's only just turned eighteen and would much prefer a younger gentleman, I'm sure.'

'Perhaps, but Lord Rupert would be considered eligible, surely?' Georgiana persisted, determined to keep Lady Pickering's attention focused on that particular gentleman so that she might discover more about him, for she was well aware that the

Dowager, thus far, had had little opportunity to do so. 'He is the Duke of Merton's brother, after all.'

'True,' Lady Pickering conceded, before adding, 'But not his heir, remember. Merton has a son. Apart from which Lord Rupert is an inveterate gambler. Merton makes him an allowance, of course. But even so, it is a wonder how he's managed to keep the duns from his door. He's been known to lose hundreds in a night's sitting and not so much as bat an eyelid.'

Lady Pickering's attention was captured by a new arrival. 'Ah! Now here is someone far more eligible. Or at least he would be if he hadn't earned himself the reputation of being a hardened cynic where the fair sex is concerned.'

Georgiana glanced across at the door in time to witness the Dowager greeting the two late arrivals, and only just succeeded in suppressing a squeal of vexation. Not only had Lord Fincham, perversely, decided to attend himself, he had also dragged his good friend Charles Gingham along to bear him company. This, she accepted at once, could prove dangerous indeed. Mr Gingham was one of the few people who might so easily recognise her, and if the Viscount had not already prepared him…?

For a moment or two she toyed with the notion

of fleeing the ballroom by way of the French windows, but curbed it. Surely it was better to brazen it out now, she reasoned, rather than attempt to avoid future encounters with his lordship's close friend?

While she was still debating on which course of action to take, the set of country dances came to an end and Sophia decided the matter by coming over to her side.

'What a charming gentleman Mr Beresford is, Georgie. So very handsome. I do much prefer gentleman with blond locks!'

'Yes, I can perfectly understand the preference,' Georgiana responded, tongue-in-cheek. 'I rather fancy I'm rapidly going off gentlemen with my particular coloured hair.'

'If that is so, pray refrain from revealing it, my dear child!' Lady Pickering advised, suddenly appearing a little flustered. 'For there is just such a one approaching.'

Georgiana didn't need to turn her head; she knew it could only be Fincham. Out of the corner of her eye she saw his companion momentarily check in his approach and could almost hear his faint gasp of astonished recognition. Yet, when he stood before her, taking her hand briefly in his own, as Lady Pickering performed the introductions, he blessedly betrayed not a sign of ever having met her before, and neither, which came as no surprise to Georgiana whatsoever, did his lordship.

After the coolest of nods in acknowledgement of her presence, he engaged a suddenly overawed Sophia in conversation before requesting her hand for a set of country dances. Then, after exchanging a few pleasantries with Lady Pickering, he sauntered away without having exchanged so much as a single word with Georgiana.

'Might I have the honour of partnering you a little later in the evening, Miss Grey?' Charles Gingham asked, thereby successfully putting an end to the faintly embarrassing silence that had ensued after his lordship's rather abrupt departure, and although she responded graciously enough, she felt she would attain scant pleasure from the exercise.

Once again the Viscount had successfully put a damper on the evening as far as Georgiana was concerned. Yet stubborn pride prevented her from revealing the fact. Her first impulse was to accept every invitation to step on to the dance floor in an attempt to appear joyously unconcerned by his cool indifference, but then she thought better of that course of action. Lord Fincham was far too astute and would see through feigned gaiety in a trice.

So, instead, she decided to occupy her mind and her time by being of the most help to the Dowager Countess.

Consequently, she left Sophia in Lady Pickering's sole care and returned to the entrance of the ballroom to bear her ladyship company until the Dowager decided it was time to mingle with her guests. Georgiana then set herself the task of finding partners for those younger females present who seemed destined not to be asked to show their skill on the dance floor. She was content enough, too, to wander about the ballroom spending time conversing with those who preferred not to dance, whilst all the time maintaining a discreet distance from Viscount Fincham. She also deliberately avoided following him with her eyes as much as possible. Even so, she was aware when he took to the floor with Sophia and happened to glimpse also his entrance into the room set out for cards.

In many ways it was a relief to see him depart, and she didn't waste the opportunity to step out on to the terrace to have a moment alone with her thoughts and also attempt to replenish those dwindling stocks of fortitude that had become sadly depleted that evening.

Placing her hands on the stone balustrade, she

peered down at the darkened garden and smiled in spite of the fact that the aspect was as gloomy as her one and only Season was turning out to be. Not that she could totally blame Lord Fincham for the attitude he was adopting towards her. Had their roles been reversed she would have felt hurt and angry had someone taken flagrant advantage of her hospitality, and then just left without so much as a by your leave. But what could she do to rectify matters? Frustratingly there was nothing she could do without revealing the reason behind her scandalous behaviour the year before. And that was precisely what it had been, she was at last obliged to acknowledge. If Lord Fincham had exposed her, her reputation would have been in tatters.

The sound of a footfall behind her successfully broke into her unpleasant reflections and she swung round to discover none other than the Viscount's close friend stepping out on to the terrace. Immensely relieved though she was that Lord Fincham was not with him, given the choice she would have much preferred to have remained on her own.

None the less, she did her utmost to hide this fact behind a smile as she said, 'Have you come in search of me, sir, to remind me of our dance?'

Charles moved slowly towards her, his eyes

scanning her delicate features intently. Seemingly, even in the poor light, he detected something in her demeanour to suggest that what she craved most of all was solitude. 'Indeed, it was, Miss Grey. There is a set just forming. But if you'd prefer to remain out here, I shall not continue to disturb your peace and quiet.'

'I should prefer to remain here, sir,' she was honest enough to admit. 'But pray do not feel your company is not welcome,' she added, moved by his solicitude. Earlier in the evening, when they had been introduced, she had sensed an awkwardness in him, as though embarrassed by the situation and his friend's attitude. 'It offers me the opportunity to sincerely thank you for not revealing the fact that we have met before.'

His smile was distinctly rueful. 'Well, I cannot deny, Miss Grey, coming face to face with you again was something of a surprise.'

Her sense of humour came to the fore and she gurgled appreciatively. 'Shock,' she corrected, before her smile disappeared and she became serious again. 'He didn't prepare you, did he? He didn't tell you that Georgie Green had returned to town in the guise of a Miss Georgiana Grey? And I cannot help asking myself why not. Was he hoping that you would quench his thirst for revenge by exposing me to the world at large…?' This time her laughter was distinctly mirthless. 'I had thought better of him.'

'It is sometimes difficult, even for me, to know what goes on in that head of his, Miss Grey. All I shall say in his defence is that last year, when you left without warning, he was like…' he shrugged '…like a man possessed. He was almost beside himself with worry. He spent weeks and weeks attempting to find you. He even engaged the services of a private investigator. And all to no avail. You covered your tracks extremely well.'

The fact that she had been so successful brought scant consolation in view of what she had just learned. He must have truly cared to have done all he had in an attempt to locate her whereabouts.

She turned to stare out into the darkened garden again, determined not to give way to the sudden swell of emotion in a bout of tears. 'I did leave him a letter,' she revealed softly. 'Surely he must have received it? I simply couldn't have stayed any longer—he must have realised that himself.' She shook her head, silently cursing herself for every kind of a fool. 'I should never have accompanied him to Fincham Park. I should have left immediately after I had discovered what I came to London to find out.'

Sensing she was being regarded with keen interest, Georgiana turned to see Charles staring at her fixedly. She hadn't intended to divulge anything at all, but now that she had she had no intention of attempting to rectify the blunder.

'Yes, sir, there was a purpose in my outrageous charade. Just as there is a purpose in my being in London now. But to hell with it all!' she cursed in fine Master Green style. 'That doesn't mean I cannot enjoy myself a little from time to time. I do believe the supper dance is about to commence. I should very much like you to partner me, sir, and, if you are not otherwise engaged, to escort me in to supper afterwards.'

'My dear Miss Grey, nothing would give me greater pleasure.'

Lord Fincham, on the other hand, was anything but gratified when he returned to the ballroom to discover his closest friend dancing with the female who had rarely left his thoughts in many a long month. That she performed the steps with inborn grace, coupled with the fact that his friend was clearly delighted to be dancing with possibly the loveliest female present, was scarcely destined to alleviate his ever-increasing taciturn frame of mind. He swore long and hard under his breath, much to the dismay of a middle-aged matron standing nearby, before swinging round on his heels and leaving the ball without informing anyone of his intentions. After successfully hailing a passing hackney carriage, he journeyed straight to his club, where he remained for several hours, before finally returning to Berkeley Square.

A lamp, turned down low, was all that welcomed him into the hall. He had never encouraged his servants to wait up for him, not even his valet. Yet, perversely, even this adherence to his expressed wishes only succeeded in irritating him further, and so he took himself off to his library in order to find solace in the contents of a brandy decanter, only to discover, to his surprise, his good friend awaiting him.

'Good gad! I would have expected you to have sought the comfort of your bed hours ago! You still intend leaving in the morning?'

Smiling enigmatically, Charles assured him this was so, before glancing up at the mantel-clock. 'Though somewhat later than originally planned, I rather fancy.' He waited until the Viscount had collected both decanter and glass and had joined him at the hearth. 'No, I waited up for you in order to satisfy my curiosity. You are one of the last people I would have ever described as either vengeful or petty, so why the deuce didn't you warn me?'

One black brow was raised in a distinctly haughty arch. 'About what, pray?'

'Don't try that tone with me, old chap,' Charles countered, distinctly unimpressed as always whenever the Viscount feigned ignorance. 'What are you about? Is it your intention to punish her?'

This time the Viscount didn't pretend to misunderstand, and for a moment stared, narrow-eyed, down into his glass. 'Do you not think she deserves to be punished for past behaviour?'

'What particular aspects of past behaviour?' Charles once again countered. 'For saving your life, maybe? Or for turning you into a human being again, proving to you that you could still experience those more tender feelings?'

His lordship was on his feet in an instant. 'That's enough, Charles!' he warned. 'I'll admit, I was concerned about her, when she left Fincham Park. More fool me!'

'No, I don't think you were being foolish at all. But I think you're being so now. And cruel, too,

I shall take leave to add. The poor girl's enough to contend with, what with the rumours about her, without having to deal with your…attitude towards her.'

'What rumours?' his lordship demanded, his bewilderment unmistakable.

'Do you mean you haven't heard? Evidently you didn't spend too much time conversing with Lord Rupert this evening. Apparently there's a rumour abroad that she's the late Earl's by-blow. I spent some time after you'd departed conversing with Lady Pickering, and there's no denying Grenville was dashed fond of the chit, absolutely adored her, by all accounts. Apparently he was once engaged to be married to her mother. And once the spiteful tabbies got wind of that… Well, you know what they are.'

After clearly recalling the chance encounter in the park, his lordship released his breath in a string of colourful expletives for a second time that evening. 'I said something to her earlier in the week that I regretted almost directly afterwards,' he explained in response to his friend's startled look. 'It was a needlessly cruel and petty thing to have said, and was uttered in order to cast an aspersion on Ronan's evident affection for her.' He shook his head ruefully.

'After what you've just told me I suspect she must have supposed I'd heard the rumour and was referring to her.'

'That I couldn't say.' Unlike his lordship, Charles was smiling faintly as he rose to his feet. 'But what I can tell you is what you always suspected was right—there was some purpose in her coming to London last year. She admitted as much, though I don't think she intended to tell me. I'll tell you something else—she's here in town for the same purpose now. She's not here to find a husband. I watched her throughout the latter part of the evening. Although she did eventually dance with several young blades, she betrayed not the least interest in any gentleman. No, she's in town for some private purpose of her own.'

The Viscount's shoulders rose in a shrug that might easily have been taken for complete indifference by someone who didn't know him well. He even sounded dispassionate as he said, 'Well, what of it? We all have our private concerns.'

'True,' Charles agreed, moving over to the door. 'But anyone who—er—perhaps felt a degree of affection for Miss Georgiana Grey just might bestir himself sufficiently to ensure that she doesn't involve herself in further potentially ruinous escapades.

She's a girl of indomitable spirit to stand up to your peccadilloes, and therefore more than capable of placing herself in danger again…

'Goodnight, Ben,' Charles added, closing the library door quietly behind him before collecting a candle from the table by the wall. He had reached the staircase when he heard the unmistakable sound of breaking glass, a clear indication that something had been thrown against a wall with considerable violence.

'Now we shall see some sport,' he murmured, smiling triumphantly as he made his way up to his allotted bedchamber.

## Chapter Eight

'Oh, why don't you borrow some of my jewels?' Lady Sophia urged, entering the bedchamber in time to watch a simple string of pearls being fastened round a slender throat. 'Grandmama won't permit me to wear most of them, she says I'm far too young. But I'm sure she wouldn't object to you borrowing any of them. You know how very fond of you she is.' Pretty features suddenly adopted a decidedly mutinous look. 'Besides, they're mine. They were Mama's, and I'm quite happy for you to wear any of them. There's a ruby set that would go very well with that new gown of yours.'

'That's kind of you, Sophie,' Georgiana responded, smiling fondly at the girl whom for years she had looked upon with great affection. 'But I'm happy wearing my mama's pearls. Besides, I don't wish to give the impression I'm wealthy, because I'm not. I shall always be grateful to your father for funding this Season for me, but I'm far too much of a realist to suppose I shall attract a rich husband. I've far too little to offer in return.'

Sophia raised her eyes in order to meet those reflected in the dressing-table mirror. 'You're lucky in one way, though, Georgie. If a gentleman proposes marriage to you, at least you'd know for sure he was marrying you for love.'

'True,' Georgiana agreed, 'though it isn't much compensation if he doesn't happen to live up to the man of my dreams, and I'm unable to return his affection.'

'Oh, I'd forget all about your Sir Galahad, if I were you,' Sophia urged in all seriousness. 'Though, you're never likely to find anywhere near a decent replacement if you don't go to a few more parties. You haven't bothered to attend half the social events I've been to. What's more, you even turned down the opportunity to drive round the park today,' she reminded her, just as a young maid slipped into the room in order to return some freshly laundered garments to the wardrobe.

'No, well, it just so happened I wanted a word with Digby,' Georgiana confessed, while making a great play of donning a pair of long evening gloves.

'I needed to consult with him over—er—certain matters.'

'Good job you did, miss,' the young maid put in, clearly having unashamedly listened to the conversation, 'because he's in no fit state to run any errands for you now.'

Had the housekeeper been present she wouldn't have hesitated to reprimand the young servant, but Georgiana was far too concerned over what might have befallen her personal servant to concern herself about codes of conduct.

'What's happened to Digby?'

'Seemingly, he tripped down the back stairs, miss, and fell badly. He were about to go out, but he won't be going nowhere now, not on that ankle. Swollen something awful, so it is!'

'Oh, Lord!' Georgiana rose in a trice. 'Apologise to the Dowager for my tardiness, Sophie, but it's imperative I see Digby before we go out.'

Without offering any further explanation, Georgiana rushed from the chamber and down to the servants' domain, where she discovered Digby receiving the gentle ministrations of none other than the housekeeper herself in her private rooms. One glance at the swollen ankle resting on a footstool was sufficient to assure Georgiana that the young maid had not exaggerated.

'Oh, Digby!' she cried, dropping to her knees beside his chair. 'Has a doctor been summoned?'

'No need for no doctor,' he assured her, though clearly in pain. ''Tis naught but a sprain. I'll be as right as rain in half an hour or so.'

'Don't be ridiculous!' Georgiana countered. 'You'll not walk on that ankle with any degree of comfort for quite some time. Of all the things to happen today, of all days!'

''Tis worse than you think, miss,' he said in an undertone, while gesturing in the housekeeper's direction.

The inference was clear, and so Georgiana kindly asked the high-ranking member of the household staff to allow her a private word with her own servant. 'Now, what is it?' she demanded to know, once she had been granted the privacy she requested.

''Tis tonight, miss. Jem got word to me earlier, and 'e reckons them there emeralds will be passed on to the Frenchie this very night.'

'But, how can he be so sure?'

'Because one of 'is sons 'as become friendly-like with a wench that works in this certain tavern. 'E found out the Frenchie and Tate 'ave met there in a private room at the back. Seems Tate 'as booked this 'ere room for tonight. I was supposed to go there now, and this tavern wench were going to 'ide me in the back room, so as I could see what went on. Jem and 'is lads can't do it. They be keeping an eye on those three gents. They'll 'ave left the 'ouse by now, so I can't send word to let 'em know what's 'appened. I've got to do it myself, Miss Georgie. There's no one else.'

'Oh, yes, there is,' she countered, after a moment's consideration. 'I'll go in your stead. Now, Digby, don't argue,' she added, when he proceeded to do just that. 'There's no other choice.'

'But you can't go walking into a lowly tavern like that, miss,' he insisted, staring aghast at her elegant attire. 'Even if you were to go dressed as a serving wench, you'd still look out o' place. You just don't look the part.'

'I couldn't agree more,' she assured him, only to dash his hopes a moment later by declaring, 'Master Green shall go!'

Startled, Digby gaped at her. 'You've never gone and brought those dratted clothes with you?'

'Indeed, I have,' she assured him with simple pride. 'I thought when I was packing my trunk back in Gloucestershire they just might come in useful. And see, I was right! It's no good—my mind is made up,' she continued, when he attempted to make her see reason. 'Instead of arguing, find some paper and write down the directions of that tavern, while I seek out the Dowager and attempt to convince her that I have succumbed to the most wicked headache and therefore won't be accompanying her out this evening.'

She rose to her feet and stared down wistfully at the gown she had chosen with particular care. 'It's rather a pity in a way,' she confessed. 'It was one of the parties I had a real desire to attend, for certain—er—sentimental reasons.' She forced her mind back to the present. 'But it cannot be helped. Meet me at the side entrance in about an hour. Her ladyship should have left by then.'

It was almost two hours later when Georgiana descended from the hired carriage outside a squalid tavern situated in a decidedly unsavoury part of the city. She had never journeyed this far east before. On that one and only occasion, the year before, when she had ventured out of the more fashionable area, Lord Fincham had been with her and she had felt completely protected. She felt anything but safe now, but didn't allow this to deter her from entering the lowly inn.

If possible the interior was even more inhospitable. The stench of unwashed bodies, mingling with other obnoxious odours, almost made her retch as she somehow managed to pick her way over to the counter, neatly avoiding the more noisome piles of filth strewn over the floor.

A young woman with tousled hair, ill confined beneath a dirty mobcap, came instantly across to serve her. 'What can I be getting you, young sir?'

Could this be the person who was to aid her? Georgiana wondered. She certainly fitted Digby's description of the serving wench, right enough— buxom and unkempt. There was only one way to find out!

'Are you Nell?'

There was a decidedly wary look in the dark eyes that stared above the counter at her. 'Who be wanting to know?'

'Jem Fisher said you'd be willing to hide me in a certain room.'

'Did 'e now?' She was clearly unimpressed. 'Well, you ain't the cove he brought in 'ere t'other day. That I do know. You be only 'alf 'is age, if that.'

'Ah, yes, that was Digby. He's—he's my uncle,'

Georgiana added inspirationally in an attempt to win the girl's confidence, though it was clear she remained decidedly suspicious. And who could blame her? She might lose her position if the innkeeper discovered she was prepared to conceal people about the tavern. 'He had an accident earlier this evening and hurt his ankle,' she went on to explain. 'So he sent me in his stead.'

'Well, I do think it strange they should 'ave sent a boy along. Still…' she shrugged '…you'll 'ide more easy in that there cupboard than that uncle o' yourn. But first you'd best buy a drop of ale, else you'll look even more out of place in 'ere.'

'I assume the Frenchman and Tate haven't arrived yet?' Georgiana asked, after being furnished with a tankard of a decidedly unpalatable cloudy brew, which she had no intention of even sampling.

The question seemed to reassure the serving girl. 'Seems you do know what you're about, for all you looks a spindle-shanks.' Her grin revealed an array of badly decaying teeth. 'No, they ain't 'ere yet, but you'd best not tarry. Wait over there by that there door, and I'll let you through into the passageway when the landlord ain't looking.'

As good as her word Nell performed the task, before showing Georgiana into a room situated a

little further along an ill-lit passage. 'I were told to
sweep out in 'ere earlier today, so you can be sure
they be coming, but I can't say as 'ow long you'll
'ave to wait. I've moved some of the shelves so as
you can 'ide in 'ere', and, so saying, she unlocked
the door of a large cupboard, where various items
had been stacked haphazardly on the higher shelves.
The bottom half of the cupboard was empty, allowing plenty of room to sit down, if permitting little
further movement.

'Are you sure you're going to be all right in there?'
Nell looked Georgiana up and down. 'You don't
look none too sturdy to me. You ain't going to pass
out nor nothing, I 'ope.'

'I'll take leave to inform you that I have never
fainted in my life!' Georgiana assured her, slightly
nettled by the suggestion.

'In that case you'd best get yerself inside,' Nell
urged. 'I'll lock you in, and come back later when
Tate and the Frenchie be gone.'

Although she didn't care for the idea of being
locked in, Georgiana quickly accepted it was for the
best. At least no one would be able to discover her
presence. So long as the serving girl didn't forget
all about her, Georgiana felt she could endure the
close confinement for a while.

It was certainly cramped, though, she decided, after spending five minutes or so in the same position. How Digby would have coped she couldn't imagine. There was only room enough for her to move slightly in order to place an eye against a very convenient knot-hole in the door, but even so her field of vision was severely restricted. No matter how she tried she found it impossible to see the door leading to the passageway, and she could only just see the table and chairs set in the corner of the room. More disappointing, still, was that, although there was a lamp burning on the table, most of the parlour was in shadow. So unless more light was brought in later, she didn't hold out much hope of ever seeing much at all.

But at least she should have no difficulty in hearing what was said, she decided, a moment before she detected the sound of footsteps in the passageway.

The door opened, and although two male figures crossed her field of vision, she could see only as far as their waists. Frustratingly, even when they seated themselves at the table she could only see as far up as their coat collars. All the same, she was able to discern that one of the men was far more expensively attired and spoke with a decidedly French accent as he said, 'Remember, landlord, we do not wish to be disturbed, and ensure no one loiters in the passage.'

There was a grunt in response before the door closed, and a short silence ensued before the Frenchman spoke again. 'So what have you for me this time, mon ami?'

'Ha, as if you didn't know!'

Georgiana could see a brown package being pushed across the table, before the man whom she assumed must be Arthur Tate spoke gruffly again. 'And I'm to tell yer that the master weren't none too 'appy with the price you got for the last lot. Said they were worth a deal more. Said 'ow if you don't do better this time, there won't be no next. And make o' that what you will. 'E don't take kindly to being crossed.'

'Fah! This master of yours can be no expert to say such things,' the Frenchman countered, seemingly indifferent to the obvious threat. 'Now, my cousin is an expert. He told me how much to expect for those pearls. We were lucky to get what we did. But if your master thinks he can do better, then let him go elsewhere. I, Henri Durand, can always do business with others.'

The name instantly struck a chord of memory. Unfortunately Georgiana wasn't granted the time to ponder on just where she might have heard it before, because the gentleman in question began speaking again and she concentrated on what he was saying.

'Who is this master of yours who dares to doubt me? It is I who take most risks in getting the gems over to France. I get what I can for them. And you may tell him so from me.'

'Told you afore, I don't know who 'e be.'

'Oh, come now, mon ami! You do not expect me to believe that. How do you know when to get in touch with me? Someone must tell you.'

'Apart from that seedy little cove that comes a-calling at my lodgings from time to time, I sees no one. No, I'm given a sign, see? Something's left at a certain spot at the gaming 'ouse. To everyone else working there it wouldn't seem important, nor out o' place, neither. But I knows, see. I knows it's the sign that something's going to be left in my coat pocket three nights hence. We 'as to dress in livery, see, and so we leaves our own clothes in a room just off the gentlemen's cloakroom. I always sees to it my coat's nearest the door on those special nights. Most of the gents visiting the place don't bother to wait for us to find their outdoor things, they goes and gets 'em themselves. Easiest thing in the world for one of 'em to slip 'is 'and round the door and drop a package in my coat pocket.'

'And you have no idea who it might be?' The Frenchman sounded decidedly sceptical.

'No, I ain't!' the other confirmed. 'And I'll tell 'e something else, I ain't going to try to find out, neither. I were warned at the start by that there seedy cove not to go asking questions, to do my job and I'd get paid.'

Georgiana saw Tate reach for his tankard, and after a moment he added, 'The only one I knows is you. Seems to me you'd know more than me.'

'I'm afraid, mon ami, I do not. The brains behind the whole operation is most cautious, it would seem. My part is to dispose of the gems and leave the money I attain for them behind a particular portion of wooden panelling in a boarding house in Dover. Whether the lady who owns the establishment is involved, I have no knowledge, but I rather think not. Perhaps it is your seedy little comrade who is next to book the room. Who can say?'

There was a scraping of a chair on the wooden floor as one of the men got to his feet. 'But if I am to make the coast, and reach France by Friday, I must leave you, mon ami. Until next time…'

Georgiana saw the Frenchman depart without

further ado. A moment later the other followed from the room, and she breathed a sigh of relief, even though she had felt in no particular danger.

While she waited to be released from her self-enforced confinement she went over what she had learned in her mind. Uncomfortable though it had been, the experience had brought its rewards, and although she might not have discovered all that she might have wished, she knew a deal more now than she had half an hour ago. Yes, all in all, it had been extremely worthwhile!

The creaking of the door was a relief to hear, and a moment later the key was grating in the lock. 'Out you come, young sir. Master's in a foul mood tonight. If 'e catches you in 'ere I might lose m' job.'

Only too happy to follow Nell down the dim passageway and out into a side alley, Georgiana was once again subjected to the unpleasant sight of badly rotting teeth when she tossed the tavern girl a shiny gold coin.

Wanting only to put as much distance between herself and the lowly inn, she didn't linger over farewells and hurried down the alley and out on to the cobbled street. Thankfully there were few people about at that time of night. Apart from a couple loitering in a doorway, the street was deserted, save for a hackney carriage at the very corner of the road. If it was for hire, it was the greatest piece of good fortune, Georgiana decided, not thinking twice about heading towards the stationary conveyance.

The Duke and Duchess of Merton's annual ball had always rated high in the social events of the Season, and as such attracted the very cream of society. This year's entertainment was proving no exception. A stream of the most notable figures in London had been filing past the entrance to the lavishly decorated ballroom for well over an hour. Consequently, the large room had become crowded, much to the annoyance of one of the latest arrivals who had quite failed to locate the person he particularly wished to see.

Reaching for his quizzing-glass, Lord Fincham once again scanned the room and spied a pretty blonde-haired girl engaged in a set of country dances, which resulted in his irritation lessening. A further sweep of the room through his aid to vision resulted in locating not his quarry, but a rather forbidding-looking matriarch in a maroon-coloured gown, sitting by herself against the wall.

He didn't allow her somewhat unapproachable

mien to deter him, and sauntered over to where she sat, bowing with his customary elegance. 'May I have the felicity of bearing you company for a few minutes, ma'am?'

Appearing anything but impressed by the fault-less address, the Dowager Countess of Grenville merely cast a cursory glance up at the immaculately attired figure before her. 'You may, if you so wish, Fincham,' she responded, betraying scant pleasure at the prospect. 'But I think I should warn you I am not in a particularly sociable mood this evening.'

Again he was not deterred. 'Why so, ma'am? Are you perhaps finding the rigours of chaperoning your granddaughter fatiguing? If so,' he continued, when he quite failed to elicit a response, 'I wonder you do not enlist the aid of your late son's goddaughter. I'm sure she could assist you in many ways.'

Fincham discovered in those next moments that the Dowager Countess of Grenville's dark eyes could be very nearly as directly probing as his own. But rather more revealing, he fancied, for he judged in an instant that the Dowager was, in all likelihood, in Miss Grey's confidence, even before she said,

'Miss Grey has always been of immeasurable help to me, Fincham, whenever I have requested her assistance.'

'But not tonight, it would seem,' he returned, after a further confirming scan of the ballroom. 'I was expecting to find her here this evening.'

The Dowager smiled grimly. 'Yes, I'm sure you were. And, in truth, she was most looking forward to enjoying the entertainment on this occasion,' she revealed. 'Until, that is, she succumbed to a sick head just prior to our departure and begged to be excused.'

His lordship returned the compliment by staring intently at the Dowager, his mind having woken up to the most alarming possibility. 'Is she, perchance, usually subject to these rapidly developing megrims?'

'I'm rather surprised you felt the need to ask,' was the prompt response, and his lordship was on his feet in an instant.

'I must away to your town house, my lady, to ensure that Miss Grey receives my personal good wishes for a speedy recovery.'

For the first time that evening the Dowager Countess betrayed a flicker of animation. 'I cannot tell you how great a burden you have lifted from my mind, my lord.' She momentarily arrested his immediate departure by adding, 'You might find it advantageous, should you be unable to pass on your good wishes in person, to have a word with Miss Grey's manservant. He is quite…devoted to her.'

Although the butler at the Grenville family's town house had no hesitation in inviting Lord Fincham to step into the hall, he was somewhat taken aback by the abrupt demands of the distinguished visitor.

'Begging your lordship's pardon, but I cannot possibly adhere to such a request. I'm reliably informed that Miss Grey sought her bedchamber some time ago, complaining of a bad head, and gave strict instructions not to be disturbed until morning.'

'Yes, I just wager she did!' the Viscount returned, totally unimpressed by this assurance that his quarry was in the house. 'None the less, be good enough to send a maidservant up to her room without delay to inform Miss Grey that Fincham awaits her below. Should she feel unequal to the task of descending the stairs, then you may tell her I am quite agreeable to attending her in her bedchamber. And if you manage to attain a response to that…I'm a Dutchman!' his lordship added, handing over his hat and cloak to the astonished servant. 'I'll bide my time in here.'

Without awaiting a response, the Viscount sauntered across to a door on the right of the hall. Although he had never been a very frequent visitor to the house in past years, he had called upon the late Earl on the odd occasion and knew the door led to a small front parlour.

Save for the fire in the grate, the room was in darkness, so his lordship occupied his time by pushing a taper into the flames and going about lighting the candles in the various wall sconces. He had just completed the task when he detected a slight noise and turned to see a middle-aged, stocky individual limping into the room with the aid of a stick. 'I've seen you before, have I not?'

'Aye, m'lord, that you 'ave. 'Twere in the park t'other week, when I were with Miss Georgie.'

His lordship nodded, recalling the particular occasion with scant pleasure. 'You'd best sit yourself. Clearly you are in some discomfort.'

Lord Fincham waited for the servant to do as bidden before addressing him again. 'Now, so that we do not misunderstand each other, I shall make several things perfectly clear at the outset. Firstly, I am convinced your mistress is not under this roof, so pray do not waste my time attempting to persuade me otherwise. Secondly, wherever she is has something to do with her—how shall I phrase it?— somewhat unorthodox behaviour of last summer, has it not?

'Come, man,' his lordship urged, when the servant continued to gnaw at his bottom lip, clearly deeply troubled. He lowered his gaze to the swollen ankle and an idea occurred to him. 'Has she gone some-where in your stead?'

This at last achieved a result. 'I begged 'er not to go, m'lord, but she wouldn't listen. She can be an 'eadstrong little filly at times. Said she could manage, and not to fret none. All I was to do was let 'er back in by the side door later. But I'm that worried, m'lord. Anything might 'appen to 'er, even dressed as she is.'

His lordship clapped a hand over his eyes. 'Oh, my God! Don't tell me she's donned boy's raiment again. It would fool no one of real discernment, at least not for long!'

'You try telling 'er, m'lord!' Clearly the servant was at the end of his tether. 'Once she's taken it into 'er 'ead to do something, there's no stopping 'er. I could tell you things that would make your 'air curl.'

'I'm sure you could, but pray do not attempt to do so. I've enough to contend with at the moment,' his lordship returned, smiling despite the fact he was no less concerned than the servant. 'Instead, tell me where she intended going tonight. Come on, man,' he urged again, when only silence followed. 'I'm not asking you to betray your mistress's trust by revealing why she has gone. All I want to know is where she is so that I might return her safely.'

His lordship had to wait moments only before his worst fears were confirmed. 'Dear God! One of the most noisome parts of the city!'

'Yer think I don't know that, sir?' There was real perturbation in the servant's deep voice now. 'I did m'best to stop 'er, then 'elp er. I dirtied 'er face with coal dust, and gave 'er a pair of old gloves to wear to 'ide those lily-white 'ands of hers. And I suggested she take a pistol with 'er an' all. A good shot is Miss Georgie!'

His lordship was distinctly unimpressed. 'Is she, b'gad! I cannot imagine that will be of much help if she is set upon by a gang of ruffians. But I'm sure you did your best,' he added, after noting the servant's crestfallen expression. 'I do not believe I caught your name?'

'Digby, m'lord.'

'Well, Digby, let us see if I cannot bring your young mistress back safely to you.'

'What do you intend to do, if you should find 'er, m'lord?' Digby asked, thereby momentarily arresting his lordship's progress across to the door.

'Ring her blasted neck for putting me to so much trouble!'

'Oh, well, that's all right then, sir. And then bring 'er 'ome, eh? I'll be waiting at the side door, ready to let you in.'

His lordship nodded in acknowledgement, and then wasted no time in collecting his cloak and hat and going back outside to his waiting carriage. 'Perkins,' he called up to his coachman, 'we are to head back to Berkeley Square.'

'Very good, m'lord.'

'Have you, perchance, a loaded pistol within easy reach?'

'That I 'ave, m'lord', and, so saying, the coachman reached beneath his seat and handed the firearm down to his lordship.

'Excellent! And now, Perkins, we'll away homeward, but I want you to stop at the first available vehicle for hire you see. Where I intend going my own equipage would look decidedly out of place and might draw far too much attention.'

No sooner had his lordship settled himself inside his carriage, concealing the firearm in the pocket of his cloak, than Perkins was drawing the team to a halt again and he was obliged to leave the comfort of his own conveyance.

Waiting only for Perkins to move away, he then addressed himself to the jarvey, giving precise instructions where he wished to go. The jarvey's surprise was not unexpected. 'Evidently you are familiar with the locale?'

'Aye, sir,' he admitted. 'Not that I'd go there through choice, at least not at this time o' night.'

'Then we are as one, my good man, for neither would I,' Fincham assured him. 'But needs must, as the saying goes. My confounded nephew has taken it into his head to explore that part of the city, which has caused his mother a deal of distress, and so she has enlisted my aid in order to return the rascal to the bosom of his family.'

'Deserves to 'ave 'is breeches dusted, m'lord!'

His lordship smiled grimly. 'If only you knew how often I'd been tempted to do precisely that. But before he receives his just deserts, he must first be found.' Reaching into his pocket, he drew out a shiny golden guinea and tossed it up into the appreciative palm of the coachman. 'Be assured there will be more if I'm successful in my endeavours.'

The jarvey looked to be experienced in the ways of the world and of the road. 'I assume you are able to protect yourself in the event of trouble?'

'I am, sir. Keep it safe under the seat.'

'A man after my own head groom's heart, I perceive. Excellent! We must hope, of course, that we are not called upon to resort to violence.' He attempted to judge the coachman's mettle, and after a moment or two felt he might have struck lucky and found himself an ally. 'All the same, I do not expect my nephew to become a willing captive. I might be called upon to adopt rather rough-and-ready means in order to persuade him to return home.'

'Don't you worry, sir. I've a length of rope under m' seat. Never knows when it's going to come in 'andy, like. You're quite welcome to it, if it will be of any use.'

'Thank you, I'll bear it in mind. Let us waste no more time.' So saying, he scrambled into the antiquated vehicle, which had long since lost what springs it might once have possessed.

As the coach sped eastwards, his lordship soon accustomed himself to the hardness of the seat and the faintly musty interior, but wasn't in the least sorry when he arrived at his destination and was able to let down the window.

He rapidly discovered the odours in the street were no better, but quickly forgot the unsavoury atmosphere when he detected a figure emerging from a side alley. The tricorn hat and the frock coat were familiar, as was the slender figure wearing them.

'Coachman, I believe we're in luck. Be ready, and hand me down that rope!'

# Chapter Nine

Although she had made the journey in just such a conveyance herself earlier, it finally struck Georgiana as somewhat strange, as she approached the vehicle, to find a hackney carriage lingering in this part of town. A wagoner's cart—yes. Now that, she reasoned, wouldn't have seemed out of place at all, not even at this late hour. But a hired carriage awaiting custom in this impoverished area of the city, where the people could barely scrape together enough to live…? Yes, definitely odd, she concluded, but the thought of walking through hostile and darkened streets decided the matter and she stopped to address the jarvey.

'Are you for hire, my good man?' she enquired in her gruffest Master Green voice.

'I might be, young sir, iffen you 'ave the blunt to pay for your ride.'

'I have funds enough about me,' she assured him,

delving into her coat pocket in order to show him a shiny coin.

'In that case, young sir, tells me where you wants to go and then 'op aboard,' the jarvey invited.

Georgiana had opened the carriage door and had clambered half-inside before she realised the vehicle was not, as expected, unoccupied. Unfortunately by then it was already too late. The large, shadowy figure looming in the corner had moved with remarkable speed. Before she could do much else other than utter a gasp of alarm, some heavy fabric had been tossed over her head and she was being hauled the rest of the way inside the vehicle in a rather rough-and-ready fashion. A strong arm then pinioned both her own before a cord was being wound round them, holding them fast to her sides.

Panic overcame her, and without taking time to consider her actions, she attempted to extract the pistol from her pocket. How she ever hoped to put it to good use with her arms so successfully constrained didn't cross her mind for a moment, and, as things turned out, she wasn't granted the opportunity even to make the attempt.

As though divining her intentions, her captor wrested the pistol from her grasp as easily as if he'd been taking a toy from a child and then proceeded to treat her as such by administering a hearty slap to the seat of her breeches, before tossing her on to the seat opposite. Tears stung her eyes and she was smarting from the indignity of it all, but had sense enough to heed the advice when a menacingly low and threatening voice warned her to sit still and behave, unless she wished to receive more of the same.

Although he had clearly been trying to disguise it, Georgiana instantly recognised something achingly familiar in that husky whispering timbre, most especially when he then went on, in the same undertone, to instruct the jarvey to move off. Fincham! She was very nearly sure of it. And the humiliating punishment just meted out only went to confirm the strong suspicion that her silent abductor was none other than the Viscount himself! But why on earth would he want to abduct her? Moreover, why was he attempting to conceal his identity?

As the conveyance turned a sharp corner and a hand grasped her shoulder steadying her, the questions at last burst into her mind. It just didn't make any sense at all. Yet, whoever it was seated opposite had known full well that she was a female. If nothing else, she felt convinced of that much at least. He hadn't uttered so much as a gasp of surprise when her tricorn had toppled off her head in her struggles and her long hair had gone tumbling down her back.

As the carriage went round a further sharp corner, those steadying fingers once again grasped her shoulder, but not before she had felt something hard and heavy knock against her side. Could it possibly have been another pistol? Fincham's own, perhaps? She opened her mouth and was on the point of demanding an end be put to the farce at once, when common sense prevailed and she thought better of it.

All at once she detected sounds of other vehicles, which suggested they had now entered the more affluent part of the metropolis. Although it was comforting to think she was now in familiar territory, the fact that all of those favoured gamesters, and that included Fincham, of course, resided in this part of the town was hardly consoling. Clearly someone had discovered her plans for that evening. That much was blatantly obvious. Had Nell betrayed them? But even if this was so, how had her infuriatingly silent captor known her true sex? Nell hadn't known; Georgiana would have staked her life on that. Only Fincham would have known her true sex for sure, she reminded herself, as the carriage at last turned a corner and drew to a halt. This fact alone all at once gave rise to some very alarming possibilities.

The vehicle rocked as her companion alighted. Georgiana then heard a brief exchange between the two men. Although the jarvey's voice was clear and carrying, the advice he offered on unruly nephews was rather puzzling. A moment later she felt a hand grasp her arm. Then, evidently deciding she stood no chance of negotiating the step, her abductor hauled her from the seat and tossed her over a broad shoulder.

Her first impulse was to struggle and kick out with her legs, but she resisted the temptation to attempt to inflict an injury. She might so easily alert him to the pistol he'd inadvertently left in the pocket of what she could only assume was his coat or cloak. Her docility clearly pleased him, for no sooner had he turned a key in a lock and entered what she increasingly felt must surely be a particular residence in Berkeley Square than he began to whistle a cheerful ditty. He then paused to pick up what she suspected was a lamp off a table and then carried her in the same ignominious fashion a short distance further before tossing her, quite without warning, down on to something soft and bouncy.

Her faint cry of alarm succeeded in eliciting a

rumble of deep masculine laughter, which also held that disturbingly familiar ring to it. She detected the click of a door closing and then heard him moving about the room, before he finally came over to release her from her confinement. Although deep down she had strongly suspected all along her captor's identity, she was powerless to control the heart-rending pain that shot through her when the cloak was finally pulled off and she stared up into those unforgettable dark brown eyes.

In her confused and highly suspicious state, she foolishly imagined everything fitted into place. In those same frantic moments she even recalled just where she had heard that Frenchman's name before. Her reaction was instinctive and she reached for the discarded cloak. Swiftly extracting the pistol from the pocket, she managed to dart out of reach before levelling the firearm.

Lord Fincham rose slowly to his feet, understandably enough not best pleased at having one of his own weapons levelled at his chest. 'I think you had better give that to me.'

'Don't come any closer,' she warned, 'or I'll shoot you down.'

'Then you had better do so, my dear,' he silkily invited, 'for I intend to come very much closer.'

Her finger automatically curled round the trigger, but amazingly enough nothing happened. It was almost as if her body would no longer respond to the commands of her brain. Although her mind might urge her to show no mercy to the villain who was responsible for the death of her beloved godfather, something far more powerful was staying her hand. She allowed the pistol to be taken from her without putting up the least resistance and then stared up to see the unmistakable glint of smug satisfaction in those same unforgettable dark eyes.

A semblance of fight returned, enough at least to enable her to pummel his chest for a second or two before abject misery became too much to bear and she crumpled back down on to the sofa.

'Why you…? Dear God! Why did it have to be you!' she managed to cry out, before great racking sobs shook her body.

For several moments it was as much as Lord Fincham could do to stare down in disbelief. Then, emitting a sound somewhere between a growl and a grasp of dismay, he tossed the gun aside, scooped her up in his arms as though she weighed no more than a child and proceeded to cradle her in his lap.

It took some little time before Georgiana at last

began to appreciate that the hand stroking her hair away from her face and the lips brushing lightly over her forehead, murmuring words that were quite unintelligible, were, oh, so very gentle. Hardly the actions of a cold-blooded killer, she finally reasoned. She sniffed loudly and felt a handkerchief being pressed into her hand. She proceeded to make good use of it, before raising her eyes and inadvertently brushing wet lashes against the line of a firm jaw.

She felt him stiffen and repositioned her head further down his shoulder so that she might stare into his face. It offered him the opportunity to do likewise and he was pleasantly surprised by what he saw. 'My compliments, child. You are one of the few females of my acquaintance who doesn't look perfectly hideous after a severe bout of weeping. But what induced such an inexhaustible flow, I cannot help asking myself? You are not a girl easily brought to tears, I think.'

Becoming more confused with every passing second, and suddenly appreciating her unseemly situation, she eased herself a little away from him. 'This is most improper, my lord. We should not be sitting like this.'

'A somewhat insignificant detail at such a time,' he responded with gentle irony, but didn't attempt to prevent her scrambling off his lap, before he himself rose and went over to the decanters.

'Here, take it,' he urged when she made no attempt to accept the drink he had poured for her. 'It will not do you a mite of harm. It is only brandy.'

She took it from his outstretched hand, docilely took a sip and then grimaced at the taste. The fiery brew put heart back into her, none the less—at least sufficient for her to stare up into those dark eyes that had been branded into her memory for so very many long and lonely months. She had seen them hard, angry and penetrating, but they were not so now. There was a hint of gentle compassion behind the evident curiosity. But they were definitely not the eyes of a cold-blooded killer.

She sighed and shook her head, sending her silky black locks sweeping across her face, and removed the strands with a hand that wasn't perfectly steady. 'I just don't understand,' she at last admitted.

'Then we are in that respect at least in complete accord, my sweet life,' he revealed. 'Although perhaps not so absolutely in the dark as I once was,' he amended, a moment later. 'Would I be correct in thinking that your—er—somewhat unorthodox behaviour last summer and your madcap venture tonight has something to do with the death of your godfather?'

The startled glance was answer enough. 'Yes, I rather thought it might be. After my brief tête-à-tête with the Dowager at the Mertons' ball, I began to suspect something of the sort.'

'You spoke with her ladyship...? But why?'

He lifted one shapely hand and waved it in a dismissive gesture. 'I cannot recall precisely just what it was that prompted me to favour her with my company,' he responded at his supercilious best. 'But your name was brought up in the conversation, and it became perfectly clear to me that she was deeply troubled because you had failed to accompany her.'

Manfully suppressing a smile, he added, 'Consumed with curiosity as I sometimes am, and finding the ball tiresomely mundane, I decided to satisfy my inquisitiveness, and so paid a call at the Grenville town house, where I subsequently enjoyed a short interlude with your manservant.'

Although she didn't quite believe everything she was hearing, Georgiana at last began to appreciate just why Lord Fincham had been in that particular area of the city. 'Digby told you where I'd gone, didn't he?'

He couldn't mistake the thread of annoyance in her voice, and didn't hesitate to come to the servant's defence. 'Only deep concern for your well-being persuaded him to do so. But it didn't tempt him to reveal why you had gone. That I began to deduce for myself on my travels through the city. Why, I asked myself, did a young woman who generally conducts herself with the utmost propriety behave so recklessly on occasions?'

She couldn't resist smiling at this, for she well knew that very little shocked Viscount Fincham. 'Your assumption was correct, my lord,' she was more than happy to tell him. 'And I do thank you for ensuring my safe return, though I would have preferred had you not adopted such rough-and-ready means and had revealed your identity from the first. But I suppose your intention was to alarm me, thereby adding to my punishment.'

He was totally unmoved by the reproachful look he received and was even less impressed when she rose to her feet in order to place the half-emptied glass on the mantelshelf, as though she had every intention of leaving.

'And where do you imagine you are going, young woman?' he demanded, his tone distinctly bored. 'If you suppose for a moment I shall calmly sit here and permit you to leave without first receiving a full explanation of your extraordinary behaviour, you may think again.'

She resented the haughty, dictatorial attitude, which was so much a part of his character on occasions, as much as she resented the fact that she was very much in his power and that he was very capable of preventing her departure if he should take it into his head to do so.

He seemed impervious to her resentful scowl, and it was soon borne in upon her that he was determined to have his curiosity satisfied. 'Oh, confound you, Fincham! Why must you become involved? The matter doesn't concern you.'

'Of course it concerns me,' he countered, setting his empty glass aside. He then rose to his feet and grasped her shoulders to administer a slight shake. 'So let's have no more evasion! Unwittingly I became involved that day at Deerhampton.' He stared down at her intently. 'Or was our first encounter not pure chance, but design?'

The astonished expression told him all he needed to know, even before she said, 'How on earth could it have been? I had no knowledge of your existence, let alone that you were, indeed, one of the five.'

The Viscount's dark eyes became markedly more

intense. 'Ah! Now you begin to interest me greatly.' Releasing his hold on her, he collected his glass and wandered across to his tray of decanters once more. 'Tell me, child, where did you first hear that expression…? Not in London, I think?'

After silently acknowledging she had unwittingly given away far too much already, Georgiana accepted the inevitable. The mantel-clock revealed that it had turned midnight; unless she wished to be here at daybreak, she had little choice but to reveal all she knew.

Releasing her breath in a sigh of capitulation, she reached up for her own glass and made herself comfortable in the chair once more. 'It was the very day after my godfather's funeral that the Dowager Countess asked me to visit. She revealed then that her son had been alive…just…when she had reached him, and that he had managed to impart that the attack upon him must have been planned in advance. And by someone whom he referred to as "one of the five". Seemingly he had revealed to one, or all of them, that he would be returning to Gloucestershire with the Grenville diamonds, which he had carried with him to London on that occasion in order to have them cleaned.'

'Forgive me, child, for interrupting, but am I right

in thinking your godfather's carriage was attacked some forty miles from the capital?'

'He frequently broke the journey back to Gloucestershire by staying overnight with his good friend General Montague Simpson.'

'Yes.' The Viscount frowned as a distant memory stirred. 'I seem to recall hearing something of the sort, but I cannot say that I ever paid much attention. Your godfather and I were never what I should term close friends.' He returned to the chair opposite. 'But I interrupted you. Pray continue.'

'The General lives on the outskirts of a small community that's surrounded by woodland, some three miles north off the main highway to Bristol,' she explained.

'An ideal location for a robbery,' he remarked, and she nodded in agreement.

'Indeed, yes, especially if someone had prior knowledge of a carriage containing a small fortune in diamonds,' she agreed. 'To continue—a local farmer, travelling along the country lane early that morning, confirmed that four mounted strangers had passed him in the lane, riding fast. A short time later he came upon a carriage. The head groom and footman were both dead, and my godfather, slumped across the seat inside, had been barely alive. The farmer told the local magistrate that he'd heard gunfire, but hadn't taken too much notice. Apparently there are always people out rabbiting in the woods.'

He nodded thoughtfully, before betraying disapproval by remarking sharply, 'And the Dowager, having discovered about "the five", instead of informing the authorities, enlists your aid…? She must be going soft in the attic!'

'On the contrary, sir, she's as sharp-witted as ever she was!' Georgiana countered, instantly coming to the Dowager's defence. 'The authorities had already made up their minds that the Earl had simply been a victim of a gang of highwaymen, which of course was true enough, as far as it went. Her ladyship realised she needed to discover far more before anyone would take her seriously.'

Totally unimpressed, his lordship raised his eyes ceilingwards. 'Then she compounds her folly by enlisting the aid of a chit of a girl! Madness, unutterable madness!'

Georgiana took exception to this. 'I'll have you know, sir, that I've now turned three-and-twenty, not some foolish schoolgirl, and am quite capable of taking care of myself!'

'Ha! As you proved so convincingly tonight!'

Sarcasm had simply oozed from his every word, which only served to irritate her still further. 'I'll take leave to inform you as well, sir, that I have succeeded in discovering a great deal already. I'll agree it might not be the wisest thing for me to go about dressed as a boy,' honesty obliged her to concede, 'but it has proved immensely worthwhile.'

There was all at once a steely glint in his eyes. 'That's as maybe, but from this day forward, my girl, you will desist, is that understood?'

How dared he dictate to her! Perhaps emboldened by the brandy she'd been steadily imbibing, Georgiana shot to her feet, determined to stand her ground and not be dictated to by someone who had absolutely no authority over her whatsoever.

She proceeded to tell him so in no uncertain terms, only to be interrupted mid-sentence. 'None the less, you will do as I say,' he told her in an infuriatingly calm tone, 'otherwise you may be sure I shall be paying a visit to the Dowager Countess with an ultimatum—either she sends you home to Gloucestershire at once, out of harm's way, or I shall go to the authorities with what I know of the matter. That, of course, might be the most sensible course of action for all concerned. On the other hand, it might well result in alerting the guilty party, which is something the Dowager has thus far done her utmost to avoid.'

'Why you…you…!' Almost beside herself with rage, Georgiana couldn't think of anything loathsome enough to call him and did her best to alleviate the rising torrent of anger by pacing the room.

The Viscount regarded her in silence, his smile betraying a degree of amusement, not untouched by admiration. 'My dear, although you look quite magnificent when you're angry, you would profit more by giving due consideration to a further suggestion: that we work together in trying to uncover the person behind your godfather's death.'

This brought an end to her irate pacing, as he knew it would, and he found himself being regarded with an element of doubt and suspicion. 'But why should you wish to become involved, my lord? I ruled you out as a possible suspect within a week or two of having first met you.'

He slanted a mocking glance after listening to this assurance. 'That was not the impression I gained a short time ago.'

'No…well…' She had the grace to look a little shamefaced. All the same, it served as a timely reminder of what she had discovered earlier that night and she shook her head. 'Believe me, my lord, you wouldn't wish to become involved. This matter concerns people you know…perhaps some you…like very well.'

He regarded her keenly, all at once sensing she was keeping something of real importance to herself, and demanded to know what it was. She was reluctant at first, but soon realised that he would not settle for anything less than the absolute truth, and so revealed everything she had discovered that night at the tavern.

After learning all, his lordship contemplated for a moment, fully appreciating her reluctance in confiding in him. 'It is possible, of course, that there is more than one Henri Durand in London at the present time, but unlikely, I would have thought. So, I think it is safe to assume that the mysterious Frenchman is indeed Charles Gingham's cousin. What I am not prepared to accept is that Charles himself is in any way involved.'

Given the depth of the friendship, Georgiana wasn't at all surprised to hear him say this, but felt obliged to remind him, 'But, my lord, Durand did mention a cousin who had put a value on the gems. And I clearly recall you revealing once that Mr Gingham is something of an expert in that particular field.'

'And so he is,' he readily confirmed. 'But he's also a most honourable man. He would never involve himself in anything illegal. That said, I shall approach Charles on the subject of his cousin when next I see him, which I do not envisage will be too far in the future.' There was all at once a hint of smug satisfaction about his expression. 'You see, my dear Miss Grey, how beneficial it will be for all concerned if we work together?'

'Well, yes,' she was obliged to concede, as she once again returned to the chair by the hearth. 'I do appreciate you are in a much better position to be able to communicate with the three suspects, although their movements are being monitored by persons known to Digby.'

'Indeed? In that case I think it behoves me to have another word with that manservant of yours. I intend to call tomorrow in any event, so I shall do so then.'

She was somewhat startled to learn this. 'You're calling at the house…? But whatever for?'

Two black brows were raised in exaggerated surprise. 'Isn't it obvious, my darling girl…? It is so that we can announce our betrothal to the Dowager Countess together.'

Georgiana blessed providence that she had sat

down again, for she felt sure her knees would not have supported her, so shocked was she by the pronouncement. 'You are in jest, of course.'

'I've never been more serious in my life,' Lord Fincham assured her. 'Think, girl! What would happen if I suddenly started singling you out for particular attention at parties, and began escorting you in the park? It would cause a deal of speculation and the majority of the ton would be following our every move. But by announcing our engagement to the world, we'll be the cynosure of all eyes for a week or two, then interest in us will swiftly wane, and we could meet as often as we wished to consult without rousing the least suspicion. And that is imperative. We must not rouse the least curiosity in any one of our three suspects, now must we?'

'When put like that, yes, I do see. But—'

'No buts,' he interrupted, holding up a hand against further protests. 'Until the guilty party is uncovered, I too must live under a cloud of suspicion, no matter your protestations to the contrary. I have far too much pride to permit that state of affairs to continue indefinitely.' The faintly haughty look faded, and his expression was all at once intense. 'Trust me, and all will be well. You'll see.'

Getting to his feet, he helped her to hers by

grasping her wrists. 'And now, Georgie, my girl, I must return you home, otherwise you'll look anything but the radiant bride-to-be on the morrow, and that will never do. No one in his right mind would ever imagine Viscount Fincham had fallen head over heels in love with a positive fright!'

So saying, he collected her tricorn off the sofa and, displaying all the dexterity of an expert lady's maid, successfully concealed her long tresses beneath it, before leading her from the room. Which was perhaps just as well, for Georgiana was feeling too stunned by the rapid turn of events to do very much for herself.

## Chapter Ten

Sitting on the window seat in the sunny front parlour the following afternoon, Georgiana saw Lord Fincham's town carriage draw to a halt outside the front entrance. For some reason she'd imagined he would call late morning. As the hours had passed she had begun to believe she had imagined the whole thing, and that he hadn't suggested an engagement between them at all. She hadn't known whether to feel relieved or devastated. On the one hand, she couldn't deny that he could be of immeasurable help in discovering what she and the Dowager most wished to know… But at what cost to herself?

She watched him step lightly down from the carriage in that lithe, athletic way of his and mount the steps. She couldn't imagine there was a gentleman living whom she would rather marry. She had long since known that that sometimes infuriatingly dictatorial aristocrat was the very one for her, but had been sensible enough to accept that a viscount would hardly consider a mere soldier's daughter as a suitable bride, even one that would come to the marriage with a modest dowry. She had succeeded in keeping a sense of perspective for so very many months—but could she continue to do so? It wasn't a question of playing the part of a loving fiancée; acting didn't enter into the matter. The dilemma besetting her was whether she would have strength enough to do the honourable thing when the time came by releasing him from the engagement?

The butler entered to reveal what she was well aware of already. 'Should I perhaps inform her ladyship that Lord Fincham is here, Miss Grey?'

'No, that is all right. We shall be going up to see your mistress presently. Just show Lord Fincham in.'

The butler remained by the door, clearly uncertain about what to do. 'Perhaps you'd like me to instruct one of the maids to bear you company, miss?'

'No, she would not,' his lordship answered, brazenly entering the parlour, uninvited. 'Now go about your business, my good man. I have never in my life behaved like a despoiler and I have no intention of doing so now,' he added, closing the door on the outraged major-domo.

'You are an abominable person, my lord!' Georgiana told him, though quite unequal to suppressing a gurgle of mirth. 'The poor man was only doing his duty, after all.'

'If there's one thing I cannot abide it's an uppity flunkey,' he revealed.

Memory stirred. 'Ah, well, you are blessed in those who serve you,' she reminded him.

'Yes, I must agree I have been most fortunate… save for just one impertinent page I was once foolish enough to engage.'

Smiling crookedly he went across to her, drew her to her feet and then stared down into those wonderfully coloured eyes framed in their ridiculously lengthy black lashes. 'Yes,' he murmured, 'you'll do very well. I'm sorry I am so late in calling,' he went on to explain, his tone all at once more matter of fact, 'only I've been rather occupied for the past few hours.'

She smiled a little wryly. 'I'd begun to imagine you'd had second thoughts.'

He looked at her closely again, easily interpreting the uncertainty in her expression. 'You've been experiencing reservations and hoped I had, too. Well, I haven't.' So saying, he drew out a magnificent sapphire-and-diamond engagement ring from his pocket like a conjurer and slipped it onto the appropriate slender finger. 'A rather lengthy visit to Rundell & Bridge was one of my more pressing errands, as were visits to the offices of certain newspapers. Our engagement will be officially announced in several different Friday morning editions.'

'Too late to reconsider then, my lord,' she acknowledged, still somewhat bemused by the beautiful adornment on her left hand. Oddly enough an engagement ring was something she hadn't considered she must don to give credibility to the part she must play… Yes, it did make it all seem so real, somehow.

'Far too late,' he agreed softly, his eyes focusing on the gentle curve of her upper lip. For a moment she thought she could detect a slight movement, as though he was about to lower his head, then he seemed to check and took a hurried step away.

'My name is Benedict, by the way. My friends call me Ben. You'd best accustom yourself to using it. I cannot have my affianced bride continuing to address me so formally. And now, my darling girl, we'd best seek out the Dowager before that butler of hers suffers an apoplexy.'

As had happened the night before, Georgiana felt as if she were being driven by a disposition far

stronger than her own. Undeniably the Viscount
could be quite single-minded when it suited his purpose, and was undoubtedly well accustomed to getting his own way. Which could not be good for him,
she quickly decided. Therefore, sooner rather than
later, she must start exerting her own will again, if
only to stop him from becoming pompously overbearing. But for the time being she was prepared to
allow him his way in most things, if only because
he seemed to know precisely how to conduct the
charade to make it believable.

'I'm sorry, my lord, what did you say?' she asked,
aware all at once that he had addressed her.

'Ben,' he corrected. 'And I simply asked if you've
already revealed to her ladyship what you discovered last night?'

'I did consult with her earlier, yes. But I didn't
reveal our…our fake engagement.'

His lips twitched ever so slightly. 'Then let us do
so now. But I think it would be best if you leave the
announcement to me.'

She was more than happy to do so, for had the
truth been known she hadn't a clue how to explain
to the Dowager why she was willing to take such a
drastic course of action. She wasn't at all sure she

knew herself, especially as she was well aware that it would ultimately bring only heartache.

Leading the way out of the room, and up the sweeping staircase, Georgiana then headed along the passageway to her ladyship's private apartments. She was fortunate enough to discover the Dowager Countess awake, and sitting in her favourite chair, for it wasn't unknown for her to take a nap at this time of day.

Not even by the slightest widening of her eyes did the Dowager betray any surprise when Lord Fincham followed Georgiana into the room. She simply placed the book she had been reading down on the table by her chair, before declaring how very pleased she was to see him.

'For it offers me the opportunity to earnestly thank you for your—er—timely intervention last night, my lord.' She cast a brief look of disapproval at the ill-at-ease young woman at his side. 'I sincerely trust you will not be put to such inconvenience again.'

'You may be sure of it, ma'am,' he returned with such conviction that Georgiana felt slightly nettled. It was a bit of a liberty on his part to assume so much. After all, she had given no assurances, least of all to him, that she wouldn't continue working on her own, if the need should arise. His next pronouncement was even more disturbing.

'But the inconvenience I was put to in tracking her down did ultimately bring its own rewards. Before we parted company in the early hours we had reached a much better understanding. Miss Grey has done me the honour of accepting my hand in marriage.'

Georgiana hardly knew where to look and in the end stared resolutely down at her feet. He had sounded so convincing, confound him! Surely they might have told the Dowager the truth, if no one else?

'May I be the first to offer my wholehearted congratulations,' her ladyship responded, after having looked from one to the other and drawn her own conclusions. 'Pray be seated, my lord,' she continued before turning to Georgiana. 'My dear, please be so good as to pour out three glasses of Madeira so that we might enjoy a celebratory toast,' she requested, before turning to the gentleman who appeared to be very well pleased with himself, and the world at large. 'Have you fixed upon a date for the wedding, my lord?'

At this Georgiana's hand shook involuntarily, very nearly spilling the wine she was carrying back over to the hearth. 'Of course we haven't, ma'am,' she put in, not enjoying the fiasco in the least. It was turning out to be far harder than she could ever have supposed. 'We've hardly been granted much time to discuss anything at all,' she added, setting the tray down on a low table.

'That's true enough,' his lordship agreed. 'But, as a rule, I am no advocate of long engagements. I shall hold a party at Berkeley Square in a couple of weeks to celebrate our betrothal, and hope to be married before the Season is over. Much depends, of course, on resolving this matter of your son's tragic demise.'

Both the Dowager and Georgiana looked at him sharply. It was her ladyship who eventually broke the silence. 'Lord Fincham, I shall be for ever in your debt for the immense diplomacy you have shown in this matter.' A hint of a smile hovered about her mouth. 'A lesser man, I feel sure, would have been deeply shocked, especially over a particular person's behaviour. None the less, I am now as one with Georgiana in the belief that you were never in any way involved in my son's death, and would therefore suggest that the matter no longer concerns you.'

'Loath though I am to disagree with you, ma'am,

but it concerns me greatly now, even if it didn't before last night.'

Grasping Georgiana's hand, he felt it tremble slightly in his own as he drew her gently down on to the couch beside him. 'I have earned the reputation of being slightly—what shall I say?—high in the instep. I am most assuredly conceited enough to expect my affianced bride's world to revolve around me, if not before, then certainly after the wedding has taken place. I think I would be asking too much of Georgie to think only of me until the person behind her godfather's death is brought to book. Furthermore, I do happen to be well acquainted with all three suspects and am therefore in a position to uncover a great deal more than we know already.'

'I cannot argue with that, my lord,' the Dowager freely acknowledged. 'And I suppose if you are set on that course of action, I cannot imagine anything I could say would dissuade you. So it only remains for me to thank you in advance for your assistance, and…' she reached for one of the glasses, and then waited for them to take theirs '…to wish you both every happiness for the future.'

The toast was duly drunk, and not a moment too soon, for the door was thrown wide almost immediately afterwards and Lady Sophia came tripping lightly into the room.

'Oh, I do beg your pardon, Grandmama! No one told me you were entertaining visitors.'

'Not at all, dear child, your arrival is most timely. Georgiana, you'll be delighted to hear, has stolen a march on you. She has become betrothed to Lord Fincham!'

As was her custom, Lady Sophia clapped her hands in delight, before enthusing over the engagement ring and then finally looking shyly up at the tall man who had instantly risen to his feet upon her arrival.

'So you're Sir Galahad!' she declared, much to Georgiana's further embarrassment. 'He certainly fits the description, does he not, Georgie?'

Smiling at the added colour flying in his fiancée's cheeks, Lord Fincham turned to the late Earl's daughter. 'I should never aim so high, Lady Sophia. And to prove a point I must now be decidedly ungallant and desert you so soon after your arrival.

'No, there's no need to see me out, Georgie,' he added, when she made to rise. 'I know the way. I shall look forward to calling again on the morrow.'

As he descended the stairs to the hall, his lordship bethought himself of something else, and requested a hovering footman to go in search of Miss Grey's personal manservant.

After being shown into the front parlour, he occupied his time by staring out of the window and smiling to himself at the rapid turn of events that had left a special someone on the floor above in a decidedly confused state. Which was perhaps all to the good, he reflected. At least while her mind was fully occupied with coming to terms with her new role in life, she wouldn't be considering other matters that concerned her greatly at the present time.

'Ah, yes, come in, man! Come in and take the weight off that ankle of yours,' he commanded, as the very person he'd requested to see came hobbling into the room, again with the aid of a stick. 'I shan't keep you from your duties for long; not that I suppose you are able to undertake a great many at the present time.'

He waited for the servant to seat himself before continuing. 'Now, has your mistress revealed what took place last night?' he asked and received a nod in response. 'Excellent! Although I don't suppose for a moment you'll be able to consult with your associates again for a few days, when you do, ask them to look out for a small, seedy-looking fellow visiting one of the houses. He could, of course, be a servant. I'm convinced the fellow must be some sort of go-between. From what your mistress managed to discover, he's already visited this man Tate a time or two. And it's quite possible also that he might well be the one who travels to Dover in order to collect the ill-gotten gains from that certain boarding house, though why the money isn't brought directly to London is something we might discover in time.'

His eyes narrowed speculatively. 'Whoever is the brains behind it all is careful enough not to be seen with any of the other key members in the organisation. I think it behoves me to begin to study the three candidates from a completely different perspective. And I shall begin tonight by paying a visit to that particular gaming house.'

The servant didn't attempt to hide his surprise. 'You're involving yourself further, then, m'lord?'

'I have little choice.' He frowned in thought. 'Er—Digby, isn't it?'

'Aye, m'lord. Just Digby.'

The Viscount frowned again at this. 'Rather an odd sort of name. Have you no other?'

'Yes, m'lord—Goodie. But where I come from

a name like that does yer no service at all. So I've just been Digby all these years.'

'Quite understandable! Well, Digby, you might be pleased to hear that your mistress and I have become betrothed. Which means, of course, that I am in a position to take much of the responsibility for her care off your hands.'

Digby's expression of unholy relief was almost comic. 'Oh, I can't tell you what a great weight that is off my mind! Begging your lordship's pardon, but the young mistress can champ at the bit at times. She may look the image of 'er dear ma, but there's a look in those eyes of 'ers, when 'er mind's set on something, that's the dead spit of Colonel Grey. She's 'er father's daughter right enough.'

His lordship smiled softly. 'Yes, I suppose you are one of the few who would know that for sure.' He returned his thoughts to the present, and went across to the door. 'I have one or two other errands to run before evening, so I must not tarry. I dare say we shall consult again in a day or two.'

As it was the first time the Viscount had visited that specific gaming establishment since his arrival in town, his appearance was greeted with an element of surprise. Lord Rupert raised one hand in an airy salute, while his companion merely nodded in acknowledgement, as Lord Fincham approached the table. Of the third suspect there was no sign, and so his lordship began by discovering where Sir Willoughby was hiding himself.

'Oh, come now, Fincham!' Lord Chard slanted a mocking glance in his lordship's direction as the Viscount joined them at the table. 'You should know our pernickety baronet better than that. He only needs to develop a slight temperature to be convinced he's dying. He probably sneezed earlier in the day and took to his bed. Never known a fellow for cosseting himself so much!'

This was true enough, his lordship silently acknowledged. Sir Willoughby hardly seemed the sort to embroil himself in anything so sordid as robbery with violence. On the other hand, Sir Willoughby, for all his pernickety ways, was as sharp as a tack, and more than capable of organising the acquiring and disposal of precious jewels, without being directly involved in the thefts himself. No, he silently acknowledged, Sir Willoughby could not be ruled out quite yet.

And, indeed, neither could either of the other two. He cast a glance at both gentlemen in turn. Just like Sir Willoughby, either was capable of running the show, as it were. But which of the three was pitiless enough to condone cold-blooded murder in order to attain his ends? One of them assuredly was.

'We haven't seen much of you this Season, Fincham?' Lord Chard remarked, dealing his lordship into the next game. 'You weren't particularly late arriving in town. Any reason for your unsociability? You haven't taken exception to something one of us has done or said?'

His lordship smiled grimly. 'Now, what could you possibly have done, Chard, that would give me an aversion to your society, I wonder?'

Their eyes met briefly above the cards in their hands, 'Nothing, I trust.'

'I've seen him about at one or two events, as it happens,' Lord Rupert disclosed. 'You were at m'brother's do t'other night, weren't you, Finch, though you didn't stay long? Looked for you myself, and was told you'd already left.'

'Well, yes, there was someone I wished to see,' he freely admitted, signalling to a waiter to bring a bottle and glass. 'And I haven't been deliberately avoiding anyone. It's merely that my attention has been totally focused elsewhere. You see, gentlemen, I have decided upon the lady whom I shall take to wife.'

'Well, upon my soul!' Lord Rupert was the first to voice his surprise. 'I thought you, like myself, were destined to remain a bachelor. Many congratulations, old fellow! Who's the lucky girl?'

'Miss Georgiana Grey, daughter of the late Colonel George Grey.'

'Wait a moment! I've met her, haven't I? Isn't she old Grenville's goddaughter. Well, I say goddaughter. I've heard—' Sir Rupert stopped short when he saw the menacing flicker in the Viscount's eyes. 'Ah, well, yes, shouldn't pay too much attention to rumours. Ravishing girl, Fincham! Smitten myself, I might tell you.'

'Have I met her, Fincham?' Chard asked, after the waiter had deposited the bottle and glass down on the table and had moved away.

His lordship checked before reaching for the wine and then filling their glasses. 'I cannot recall seeing you at any of the parties she's attended, although there haven't been that many, I must confess. The Dowager Countess lacks the vitality she once had and has been most selective since her arrival in town, but I shall expect my fiancée to attend far more in future.' Again he looked from one to the other. 'I trust you will both do us the honour of attending our select little party to celebrate the event in a couple of weeks? But in the meantime, until it is officially announced, I trust I might rely on your discretion in keeping the news to yourselves.'

His companions might well have done so, but that didn't stop a deal of interest being shown the following afternoon when he took Georgiana to the park in his open carriage. He deliberately chose the fashionable hour and so wasn't unduly surprised by the evident curiosity they aroused. What did irk him, and what he considered a confounded intrusion into his privacy, was the fact that the Dowager Countess had insisted on Georgiana being accompanied by a young maid.

He tolerated it for so long, and then could bear it no longer, and tapped Perkins on the shoulder with a walking stick, requesting him to stop. 'We'll stroll for a while, my darling,' he told Georgiana, jumping swiftly out and helping her to alight. 'No, you may stay where you are and enjoy the ride,' he added, when the maid attempted to follow. 'As long as Miss Grey remains within your sight, you will have carried out your mistress's instructions to the letter.'

'You are quite outrageous on occasions,' Georgiana didn't hesitate to tell him, after he had ordered

Perkins to move off and remain a short distance ahead. 'And something of a hypocrite, I might add,' she persisted, when all he did was betray sublime unconcern by tucking her arm through his. 'You berate me for unconventional behaviour, and yet when I attempt to adhere to codes of conduct, you dismiss them out of hand as unnecessary. I simply cannot win!'

'There's a difference between propriety and quite unnecessary precautions,' he finally countered. 'I've never allowed myself to be plagued by duennas, companions or chaperons, and I don't intend starting now, especially not with you. Haven't I always done whatever was necessary to protect your reputation?'

He looked down with a smile that instantly softened the harsh lines of his face to such an extent that one society matron passing by in her carriage was later heard to say that she could hardly believe it was Fincham she saw, so tender was his expression.

'You and I were able to enjoy, for a short time at least, an easy camaraderie that very few in our positions are ever privileged to experience. It wasn't without its disquieting moments, I'll admit, but on the whole I look back on that time we shared with a certain…fondness.'

'And I with a deal of satisfaction,' she admitted, after studying his immaculate attire. 'Not only was I successful in discovering what I dearly wished to know, but also I succeeded in persuading you to alter your mode of dress.'

Had it not been for the betraying twitch at the corner of his mouth, she might have believed him when he said haughtily, 'I shall take leave to inform you that no one has ever succeeded in influencing my judgement or behaviour, especially not some impertinent young page.' She chose, however, not to pursue the matter and changed the subject by attempting to satisfy her curiosity on one point at least.

'I knew almost from the first,' he willingly revealed, 'at least I suspected. And I was firmly convinced of your true sex long before we had arrived in London.'

'And still you engaged me as your page.' She was unable to keep the note of censure out of her voice. 'And you call my behaviour disgraceful!'

He laughed outright at this, drawing even more attention to them. 'I cannot deny it was somewhat unusual, but you had aroused my curiosity by then, child. Besides, I just couldn't deposit you and leave you, a mere fledgling, to avoid the capital's many pitfalls.'

The conversation was evoking too many poignant memories for her peace of mind, so Georgiana decided to change the subject before sentiment induced her to reveal more than was wise.

'No, I haven't discovered a great deal,' he responded in answer to the question. 'I managed to run both Chard and Gyles to earth at the gaming house, but Trent wasn't there. Whoever is behind it all isn't stupid. He'll not be easily unearthed. He's too careful by half. You must be patient, my darling.'

The glance she cast up at him held more than just a hint of disquiet. 'Sir, it is good of you to assist the Dowager and me in our endeavours, and I don't want you to imagine that I'm not immensely grateful. All the same, I cannot help but own to a feeling of guilty unease for involving you in this matter. I know you and my godfather were not close companions. You've admitted as much. But I've gained the impression that you are perhaps friendlier with those other three, therefore I cannot imagine you'd attain much satisfaction from bringing the guilty one to justice.'

'I shouldn't gain any,' he freely admitted. 'And

you're quite right in your assumption—I have so-cialised more with them than I ever did with your godfather.' He shrugged. 'I suppose that's because they're nearer to me in age, and therefore we have more in common. But don't run away with the idea that I'm bosom-friends with any one of them, be-cause I'm not. We socialise only during the Season. We never meet at any other time.'

'Yes, but—'

'No buts,' he interrupted. 'My mind is made up. Besides, this state of affairs cannot be allowed to continue. The next robbery to take place just might involve one of my own relations, or a close friend. Then I would very much regret not bringing the guilty party to book.'

No sooner had he spoken than he was acknowl-edged by none other than the sister-in-law of one of the suspects, out taking the air with her daughter in an open carriage, which instantly turned Georgiana's thoughts in a new direction by reminding her of what she had been obliged to forgo earlier that week.

'What was it like, Ben…the Mertons' ball, I mean?' she didn't hesitate to ask him. 'Was it as splendid as last year's? I shall never forget that ball-room—all sparkling light and fragrant flowers.'

Although well pleased at her use of his given

name, he couldn't work up much enthusiasm for the topic of conversation. After so many Seasons in town he could only assume he had grown inured to these grand affairs, as they no longer impressed him. 'Well, I wasn't there for long, and didn't pay too much attention,' he responded, having difficulty in summoning up an image of the room when last he saw it.

'Oh, but surely you must have noticed the decoration,' she persisted, determined to have her curiosity satisfied. 'Last year her Grace decorated the walls with artistic swathes of apricot and cream silk to match her daughter's gown. Very clever, I thought.'

'Oh, God, yes, now I recall!' He clapped a hand over his eyes as though to obliterate the image his mind's eye was conjuring up. 'This year it was worse. The chit was wearing primrose. Nauseating colour! I felt quite bilious and was glad to leave.'

She strongly suspected he was exaggerating. All the same, she couldn't suppress a gurgle of mirth, which resulted in several other passers-by glancing curiously in their direction.

'Mind you, it's a timely reminder,' the Viscount continued, betraying a deal more interest now. 'I'm not having the reception rooms at Berkeley Square resembling a confounded haberdasher's window! You can have as many flowers as you want—cartloads of 'em for all I care. But no swathes of silk, for pity's sake, especially not matching the colour gown you'll be wearing for our betrothal party.'

'But you don't know what I shall choose to wear. I haven't decided myself yet,' she pointed out.

'Ah, but I have,' he astounded her by revealing. 'It wasn't too difficult a matter to discover where you'd had other dresses made. I merely visited the same modiste and asked her to make you a further evening gown. She was more than willing to oblige me when she realised it was for the divine Miss Grey, whose slender form so perfectly displayed her creations.'

Georgiana didn't know whether to feel flattered by this unexpected show of interest, or downright annoyed over his interference. She at once appreciated, though, that a crowded park was hardly the ideal place to point out that it had been a bit of a liberty on his part to decide what she should wear to the party—fake engagement though it was!— and so decided to accept the unexpected gift with a good grace.

'And that reminds me of something else I wished to say to you,' he went on, thereby denying her the opportunity to voice any gratitude. 'Tomorrow, our engagement will become common knowledge. If I know anything the door-knocker will never be still, so it's unlikely I shall be granted the opportunity to visit you. And if you take my advice you'll remain indoors yourself, or risk being pestered to death by the vulgarly curious, who'll all want to get a look at you. But the following day, I'd like you to visit Berkeley Square. We must start organising this confounded party of ours. I'll send the carriage for you. Bring that manservant of yours along. He'll be chaperon enough for the journey. Besides, I want to have a word with him.'

'Yes, of course, I'll come,' she responded, slightly disappointed not to be seeing him again until then, but perfectly understanding the reason why not. Something else then occurred to her. 'It will be interesting to visit the house again, if only to see the servants' reactions.' She smiled wistfully. 'I wonder how many of them will recognise me?'

'Brindle's sure to do so,' he returned with conviction. 'Turns out he did penetrate your disguise, eventually. But, as for the others…?' He shrugged, appearing quite unconcerned. 'Who can say?'

'Dear Brindle… Yes, I look forward to seeing them all again.'

# Chapter Eleven

Although she had expected the official announcement to cause a ripple through London society, never in her wildest imaginings had Georgiana supposed she would become something of a celebrity overnight. Not long after the Friday editions of the morning newspapers had been pored over at breakfast tables across the capital the door-knocker at the Grenville town house was never still. After having captured one of the richest prizes the Marriage Mart had to offer, she had been catapulted up the social ladder, going from a Little Miss Nobody, hardly of more consequence than a paid companion to the Dowager Countess and her granddaughter, to the singular young woman who had succeeded where so many others down the years had failed.

A lesser person might have allowed the outburst of attention to go to her head. Like the Dowager Countess, who sat in her favourite chair in the drawing room, serenely welcoming the never-ending stream of visitors throughout the afternoon and early evening, Georgiana herself was determined to maintain her objectivity.

The following day, though, when she was informed his lordship's own town carriage stood at the door, she couldn't wait to escape from the house, and the insincerity of those who all at once had developed a desire for her society.

Digby, almost fully recovered from his injury, accompanied Perkins round to the mews, leaving Georgiana to enter that Berkeley Square house, which she knew so well, by herself. She couldn't deny when she raised the knocker that she felt slightly apprehensive at the possible reaction of the servants. But she need not have worried. Brindle, a prince among butlers, behaved impeccably, not even by so much as a slight raising of one greying brow betraying the fact that he had ever set eyes on her before that day. After bowing her into the hall, he offered his sincerest congratulations on her betrothal to his master, before informing her that his lordship awaited her in the breakfast parlour.

Georgiana glanced at the excellent time-keeper, taking pride of place in the corner of the chequered hall. It wanted only a few minutes to one. 'Great heavens! What a slug-a-bed! I broke my fast quite some time ago.'

'As is his lordship's custom when he remains away from home all night, he breaks his fast somewhat later than usual.' There was a hint of a twinkle in the grey eyes as he added, 'His lordship assured me you would have no trouble finding your own way to the breakfast parlour, Miss Grey.'

Even this attempt at humour on Brindle's part failed to take the sting out of what he had unwittingly divulged a moment before. Georgiana was only too painfully aware that whenever the Viscount remained away overnight it was more than likely he had spent it in the arms of his mistress. It oughtn't to have mattered a whit to her whether he kept a mistress or not. Unfortunately it did. The knowledge was as painful now as it had been the year before when she had first learned of the 'Divine Caroline'.

She turned and headed down the passageway that led to the breakfast parlour, determined not to reveal the hurt and anger coursing through her. With the best will in the world, though, she was unable to conceal the shock at discovering his lordship not alone, and stopped dead in her tracks, as her eyes focused on the fair locks of his companion.

'Ah, Georgie!' After making use of his napkin, his lordship rose immediately to his feet. 'Come in, my darling. It isn't like you to be so shy. There's someone here simply longing to meet you. Lady Eleanor Fincham, my fiancée, Miss Georgiana Grey.'

She then found her hand being warmly taken and held by a statuesque female in her early thirties, whose warm smile was mirrored in a pair of soft grey eyes. 'I cannot tell you how much I have been looking forward to making your acquaintance. I didn't hesitate to accept the invitation to come to London, after reading Ben's letter.'

Georgiana then discovered those grey eyes could twinkle merrily, betraying a lively sense of humour. 'Though perhaps I ought to say I was summoned to the capital. Apparently, I'm to play the duenna, so that you may visit the house as often as you wish to arrange the party, without giving rise to a deal of gossip. I'm to remain until after the event, so please do not hesitate to make use of me whilst I'm here.'

Lady Eleanor then turned to her brother-in-law and attempted to scold him for keeping so much to himself. 'You quite failed to tell me how lovely your future Viscountess is,' she reminded him, before demanding to see the ring and then uttering a gasp of delight. 'I've known him for years and never realised until now how much of a romantic he is! Only a man deeply in love would think of choosing sapphires for you, my dear.'

As had happened all too often in recent days, Georgiana hardly knew how to respond, and was spared having to do so on this occasion by his lordship's timely intervention. With a suspicion of a smile he suggested the ladies repair to the library and begin writing the invitations without delay.

'And I would also suggest you leave the writing to Georgie, Eleanor. Unlike your spidery scrawl, she writes a most elegant copperplate.' There was a decided glint in his eyes. 'I still treasure the letter she wrote to me last summer and consider it the finest example of a lady's handwriting I've ever seen.'

Once again Georgiana was at a loss to know what to say. She knew precisely the letter to which he was referring. And to think he had kept it all this time was rather touching.

'There's no need to look so embarrassed, my darling,' his lordship continued, once again filling the breach. 'Never let it be said that Fincham did not give praise where it was due. And now, ladies,' he added, after finishing his coffee, 'I shall leave you to your own devices. I jotted down a list of those whom I think we should invite, Georgie, but add to it if you consider I've missed someone off. It's all ready for you in the library, with the pile of invitation cards.'

He went over to the door, but turned back to add, 'By the by, did that manservant of yours accompany you here?'

'Yes, he went round to the mews with Perkins.'

'Excellent! I'll run him to earth there. I should be back in an hour or so. But until then I shall leave you in Eleanor's very capable hands.'

'Good heavens!' His sister-in-law rolled her eyes in dismay. 'The man cannot sit still for five minutes. I arrived here yesterday and have hardly seen anything of him! Still…' she shrugged '…he must have a hundred and one things to do if he wants the party organised in less than two weeks. So perhaps we'd best repair to the library, as he suggested, and do our bit.

'Now, I'm here to help all I can,' she continued, as she led the way across the hall, little realising that the young woman beside her was very familiar with the layout of the house, and had been in each and every room. 'But I have no intention of interfering.'

'I shall be glad of your help, my lady,' Georgiana

assured her. 'I assisted the Dowager Countess in arranging the ball for her granddaughter and realise how much work is involved.'

'Eleanor, please. I do not intend that there should be any formality between us. Why, I'm beginning to look upon you as a sister already. And am determined we shall be the very best of friends!'

An hour later Georgian felt as if she'd known Lady Eleanor all her life. She loved her frank, open manner, which was not so dissimilar to her own. Although, by her own admission, she no longer socialised as much as she once did, and rarely journeyed to the capital, Eleanor seemed to know something about most all of those whom the Viscount had invited to the party.

One name, towards the end of the list, caused her to betray a moment's disquiet. 'Now, why on earth has he included them, do you suppose?' she murmured, and then seemed to realise she'd spoken her thoughts aloud and appeared faintly embarrassed.

Georgiana glanced again at the list, and the names of Lord and Lady Wenbury seemed to jump off the page. Instantly memories of gossiping round a certain kitchen table came flooding back.

The previous year when she had first learned of

the 'so-called' love of the Viscount's life, she had felt nothing, except perhaps a deal of sympathy towards the man who had been heartlessly tossed aside by the woman he had loved. As far as she could recall his lordship had never once given her the impression that he suffered from unrequited love, and she supposed that was partly the reason why, up until now, she had felt more curiosity than any degree of jealousy towards the woman who had so callously jilted him. She couldn't ignore, though, that almost overnight everything had changed, and now she very much resented the idea of his old love attending the party—of any past flames attending, come to that.

Clearly Lady Eleanor did not hold Lord Wenbury's wife in high regard and, given her obvious regard for her brother-in-law, it was perhaps understandable why not. Yet, for reasons known only to himself, Ben had wished the Wenburys to attend, and she, at least, must accept the situation with a good grace. She must never allow herself to become overly sensitive and must attempt never to brood over insignificant details. The whole engagement was a confounded sham, anyway, she reminded herself, once again lifting the quill from the standish. And she must never foolishly lose sight of that fact…ever!

* * *

When the day of the party finally arrived, and she was at last journeying to the Viscount's town house for the celebration itself, Georgiana believed she had her every wayward emotion well under control, and had her mind firmly focused on the only reason for the engagement.

She'd been granted numerous opportunities during the past days to judge Ben's attitude towards her, and she had come to the conclusion it could best be described as still bordering on sibling affection. There was naught of the lover in his manner towards her. The only time he ever attempted to touch her more than fleetingly had been on those occasions when they had danced together. She could only be grateful those instances when they had attended the same party had been blessedly few during the past week or so, for it had been only then, when he had been close, tall and strong beside her, that she had become too conscious of his masculinity, of his innate power to attract her. It had been only then she had felt her resolve weakening, which had resulted in her wanting to put as much distance as possible between them.

Yet, on other occasions she had had cause to be grateful for his presence; such as that time at

Berkeley Square when Ronan had escaped from the kitchen area, and had come bounding across the drawing room to greet her, quite blatantly ignoring his master and Lady Eleanor in his eagerness to reach his goal.

'Struck up an immediate partiality for her company from the first,' his lordship had remarked in response to his sister-in-law's surprised look. 'There have been times I think the ungrateful cur actually prefers her to me!'

His mock outrage had instantly averted what might have been a slightly awkward moment. Lady Eleanor had just chuckled and not asked for any further explanation for the dog's astonishing behaviour. Then there had been that other significant incident when Georgiana had had her first encounter with Cook after so very many months. Clearly Brindle had never betrayed his master's trust by revealing what he knew to any other member of staff, for Mrs Willard's jaw had dropped perceptively and she had just stared across the room in stunned disbelief, until his lordship had again, showing great presence of mind, intervened.

'Struck dumb by your future mistress's loveliness, no doubt. Perfectly understand! But surely you didn't expect your lord and master to become betrothed to a bracket-faced creature?'

Once again his timely intervention had averted what might so easily have turned into a most embarrassing moment, especially as Lady Eleanor had again been present at the time. Cook had seemed to collect herself almost at once, and during all subsequent meetings between them had not attempted to allude to the fact that they had known each other the year before in vastly contrasting circumstances, though that wonderful rapport they had enjoyed back then had soon re-established itself.

So could anything go wrong tonight? Georgiana couldn't help wondering, as she stepped lightly down from his lordship's carriage. She sincerely hoped not, but was too much of a realist to sit back on her laurels. The Viscount would be on hand, of course. But that was not always necessarily a good thing, she reminded herself, as she reached out her hand to make her arrival known.

Brindle, bowing her into the hall, for once betrayed his emotions in a look of absolute appreciation, which was no less marked than those she had received from the Dowager and Lady Sophia before she had left the Grenville town house a short time earlier.

There could not have been a gown in the length and breadth of the land that would have suited her better. Gloves, silk shawl and slippers were all dyed the exact same shade as the beautifully fashioned deep blue dress, a colour undoubtedly chosen to emphasise the unusual hue of her eyes. Whether or not the Viscount, or the modiste, had decided upon the exact shade, she had no way of knowing.

'His lordship desires a private word with you in the library,' Brindle informed her, throwing wide the door leading to the book-lined room.

Georgiana wasn't in the least surprised. She had received a brief note earlier in the day from Brindle's master requesting that, apart from the engagement ring, she don no jewellery for the occasion, as all necessary adornments awaited her at his home. She had supposed he had chosen something from the family jewels for her to wear, for which she could only be grateful as her own selection was woefully inadequate for such an occasion as this, concocted though the engagement was.

As she entered the room Georgiana almost stopped dead in her tracks as her eyes focused on the tall figure of the master of the house standing, sentinel-like, by the window. She'd seen him in formal evening attire on numerous occasions in recent weeks, but never had she seen him looking quite so magnificent. Tall and well muscled, his physique was admirably well suited to the new style of dress advocated by Brummell. His only adornments, apart from his quizzing-glass, was a large diamond nestling in the folds of his cravat and a simple gold signet ring on his right hand. Undeniably, there was about him that certain haughty air of a man who knew his own worth; and although he might never be considered strictly handsome, he cut the strikingly unforgettable figure of a gentleman of breeding and good taste.

After dismissing Brindle with a nod of his head, his lordship sauntered towards her in his usual gracefully athletic way, his gaze not missing the smallest detail of her own attire. Not for the first time he was struck by the slender shapeliness of her figure, and again it crossed his mind to wonder just how she had managed to conceal her feminine charms so adequately during those weeks she had acted the page. Some sort of chest binding, he could only suppose. Now, however, was not the appropriate time to attempt to satisfy his curiosity and risk discomposing her. Tonight he needed her to appear perfectly relaxed, and so he merely said, 'Perhaps now you can appreciate just why I was so against decking the reception rooms out in swathes of silk to match your gown.' He shuddered. 'I should have felt I was yet again enduring a wretched Channel crossing!'

Her immediate gurgle in response was exactly what he would have expected, and he found himself smiling too. 'Come over here, I have something for you.' He reached for the velvet-covered box on the top of his desk and flicked open the lid to reveal an array of sapphires and diamonds lying on a bed of silk. Her reaction was once again what he might have expected. Her perfectly shaped lips parted and her eyes widened in disbelief.

Before she had recovered from the shock sufficiently to speak, he was already clasping the necklace about her throat, his fingers unavoidably brushing the nape of her neck as he did so. Her reaction this time did not please him. She had stiffened...visibly so!

He was not a male accustomed to the fair sex flinching at his touch. The opposite was, in fact, very much more the case. Every female with whom he had enjoyed more intimate relations had actively encouraged his advances. He'd enough experience to be very sure that Georgiana wasn't indifferent to him. From the first there had always been a wonderful rapport between them, largely based on trust and respect, not to mention common interests. Furthermore, he'd touched her dozens of times without her cringing from him as though he were some kind of sexual predator, for heaven's sake! All the same, he couldn't deny that he'd caught a certain wariness in her expression from time to time during more recent days.

'What's wrong?' Grasping her shoulders, he turned her round to face him squarely and then placed one hand beneath her chin so that she had no choice but to look him in the face. 'And please don't insult my intelligence by denying it. It's patently obvious something's troubling you.'

She moved away and he didn't attempt to stop her. 'If you must know,' she said after a brief silence, 'I'm finding it all a bit of a strain.' Her sudden shout of laughter was distinctly mirthless. 'You might find this hard to believe, Ben, but lying doesn't come easily to me.'

'I do not find that hard to believe at all,' he assured her. 'I could always tell when you were lying to me, Master Green.'

The name succeeded in evoking many bittersweet memories, and Georgiana wandered over to the hearth and stared up at the portrait that had so captured her attention all those many months ago. 'You brought me in here that first evening, remember? I never imagined then that I would be standing here almost a year later attempting to convince the world that we…'

As her words faded he went across to her and grasped her arms. Thankfully, this time she did not recoil at his touch, but her expression was hardly encouraging. He administered a small shake. 'I shall take leave to inform you, my girl, that you'll fool no one into believing you're a happily engaged female when you're wearing that woebegone face.'

She couldn't help smiling at this. And he was perfectly correct, of course! If she wished to succeed in her aim, she must play her part to the full. So long as she maintained that all-important sense of proportion and didn't attempt to persuade herself it was real.

'You're right, of course,' she agreed, echoing her thoughts. 'And what female wouldn't feel deliriously happy with a king's ransom in gems adorning her throat.' She peered down at the bottommost stones that almost reached the cleft between her breasts. 'They are truly magnificent, Ben. Are they part of the family jewels?'

'Certainly not!' He had sounded affronted. 'They

are my betrothal gift to you. However, I should prefer if they remain here in this house, if you have no objection. Of course, you may wear them as often as you wish.'

Georgiana was too stunned to be able to formulate any kind of response, let alone take time to consider why he might wish to keep them here at Berkeley Square. In fact, it was as much as she could do to don the matching earrings when commanded to do so.

'And now, my darling, I think it best if we repair upstairs without further ado. Eleanor and Charles will be awaiting us; we must be ready for when the first of our dinner-guests arrive.'

Much later that evening, when she stood beside the Viscount at the entrance to the large drawing room, Georgiana felt she had managed to regain at least some of her self-possession. The dinner party had been a most enjoyable affair. She'd been more than happy for Lady Eleanor to preside over the table as hostess, which of course had enabled her to relax far more and enjoy the company of the Viscount's good friend Charles Gingham, who had sat on her immediate left.

Now, of course, the most crucial part of the

evening had begun. Two of the suspects had already arrived and were ensconced in the room set out for cards. The third, bewigged, and dazzlingly attired in a coat of gold brocade, satin knee-breeches and high-heeled buckled shoes, was at last mincing his way along the passageway towards them.

'God in heaven, Trent!' his lordship exclaimed in disgust. 'Never tell me you've been dipping into the rouge pot!'

'Had to, dear boy,' Sir Willoughby responded, not visibly chastened by the Viscount's evident disdain. 'Positively washed out I look without it. I swear that demmed chest infection very nearly took me off!'

He then felt for his quizzing-glass and through it peered for several moments at the gems adorning a slender throat before transferring his gaze to the feature that so perfectly matched the exquisite stones. The next moment his own eyes widened, and the aid to vision slipped from his fingers. 'Good gad!' he exclaimed. 'It cannot be!'

'Quite right, Trent, it cannot,' his lordship concurred in a dangerously quiet tone. 'And you would be wise to forget that you ever thought it could have been.'

'Forgotten already, dear boy,' he returned airily, before sauntering into the room.

'Don't look so crestfallen,' his lordship chided gently. 'People might suppose we've had a lovers' tiff.'

'But he recognised me, Ben. What dreadful ill luck! I would never have supposed for a moment that he was so observant.'

'Don't let that foppish air fool you, my darling. Sir Willoughby Trent is quite remarkably astute. Very little escapes him.'

'Really?' Georgiana began to view the baronet in a new light. 'So he's quite capable of organising these jewel thefts.'

'Oh, more than capable,' he concurred. 'But I rather fancy he isn't the one. I haven't ruled him out quite yet, but he's definitely bottom of the list. And don't allow the fact that he recognised you trouble you unduly. He won't say anything.'

'But how can you be so sure?'

'Because he has a rather perverse sense of humour. If he revealed your little secret, he would risk being disbelieved, besides denying himself the pleasure of tormenting you in the future. Furthermore, I know a thing or two about him that he definitely wouldn't wish spread abroad. So put it from your mind and go and mingle with our guests. I do believe the Dowager and her granddaughter would appreciate a few words with you, as would several others. I'll remain here to greet any late arrivals.'

She was only too willing to oblige, and until the time came for her to partner Ben and lead the first set of country dances, she believed she maintained the role of a newly engaged young woman to perfection.

At least Lady Sophia evidently detected nothing amiss when she claimed Georgiana's attention the instant the dance came to an end. Her over-enthusiastic partner had inadvertently torn her flounce and Sophia wished to repair the damage at once.

'You see, I'm supposed to be dancing with Mr Beresford next, Georgie, and I don't want him to see me less than perfectly groomed,' she revealed shyly. 'I cannot thank you enough for inviting him. I do so much prefer him to any other gentleman of my acquaintance!'

'I know you do, Sophie. And so does your grandmother.' She cast the girl a sympathetic smile. 'I know she approves of Beresford. After all, why should she not? He has no title, but he comes from a good family and he isn't exactly impoverished. But have a care, my dear, because I do not believe the Dowager will give her blessing to a serious attachment between you, at least not this year. Next might be different. She wants you to enjoy the society of many young gentlemen before you finally think seriously about marriage.'

Lady Sophia sensibly seemed to accept this. 'And when I do finally become betrothed, I should like a party just like this one, not some grand ball where you hardly know anyone. Tonight has been lovely. Everyone I've spoken to thinks so.'

This was gratifying to hear, for Lady Eleanor, the servants, Ben and she herself had worked so hard to make it a success. And so it was proving to be, despite the odd disappointment and the occasional disquieting moment.

After seeing Lady Sophia into the ladies' withdrawing room, where a young maid was on hand to assist in just such an emergency as a torn flounce, Georgiana, almost without thinking, continued along the passage to a small bedchamber overlooking the Square. It had been her very own room during those few short weeks she had stayed in the house the previous spring.

Pushing wide the door, she was gratified to discover nothing had changed. Seating herself on the windowsill, as she had done many times in the past, she stared out across the Square in time to see a smart carriage depositing its passengers at the house opposite. She couldn't help wondering whether the party taking place there was as enjoyable as her own was, amazingly enough, turning out to be. It was true she had suffered a disappointment when organising the event, when she had discovered that Charles Gingham wouldn't be bringing his young wife along, but she had quite understood. Apparently, poor Louise was increasing again and not having such an easy time of it on this occasion.

The encounter with Sir Willoughby Trent had unnerved her for a time, as indeed had her first-ever encounter with the supposed love of his lordship's life. All the same, it was rather strange that when she had met Lady Wenbury face to face she had not experienced even so much as a twinge of jealousy.

Although perhaps not in her first flush of youth, Lady Wenbury was undeniably strikingly lovely. From her perfectly arranged fair locks to her satin-shod feet, she bore all the perfection of a London modiste's fashion plate. Accompanying her had been her spouse, a portly gentleman of average height who, in stark contrast, carried his clothes very ill. Yet, it wasn't so much the baron's appearance that surprised Georgiana as the Viscount's attitude towards him.

Not even by so much as a slight frostiness of tone

had his lordship betrayed that he had felt the least animosity towards the middle-aged man who had married the woman he himself had very much desired to wed. In fact, he could not have been more welcoming or genial in his greeting. His attitude towards the baroness had been even more surprising. Apart from a remark clearly meant in jest, which had resulted in her tapping his arm flirtatiously with her fan, while favouring him with a provocative smile, he had shown no interest in her whatsoever.

Quite the contrary, in fact! Not once had he attempted to seek her out for a private conversation, nor had he seemed to search her out with his eyes. It was almost as if Lady Wenbury meant absolutely nothing to him now. At least he hadn't appeared to consider her in any way more important than any of his other guests. So why had he made a point of inviting the couple?

'What on earth are you doing skulking away in here?' that deeply attractive and, oh, so familiar voice demanded to know, making her start guiltily. 'Our guests will soon begin to wonder where you are, as I myself would have done had I not happened to glance out of the drawing room and catch you wandering along the passageway.'

Good heavens! He might not have been watching

Lady Wenbury, but he was certainly keeping his eye on her! As she didn't know whether to feel flattered, or slightly alarmed, she decided it might be wise to be truthful, given that he had already revealed he knew very well when she was attempting to conceal something from him.

'It just so happens I wandered in here without thinking. This used to be my room when I resided here,' she reminded him.

'Well, it won't be again,' he returned abruptly, which resulted in her wistful little smile vanishing in an instant. As he moved towards her he watched it replaced by a look that appeared to encompass both wariness and sadness. 'What's troubling that pretty little head of yours?' he queried with the same gentleness as he traced the fine bones of her face with his fingertips. 'Have I ever told you how very…lovely you are?'

As he spoke his head lowered, his intention clear. Georgiana knew it was madness; somehow, though, she didn't seem able to move, and when his arms had stolen about her and his mouth had at last fastened on to hers, she couldn't have moved even had she wanted to. And the most worrying fact of all was that she experienced not the slightest desire to do so!

Like some master puppeteer, he had her completely under his control. Exerting only the slightest of pressures he succeeded in forcing her lips apart and, as though operating some invisible strings, persuaded her to raise her arms and place her hands on his shoulders. In those delicious moments of experiencing this their first kiss, she felt she could deny him nothing and was more than happy for him to maintain complete control. It was only when he at last raised his head and the tender, invisible manipulation was finally broken, that a degree of common sense at last prevailed.

Even he spoke with less than his customary aplomb as he said, 'I think it might be wise to return to our guests now before the temptation to enter quite a different bedchamber becomes too strong. Besides which, someone has arrived who particularly wishes to make your acquaintance, and as he has attained considerable influence in—er—certain quarters, it wouldn't do to offend him.'

Still somewhat bewildered by what had just taken place, and most definitely not in full possession of her faculties, Georgiana was once again content to be guided by him. Like some docile child, she accompanied the Viscount back into the drawing room, where he took her straight over to the celebrity whose attire was every bit as impressive as his own. He then left her with the young gentleman of renown, with the strong warning that he would be watching closely from the other side of the room.

Chuckling at his distinguished guest's witty response, the Viscount collected a glass of champagne before stationing himself in the doorway between the two reception rooms so that he might watch the dancing for a while. He was swiftly thwarted in this desire by a tap on his shoulder and he turned to discover his good friend Charles Gingham at his heels.

'Where's that divine fiancée of yours? Entertaining some young sprig on the dance floor?'

'No, she's over there,' his lordship responded, gesturing to a certain spot in the drawing room, 'entertaining that particular sprig in conversation. And doing an excellent job of it, if the Beau's expression of rapt attention is anything to go by.'

'Good gad! How on earth did you manage to get Brummell here?' Charles looked about in some alarm. 'He hasn't brought Prinny with him, has he?'

'Good God, no! Never having been a devotee of the Regent's, I avoid the Carlton House set as a rule, with one exception. Although we differ in our political affiliations, George Brummell and I do have certain things in common, young though he is.'

'Well, he clearly appreciates your choice of future bride,' Charles responded, 'and I don't suppose for a moment it is simply because he has developed a penchant for that particular name.'

The Viscount was not slow to follow his friend's train of thought. 'Ah, yes, his very good friend the divine Duchess of Devonshire! Undoubtedly a lady of great charm, but not one of outstanding beauty. At least I never considered her so, and that was long before her tragic disfigurement.'

'But your own Georgiana is clearly very much to your taste,' Charles parried. 'Though at one time I would never have supposed it could be so.' He gave a sudden bark of laughter as a distant memory returned. 'If I recall correctly, your future bride was to be divinely fair and dutifully biddable—traits one could hardly attribute to Miss Grey, if you don't mind my saying.'

There was a suspicion of a twitch at the corner of his lordship's mouth. 'As you are clearly fast falling into a rollicking mood, I shall refrain from trying to maintain a sensible conversation with you. But perhaps if you have recovered sufficiently for a rational discussion you might care to join me in the library before we retire. There are one or two matters I should like to share with you.'

# Chapter Twelve

'Damnably enjoyable evening, Finch!' Charles declared, when they had finally repaired to the library to enjoy a glass of brandy before retiring. 'All the guests thought so. Georgie, bless her, has certainly silenced any critics who might have wrongly supposed she lacked the necessary social skills for her future position in life. The dinner menu couldn't have been bettered in my opinion, and the reception rooms, with those beautifully arranged flowers, looked an absolute picture! She did you proud, old fellow.'

There was a hint of smug satisfaction in the Viscount's expression. 'Yes, she has worked hard this past week or so. I never doubted her ability to organise the event. And, of course, it was one way to keep her fully occupied and therefore less inclined to indulge in ill-judged behaviour.'

'Eh?' Charles was clearly startled to be told this.

'Is she likely to do so, then? Not been gadding about in boy's raiment again recently, surely?'

'Afraid so, old fellow.' There was a distinct menacing gleam in his lordship's dark eyes now. 'But she won't again, if she knows what's good for her. That said, I'm forced to own there was perhaps some justification for her having done so. And that is why I wished to speak to you now.'

It was clear he held his friend's full attention, so the Viscount wasted no time in revealing almost everything he knew concerning the seventh Earl of Grenville's death. 'So we are left with three possible suspects, and I am at present attempting to eliminate two of them.'

Charles shook his head. 'Do you know, I was only talking to Louise and Mother about this recently, Finch, wondering if these robberies were in some way connected. But how the deuce are they disposing of the jewellery? No one in London would be stupid enough to purchase any of it, surely?'

'No. It's going across the Channel. And that is where I would appreciate your assistance, my friend.' His lordship's gaze was unwavering. 'I'm inclined to believe, you see, that your cousin Henri might well be involved in this business.'

Not even by the slight raising of one fair brow did

Charles betray surprise at learning that. 'I assume you have proof.'

'Only what Georgie herself managed to discover. That said, I believe he's over in France as we speak, attempting to dispose of Lady Chalmondley's emeralds. There's plenty of smuggling going on, and many who'll risk taking a passenger across to France for a price. I'm having a particular Channel port watched for his return. His movements will then be closely monitored for the foreseeable future. And it is with regard to Henri that I believe you might be of some help.'

'Of course, I'll do what I can. But I haven't had any contact with him in…oh, must be five or six years,' Charles reminded his lordship. 'I believe he still resides in the capital, but I couldn't tell you where, exactly.'

'It shouldn't be too difficult to discover where he's lodging. I'll write to you in a week or so. Then you can make casual contact, and see what you can discover from him without arousing his suspicions. Seemingly, a relative of his is involved in disposing of the gems.'

'He has a number of French cousins,' Charles pointed out. 'I've never been acquainted with any of them.'

'That's of no importance. Just make contact with Henri again on his return and see what you can discover. Any small detail he lets fall could turn out to be important and might ultimately lead to the brains behind it all.'

Charles shook his head, evidently having some difficulty believing everything he was hearing. 'And you say Georgie herself discovered Henri's involvement. How the deuce did she accomplish that?'

'Would you believe by visiting a—er—lowly tavern in the east of the city, where it was arranged that the booty would be handed over to your cousin?'

'Good gad!'

'Quite!' his lordship agreed, smiling faintly. 'It just so happens it was on that particular night I persuaded her to become engaged.'

'Eh…?' Again Charles didn't attempt to hide his astonishment. 'Do you mean she didn't wish to become betrothed?'

His lordship considered for a moment. 'I'm not altogether sure, old friend. What I can tell you is that she'd never considered a marriage between us.' His smile faded and he was suddenly serious. 'You see, Charles, Georgie believes the engagement to be bogus and that my only interest is to prove beyond doubt I had nothing whatsoever to do with

her godfather's demise. You must remember I was
one of the—er—so-called "favoured five".'

Charles was clearly all at sea now, and it showed.
'But surely she doesn't suspect you?'

'No, she doesn't,' his lordship responded with absolute conviction.

'Then why on earth don't you tell her the truth?'

'What…? That I've been in love with her almost
from the first?' The Viscount's smile had a decidedly bitter curl. 'I'll tell you why, Charles… It's
because I'm a damnable coward, that's why! Past
experience has left me distinctly wary about revealing my feelings to a member of the fair sex.'

'You're thinking of Charlotte, naturally,' Charles
returned softly. 'I did wonder why you had invited
Lady Wenbury tonight. Surely you weren't compar-
ing the two?'

'Assuredly not! To me Georgie is far above in
every respect the woman I now consider merely
a youthful indiscretion. But I'm not so foolish as
to suppose she hasn't at some point learned of my
association with the baroness, and all the foolish
conjecture that resulted after her rushed marriage
to Wenbury. I believe Georgie now realises I'm not
suffering any regrets about what happened. Quite
the opposite, in fact! I consider I had an extremely

lucky escape. I can never thank you enough for dragging me over to France all those years ago.'

His lordship was silent for a moment, staring thoughtfully down at the amber liquid in his glass. 'I've experience enough and am arrogant enough to believe Georgie cares for me very deeply. None the less, she is not certain of my feelings towards her or of my genuine motives for wishing the engagement to take place. Why, she must be asking herself, does a gentleman present a lady with a fortune in gems, only to insist they remain in his charge, if he intends her to keep them? And why too does he never bestow other tokens of his affection, except rarely, when natural inclination overcomes resolve?'

Again there was a hint of smug satisfaction in his smile. 'Yes, I have succeeded in maintaining poor Georgie in a state of delicious confusion during these past couple of weeks, and I intend to do all in my power to keep her there, at least for the time being. While her mind is focused on attempting to comprehend my diverse behaviour, she will be less likely to concern herself with other matters.'

Undoubtedly the Viscount would have derived much satisfaction from the knowledge that his betrothed had spent much of that night pondering over his perplexing behaviour: one moment the gentle, persuasive lover, the next the dour elder brother determined to keep a younger sister under strict control.

Those hours of wakefulness had not been in vain, however. Although when she rose from her bed the following day she might not have been any clearer in her mind as to why his lordship's manner towards her could be so contrasting, she was very sure that he had done his utmost to keep her involvement in a very important matter to the absolute minimum.

During those days leading up to the engagement party, she had been too preoccupied with organising the celebration to concentrate more than fleetingly on those events surrounding her godfather's death. Even so, it had occurred to her on several occasions that Digby had been spending a deal of time with his lordship. She didn't so much begrudge her servant liaising with the Viscount as resent her deliberate exclusion from those various meetings where information must undoubtedly have been exchanged.

Consequently, when she met the Viscount at the prearranged time in the park later in the day, she was determined to involve herself again in unmasking the mastermind behind the robberies, a fact that would undoubtedly have caused his lordship some disquiet had she been foolish enough to admit as much. However, if there was one thing she had learned in all her dealings with Lord Fincham it was that sometimes it was very wise to keep one's own counsel.

So she merely greeted him cordially by announcing her intention of purchasing a suitable mount so that she might enjoy her favourite form of exercise while she remained in the capital. 'I'm assured Tattersall's is the place to go.'

'But not for a lady,' he returned discouragingly. 'The fair sex is not welcome there. Nor should any member of it attempt to cross the portals of that all-male preserve if she wishes to retain her good name.'

Much as she might resent the domination of the male in society, Georgiana had sense enough to accept that matters would not change overnight; if she wished to continue to be looked upon with approval in the polite world, then she must not flout those rules governing the behaviour of her sex.

That accepted, there were other ways to achieve one's objective, she mused, a solution to the dilemma having quickly occurred to her.

Unfortunately his lordship, silently considering how utterly charming she looked in her fashionable bonnet trimmed with blue ribbon, just happened to detect that unmistakably speculative glint in her eyes and wasn't slow to interpret the meaning behind it. 'Don't you dare contemplate involving Master Green, my girl!' he advised in a dangerously low undertone. 'I'll acquire a suitable mount for you.'

Such blatant interference in her affairs ought to have annoyed her intensely. Perversely, it had the opposite effect. She felt more amused than anything else. Clearly the gentle lover of the night before had been replaced by the strict elder brother again. But maybe it was for the best, she reasoned. And a deal safer! After all, she'd experienced often enough his overbearing moods and had succeeded more often than not in managing him without too much trouble. The ardent fiancé, on the other hand, was an unknown quantity and, therefore, far more difficult to deal with.

'Very well,' she agreed amicably, surprising him somewhat. 'But on the strict understanding I reimburse you for the cost,' she added, proving at a stroke that she was not prepared to bend to his will over everything. 'I mean it, Ben,' she continued, when he looked directly ahead, smiling a little smugly, as was his wont when he believed he had attained the upper hand. 'The horse shall belong to me. I fully intend to take the animal back with me to Gloucestershire at the end of the Season.'

Although this determination clearly didn't please him, he merely said, 'We'll discuss the matter more fully when the time comes. Instead, tell me what you made of society's latest darling?'

'Brummell, you mean?' She took a moment to consider, while smiling at clear memories of the interlude with the famous beau. 'Well, although he's still young, a matter of a year or so older than me, he's undoubtedly made a name for himself. He's very ambitious. He's clever and extremely witty. He's attractive, despite his nose having been broken. A fall from a horse, I believe he said. He succeeded in keeping me in a high state of amusement with his wicked observations about some of those present.'

'Yes, I saw you were enjoying his company hugely.' He didn't sound altogether pleased. 'Dare I ask what he said about me?'

A teasing glint added an extra sparkle to her eyes. 'Oh, I couldn't possibly reveal everything he said. But on the whole you fared better than most. I think he rather likes you, even though your political views are vastly contrasting. Naturally he approves your style of dress. Which is more than can be said for

Lord Wenbury. He compared him to an oversized wasp, would you believe?'

'Ah, yes, poor Eustace! Never had any taste in clothes, nor the figure to carry 'em, come to that.'

She looked up at him sharply. Although he'd been disparaging about the baron's style of dress, again there hadn't been so much as a hint of resentment in his voice towards the man who had married his old love, which only went to substantiate her belief that he did not wear the willow for the baroness.

'I believe I overheard Lord Wenbury say that he and his wife were bound for Lady Kilerton's soirée this evening. The Dowager Countess has a fancy to attend. And I think I shall go, too, as Lady Eleanor said she would be among the guests. It will offer me the opportunity to say a final farewell. She intends to return to the country tomorrow, so I understand.'

He confirmed this with a nod. 'But I shall not be escorting her. My time will be better spent at my club, I think, or at another gaming establishment.'

Perhaps that was true. None the less, Georgiana had no intention of taking a back seat any longer and that night was bent on starting her own investigations anew. Firstly, though, she was determined to bestow her heartfelt thanks on the lady whom she had come to look upon as a true friend and who had been such a support during the past couple of weeks.

Slipping into the vacant chair beside Lady Eleanor, Georgiana didn't waste time in giving voice to her appreciation or declaring her sadness at losing her new-found friend's companionship so soon. 'Heaven only knows when we'll see each other again.'

'Oh, don't you worry on that score. I have every intention of visiting Fincham Park frequently once the new mistress is in residence!' The widow did not miss the forlorn expression that just for one unguarded moment passed over delicate features. 'Why, Georgie! Whatever's amiss? You and Ben haven't quarrelled, have you? I know he can be tire-somely dictatorial on occasions, but his heart's in the right place.'

'Oh, no, no, nothing like that,' Georgiana hur-riedly assured her. 'It's just…well… We have made no firm plans to marry. So it might be ages before you and I see each other again.'

'I'll wager if Ben has his way you'll not be enjoy-ing a long engagement.'

'No, I doubt we shall,' Georgiana agreed wistfully. 'But I should still like to maintain contact with you.

You're the only real friend I've made since coming to town.'

Lady Eleanor gave the younger woman's hand an affectionate squeeze. 'There's nothing to stop you visiting me whenever you wish. My daughter and I shall love having you as our guest. If Ben's overbearing ways ever become too much, and you wish to have a break from him for a week or two, or even longer, come and stay with me. You'll be safe from his tyranny there.'

'You never know, I might just take you up on that offer one day,' Georgiana responded, before some new arrivals captured their attention.

Lady Eleanor was not slow to voice her disfavour. 'I'd forgotten they were coming.'

'You don't approve of Lady Wenbury, that's plain. And, given your sisterly affection for Ben, under-standable. I do not know her well enough to have formed an opinion. That said, I found her gracious enough yesterday evening.'

A sound suspiciously like a snort was the response to this. 'Oh, yes, she's acquired all the social skills, I'll give her that. And I'll go as far as to say, even after presenting Wenbury with his first child last year, she's still a fine-looking woman, though not quite as lovely as she once was. There's no denying

Charlotte Vane was quite breathtakingly lovely in her youth—the face of an angel and the figure of a goddess. And the heart of a conniving harpy! My one consolation is that Ben instantly saw her for what she was when she married Wenbury. What a lucky escape for him, it was to be sure! And look at him now—he has you!'

Georgiana found herself quite unequal to meeting her friend's admiring gaze and was fortunate enough, a moment later, to catch sight of someone of far more significance to divert her thoughts.

'Gracious, me! Sir Willoughby Trent is one of their party. Now, I find him of far more interest.'

Lady Eleanor was clearly startled. 'Do you, my dear?'

'Perhaps I should say…diverting,' Georgiana returned, quickly correcting her blunder. 'What do you know about him? Why does one never see him with his wife?'

'Ah well, that much I can tell you! Sir Willoughby happens to be married to a cousin of an acquaintance of mine, the wife of a local squire, who lives close to Ben, as it happens.'

Georgiana gave a start as memory stirred. 'Not Squire Wyndham, by any chance?'

'Why, yes!' Lady Eleanor again betrayed

amazement. 'Never tell me you've met him? He so rarely comes up to town.'

'No, I've never met him,' Georgiana was able to reply with total honesty, though sensibly keeping her gaze averted. 'Ben mentioned his name in passing once. All I know is that he has two daughters.'

'Yes, that's right. The younger girl, Mary, is a sweet-natured child. Her elder sister Clarissa is quite another matter!'

Once again it was clear that she and Lady Eleanor held similar views. Unfortunately Georgiana could not own to the fact, at least not on this particular occasion. So, instead, she turned her companion's thoughts again to Sir Willoughby.

'As I said, he married Lady Wyndham's cousin quite a number of years ago. She's a good deal older than he is—by some ten years, if my memory serves me correctly. He was an only child, quite pampered by an adoring mother. I think his wife may have taken her place. But for all that the marriage, I think, is a happy one. Lady Trent dislikes town life, and is content to remain in the country. For his part Sir Willoughby likes to spend a little time in London and strut about in his diamond-buckled shoes, just to prove that he's a worthy of some substance. But to be perfectly honest, I think he's happiest at home being spoilt by his doting spouse.'

Perhaps Ben was right, Georgiana reflected, as she watched, to rapturous applause, a rather large female seat herself at the pianoforte to begin the evening's entertainment. Sir Willoughby Trent just didn't seem the type to involve himself in robbery and murder. Besides which, anyone who walked around in diamond-studded shoes was hardly short of a guinea or two. No, the mastermind was not Sir Willoughby, she decided, mentally crossing him off the list.

Later that same evening the Viscount, oddly enough, was coming to the same conclusion about another of the suspects. Having arrived at his club quite early, he had settled himself at a discreet corner table, where he had been obliged to wait quite some time before his patience was rewarded by the arrival of at least one of the questionable trio.

'Ah, Gyles! Care to join me in a hand or two of piquet?' he invited.

A rueful expression washed over Lord Rupert's face. 'Best not, old fellow. Pockets to let, and all that. Had a run of the most ill luck lately. Besides,

I've enough IOUs floating about the metropolis at present without adding to the blighters.'

His lordship wasn't slow to appreciate the situation. 'Merton cutting up rough, is he?'

'Worst he's ever been,' Lord Rupert confirmed. 'That dratted brother of mine has always had an uncertain temper. But I thought he was going to suffer an apoplexy this afternoon when I dropped in to touch him up for a loan.'

His lordship, though sympathetic, could well appreciate the stance the Duke of Merton had taken. Lord Rupert Gyles was universally considered a genial soul for the most part, but there was undeniably an irresponsible streak in his nature. He had always enjoyed the finer things in life, and had lived beyond his means for years.

'Dare I ask how much?'

The Duke's brother had the grace to look a little shamefaced as he revealed what he owed.

His lordship pursed his lips in a silent whistle. 'In that case you'd best join me in a glass of wine, and we'll play a hand or two merely for love.'

'Ha! That's all very well for you to say,' Lord Rupert scoffed, readily accepting the invitation, all the same. 'You've that in abundance, too. Lucky dog! Any fool can see that. I must say, though,' he continued, after fortifying himself from the contents of his glass, 'you've found yourself an absolute darling there... And those gauds she was wearing! I don't suppose you'd consider loaning them to me for a week or two so I can clear my debts? I'd return them to you, as soon as I was on my feet again, as it were.'

'Assuredly not!' Although his lordship was instantly alert at mention of the sapphire necklace, he quickly appreciated his companion was in jest, as he'd never attempted to borrow so much as a penny from him before. 'Do you know, Gyles, you could do worse than find yourself a wife and settle down.'

The advice was not well received. 'Oh, not you too, confound it! That's exactly what that dratted brother of mine insists I do. He wants me to leave London in the middle of the Season and return to the ancestral pile in order to court a rich widow who's recently moved into the area. A rich widow with two brats hanging on her apron strings, I might add!' He visibly shuddered. 'Can you see me happily settling down in that situation?'

'You won't know what it's like until you try.'

'Oh, come on, Finch. I'm a bachelor, born and bred. Happy as can be in my rooms overlooking the park, with just my faithful valet Barns to take care of my needs. Besides…' he shrugged '…I consider there's something rather sordid about marrying just for money. I know plenty of people do—Chard, to name but one. He must have run through his wife's fortune years ago, the way he plays. And what's he left with…? A wife he can't bear the sight of and keeps hidden away in the country! No, that's not for me. I've got my faults, plenty of 'em, but I've some principles too. I wouldn't saddle myself with a wife, just for money. It's so damnably degrading! It'd be dashed unfair on the filly, too.'

After silently contemplating everything he'd heard, his lordship said, 'I don't see as you've any choice, Gyles. You'll have the duns after you, if you remain in town. And you never know, there's just a possibility you might actually like the widow when you meet her.'

As the following day, maintaining the trend of the past week or so, was another fine one, Georgie was only too happy to accept the Viscount's written invitation to meet in the park again at the fashionable hour. As they strolled along, acknowledging their many mutual acquaintances, she casually alluded to the matter of the jewellery thefts, and voiced her agreement with him where Sir Willoughby Trent was concerned.

'He just happened to attend Lady Kilerton's soirée last night, so I had plenty of opportunity to observe him at leisure.'

He slanted a sympathetic glance. 'Was it such a devilishly tedious affair, my darling, that you found the sight of the powdered and painted baronet of more interest?'

She couldn't forbear a chuckle at this. Ben was notoriously critical when it came to judging the accomplishments of his fellow man, and as a rule avoided such entertainments as soirées like the plague.

'I must confess we were obliged to listen to one or two, as you are wont to call them, screech owls performing, and a couple of distressingly poor performances on the pianoforte. Not to mention Lord Wenbury's love poem, which very nearly sent me into whoops. But apart from those lamentable contributions it was a most enjoyable evening.'

She risked a swift glance up at him in order to assess his mood. She strongly suspected that if she were to display a deal of interest in his own investigations, she would discover nothing at all. So she asked as casually as she could, 'And how did your evening fare?'

'Most instructive, as things turned out. After a deal of consideration since leaving White's last night, I'm now prepared to cross Sir Rupert Gyles off the list. It just so happens I considered him almost on a par with Sir Willoughby as the most unlikely suspect. Had it not been for the fact that it's common knowledge that he lives beyond his means much of the time, but always manages to come about eventually, I would have dismissed him at the outset.'

Although not doubting his judgement, she was curious. 'What ultimately convinced you of his innocence?'

'Discovering, amazingly enough, that Sir Rupert has a rather quaint streak of chivalry running through him. He considers marrying merely for money beneath contempt, and cited Chard's situation as what typically happens when people do.'

Georgiana listened with interest when Ben then went on to disclose the Duke of Merton's ultimatum, and solution to his brother's woes. 'And do you suppose he will marry the widow?'

'That remains to be seen. But I strongly suspect Lord Rupert will leave the capital within days in order to avoid the duns, and be forced to rusticate at the ancestral pile for several weeks, as he's no country property of his own. Whether he does change his mind and make contact with the widow is another matter. My point is, my love, that beneath that veneer of idle insouciance beats the heart, surprisingly enough, of a man of high principles. So, I put it to you, if he would not wed merely to get his hands on money, is he likely to condone murder in order to get himself out of debt?'

After taking a moment only to consider, Georgiana shook her head. 'I wouldn't have thought so, no.'

'Precisely my own conclusion,' he concurred. 'Furthermore, if he were the one involved, he would hardly be leaving London when he was expecting some time soon his lion's share of the money from the sale of those emeralds... So that just leaves Lord Chard.'

Easily detecting the note of uncertainty in his voice, she looked up at him sharply. 'There's some doubt in your mind, I can tell. You don't suppose the Dowager misunderstood my godfather's dying words, and that it had absolutely nothing to do with any of "the five" at all?'

'No, I wasn't thinking that,' he assured her promptly. 'The only reason I doubted it could be Chard was simply because it was universally acknowledged that he had married a wealthy cit's daughter. But something Lord Rupert remarked on yesterday has given me cause to wonder.'

Raising his eyes, the Viscount stared resolutely ahead at some distant spot. His dark brows drawn together in thought. 'Just let's suppose for a moment that the vast fortune the wife had been rumoured to have brought to the union had been exaggerated. Supposing Chard's excessive gaming—and he has been known to lose vast sums at one sitting—had run through his wife's dowry some time ago... what then? Unlike Lord Rupert, who has been in dun territory a dozen and more times since leaving Oxford, Chard has always been prompt in paying his debts.'

'Then he must be getting financial help some-where else.'

'Quite so!' he agreed. 'Chard is far too astute to place himself in the hands of the money-lenders. So unless there is someone he can call upon in times of need...?'

'We have our man,' Georgiana finished for him.

'We do, indeed, my darling. But proving it is a dif-ferent matter entirely. Remember, he does not soil his hands with the robberies themselves. It's my belief that, like my good friend Charles Gingham, the man at the top is something of a connoisseur when it comes to judging fine gemstones. He wishes to satisfy himself as to their worth, and then promptly passes them on to Master Tate at the gaming house, and then ultimately to Henri Durand.

'Ah, by the by! I've enlisted Charles's help in the matter,' he went on to reveal. 'He is to make contact with his cousin upon Henri's return to town. Which, as I've already mentioned, shouldn't be long delayed now, I wouldn't have thought. I do not hold out much hope of Charles uncovering very much at all, but one never knows.'

Once again he stared thoughtfully at some distant spot. 'I cannot help thinking that the one we really need to unearth, if we stand the remotest chance of bringing Chard to justice, is this go-between, the seedy, shadowy figure who first made contact with Tate and, I suspect, Henri Durand also. Where does he fit in to it all? More importantly, where does he reside when not carrying out his master's orders? Definitely not with his master in town, that I do know. There's no one in the house who fits that description.'

But how did he know? Georgiana wondered, but refrained from asking anything further. To do so she felt sure would be a grave mistake. He seemed willing enough to pass on snippets of information.

None the less, if he thought she had any intention of involving herself further...?

No, her best bet, she finally decided, was to tax Digby about precisely what had been going on since her venture to that lowly tavern in the east of the city. But even with him she was very well aware that she would need to use cunning in order to achieve her objective!

# Chapter Thirteen

As another week drew to a close, a week in which she had been out most every evening enjoying the pleasures the capital had to offer the privileged few, Georgiana was looking forward to spending a quiet afternoon and evening at home for a change, with just the Dowager and her granddaughter to bear her company. She wasn't even expecting Lord Fincham to pay her a visit, either, as he had informed her the evening before, when she had conversed with him briefly at a party, that he had made arrangements to meet with his man of business, and so had every expectation of being occupied for much of the day.

Consequently, it came as something of a surprise when, midway through the day, Digby sought her out to say that his lordship's head groom had called and had left a grey mare round at the stables.

True to his word, the Viscount had found her the perfect mount, as she swiftly discovered when she put the mare through her paces in the park, the faithful Digby, mounted on one of her ladyship's carriage horses, dutifully bearing her company.

'She's utterly adorable!' Georgiana declared, after completing a circuit of the park. 'And not an ounce of malice in her anywhere. Puts me in mind of an animal I saw in Hampshire last summer.'

Other very special memories then returned, and she was reminded again of her transformation within a twelvemonth from page to fiancée. The real reason behind the metamorphosis quickly followed, forcing her to concentrate on the present and some recent disturbing happenings.

As a result she favoured her companion with a considering look. This was the first occasion she'd spent any length of time with him for almost three weeks. He wasn't wholly to blame for that, of course, she was obliged silently to concede. In truth, she had been occupied much of the time herself since her mock engagement to the Viscount had been announced. More recently, most of her days had been spent accompanying the Dowager and her granddaughter out making social calls, or receiving the numerous visitors to the house, and when she had managed a few minutes to herself, and had sought

Digby out, she had always been told that he was out on some errand or other.

Of course she knew well enough what was keeping him so occupied, and was immensely grateful for all he was attempting on her behalf. Increasingly, though, she felt he was doing his utmost to avoid too much contact with her; it wasn't too difficult to guess at whose instigation.

'I am glad I still have you to bear me company, although,' she continued artfully, absolutely determined not to be kept in the dark over any possible recent developments a moment longer, 'I do not tend to see very much of you these days. Why, I declare we haven't exchanged more than a dozen words in the past couple of weeks or so!'

If he suspected there was an ulterior motive in the topic of conversation he betrayed no sign of it. 'Well, miss, you've been gadding about a good bit yourself of late… And me? Well, you knows what I've been doing.'

'Yes, and immensely grateful to you I am, too,' she wasn't slow to assure him, before adding, 'That doesn't alter the fact, though, that I miss not having you around. And, of course, now I have my very own mount to ride, I'm going to need you to accompany me out regularly. I have no intention of having the Dowager's taciturn groom bearing me company.' Again she cast him a surreptitious sideways glance when he offered no comment. 'So, I suppose what we must do is find someone else to take over your—er—other commitments.'

This finally brought about the response for which she had hoped. 'Oh, no, you can't do that, miss!' There was an unmistakable note of alarm in his voice. 'It just so 'appens his lordship were saying, only t'other day, we're at last seeing some results. 'Is lordship wouldn't want any one else involved, that I do know. 'E's quite 'appy with Jem Fisher and 'is boys. Why, 'e's even sent one of the lads to Dover to keep watch on goings-on there. 'E expects to 'ear from 'im any day now, as the Frenchie 'as already returned to town.'

Had he, indeed? His lordship might at least have informed her of that development! How much more was he keeping to himself…and why? Georgiana couldn't help wondering. Was he merely doing his level best to prevent her further involvement…or was there something he was determined she shouldn't discover?

After the lengthy meeting with his man of business, during which, among many other things, he had made a fundamental adjustment to his will, naming his fiancée, Miss Georgiana Grey, as main beneficiary to his private fortune in the event of his death, the Viscount found his good friend Charles Gingham awaiting him in the library.

'The ever-efficient Brindle has attended to your needs, I see,' his lordship remarked, pouring just one glass of wine before joining his friend by the hearth. 'I assume you're here in response to the letter I sent early this week.'

Charles nodded. 'And no doubt you'll be pleased to hear I've already made contact with my degenerate cousin, as you requested. But I'm afraid I discovered nothing to the purpose. And to be perfectly candid, Ben, I don't think I'm likely to uncover much more than you already know. Henri might be a lazy, un-principled wretch, but he isn't stupid. If I suddenly begin to develop a desire for his company again, after all the years of ignoring his very existence, he's bound to become suspicious.'

'Assuredly,' his lordship agreed. 'So you can tell me nothing.'

After sampling his wine, Charles confirmed this with a shake of his head. 'I did, however, conduct a brief conversation with his landlady, who revealed that Henri has been away on business on three or four occasions within the past twelve months or so, and has stayed away a fortnight or more at a time, as a rule. But whenever he returns he always pays any arrears in rent, so she isn't complaining.'

'And evidently Henri let nothing slip during your reunion?'

Again Charles confirmed this with a shake of his head. 'I'll say this for him, though, he's got himself a comfortable little situation there. Although not located in the most fashionable part of town, his rooms are quite charmingly furnished. So he's making himself a reasonable income somehow.'

'I expect he's several irons in the fire, as it were,' the Viscount responded, 'and none could bear too close a scrutiny, if I'm any judge.'

Charles readily agreed with this before giving a start. 'There was something he did let fall, now I come to consider it. He mentioned he intended to be out of town again for a few days next week, attending the races. Which suggests, does it not, that no further robberies have taken place, or are planned. Not that I suppose for a moment he was actively involved in the robberies themselves.'

'Oh, no, I shouldn't imagine so at all,' the Viscount concurred. 'The real case-hardened men would have been chosen for that purpose, those who wouldn't balk at the use of violence to attain their ends.'

Charles was silent for a moment while he studied his friend closely. 'You know who's behind it all, don't you, Ben?'

'I believe so, yes. But I need proof, Charles, before I disclose the name of the culprit… And that might be the hardest to achieve, unless one can tempt him to show his hand,' he responded, his eyes sliding briefly across to the impressive oak desk, and its one particular locked drawer. 'But, no matter,' he added, his mind swiftly turning to something else. 'How long do you propose remaining in town?'

'Only until tomorrow. My mother's brother is gracing us with his company for a week or so.'

'Ah, Uncle, the Bishop!' The Viscount cast an amused glance up at the plasterwork ceiling. 'In that case I must deny myself the pleasure of your company. Assuredly you must return to play the genial host, or risk eternal damnation!'

Brindle, that highly efficient ruler of the household staff, had been in service throughout his life and, as such, had become something of an expert when it came to judging his fellow man. Consequently, he had no hesitation, the following day, in ordering the low-bred individual who had had the temerity to present himself at the front entrance to take himself round to the rear. All the same, years of experience persuaded him the lowly caller was no tradesperson. Furthermore, there had been just something in the individual's mien to suggest that he was, against all the odds, possibly acquainted with his lordship, and that he had called for a definite purpose, which he would disclose only to the master of the house. Brindle, therefore, had no hesitation in making the caller's arrival known to his master.

'As the visitor didn't state his business, did he, perchance, give a name?' his lordship enquired, without looking up from the letter he was engaged in writing.

'Jeremiah Fisher, my lord.'

This information had an immediate effect upon the Viscount. Losing complete interest in the composition of the missive, he threw down his pen and rose at once to his feet, requesting to see the man in question without delay as he did so.

'Before you go,' he added, bethinking himself of something else, 'have we anything in the house you consider suitable for our visitor to drink?'

Brindle sniffed quite pointedly. 'I rather fancy rum will suffice, your lordship.'

'Excellent! Then bring in a bottle and a couple of glasses,' the Viscount returned, smiling faintly at his diligent servant's evident disapproval.

Brindle had been the family's butler as far back as his lordship could remember, and had always been a stickler for maintaining standards of behaviour. Only one very special person had ever induced the very correct major-domo to deviate from strict codes of conduct and adopt a more tolerant approach. No mean feat, his lordship silently acknowledged, as his visitor was shown into the library.

After dismissing the butler, and dispensing the strong liquor himself, his lordship settled his guest in one of the comfortable chairs by the hearth. 'You have something of importance to tell me, Fisher?' he said, not wasting time on unnecessary pleasantries, which he felt sure wouldn't be appreciated anyway.

Fisher nodded. 'My lad Jack got back night afore last. And an eye's been kept on a certain cove ever since.' He paused to toss the rum down his throat, and then gave an appreciative, near-toothless grin. 'The lad stayed in that boarding 'ouse, keeping watch as you ordered. Almost a week 'e were kicking his 'eels in Dover afore the Frenchie turns up again. Knew it were 'e on account of 'im 'aving that there particular room in the boarding 'ouse. 'E only stayed the one night, then 'e ups and gets the stage back to Lunnon. My lad bides 'is time there as ordered, and the following week it were, this 'ere cove arrives and stays in the very same room as the Frenchie. Then 'e leaves the next day, and m'son follows. The cove stays overnight at Canterbury, then goes on the next day as far as Rochester. Then he collects a gig from a local inn and travels the few miles to this 'ere big 'ouse, by name of Chardley Court.'

'Not wholly unexpected,' his lordship remarked grimly. 'Can you furnish me with a description of this man?'

'Can do better than that, sir,' Fisher replied, staring rather pointedly down at his empty glass. ''Is name be Ivor 'Encham, and 'e be steward at Chardley,' he divulged, after the Viscount had obligingly refilled his glass.

'The following week 'e picks up the stage again at Rochester, and travels on to Lunnon, where he puts up at an inn. I were trailing him the following day, and I don't think I need tell 'e at which 'ouse 'e calls at first.'

'Lord Chard's town house,' his lordship responded, gaining scant pleasure from knowing his suspicions had been correct. 'Then I imagine he paid a call at the lodgings of our friend Arthur Tate.'

Jem Fisher confirmed this with a nod of his head. 'Then back 'e goes to the inn and buys a ticket for the stage back to Rochester.' Again he emptied his glass in one swallow. 'Don't suppose you'll be wanting me and the boys n'more now, m'lord,' he said, casting a longing look at the bottle on the table between their respective chairs.

'Help yourself, Fisher,' his lordship obligingly invited. Rising to his feet, he then went across to his desk and drew out a leather purse, which he tossed into the appreciative hand of his visitor. 'No, I do not believe your services shall be required further,' he confirmed. 'But should I chance to change my mind, I'll get Digby to make contact with you again.' He sighed before emptying his own glass. 'I think it behoves me now to make contact with a highly conscientious personage of my acquaintance closely associated with Bow Street.'

A distinct look of alarm flitted over the visitor's snub-nosed face as he tossed the third glass of rum down his throat and got to his feet. 'Well, as me and the lads does our best never to 'ave no dealings with that place, as yer might say, I'll bid yer good day, m'lord.'

In spite of the fact that he didn't relish what he must now attempt to do, his lordship couldn't help smiling at his roguish visitor's droll sense of humour as he once again seated himself at his desk. Delving into the same drawer that had contained the leather purse, he drew out a velvet-covered flat box. After flicking open the lid, he considered its sparkling contents for a few moments, before reaching again for his quill and composing two brief letters.

Like her Grace the Duchess of Merton, Lady Lavinia Radcliffe had been for many years one of the capital's most accomplished hostesses. Her annual ball, held in mid-May, had long been considered one of the highlights of the Season. Only those making up the cream of society were ever invited. Consequently, invitations were highly prized.

As the Dowager Countess and Lady Lavinia had remained close friends since girlhood, invitations to the prestigious affair had been sent to the Grenville town house several weeks before. This, quite naturally, had come as no surprise to Georgiana. Nor had the hurried note, written in his lordship's bold, if slightly untidy, handwriting, requesting her to don the sapphire necklace for the occasion, which he had duly sent to the house earlier in the day. After all, the Radcliffe ball was one of those lavish events where all present would be dressed in their finery.

She chose, however, not to don the dark blue gown she had worn for the engagement party, lovely though it was. She plumped, instead, for the cream-and-rose coloured creation she had intended to wear to the Merton ball earlier in the Season, a choice that instantly won a look of approval from Lord Fincham when she arrived at the Radcliffes' town mansion to discover him surprisingly already there.

'My, my! It isn't like you to arrive so early in the evening,' she teased him. 'It's your custom to be one of the last to arrive so that you can make an impressive entrance.'

Lady Sophia, who had long since lost any shyness when in his lordship's company, chortled appreciatively at this. Even the Dowager couldn't forbear a smile. Only the Viscount appeared not in the least amused.

'It would seem, my girl, you have become distinctly pert in recent days. Clearly it behoves me to spend more time with you in order to improve your manners. And I shall begin so doing without delay.' He turned to the Dowager. 'With your permission, ma'am, I shall relieve you of my fiancée's pernicious influence for the next half an hour or so.'

Although she wasn't in the least alarmed to have her arm securely imprisoned round his lordship's, Georgiana was curious to know why he was so intent on spiriting her out of the already crowded ballroom. 'Is there something you wish to discuss with me in private? Have there been any further developments?'

'No, not really.' All at once his gaze grew markedly keener. 'God, how I've missed you these past days!'

And how she wished he wouldn't say things like that to her! How she wished, too, he wouldn't look at her in that intensely intimate way, as though branding her his own with his eyes. She could almost believe that he meant it. And perhaps he did in a way. After all, hadn't they always rubbed along wonderfully well for the most part? But to read anything more into it than genuine fondness would be dangerously foolhardy, she reminded herself.

'And to prove it, I wish you to partner me in a game or two of whist, just for a short while,' he surprised her by announcing, his tone once again reverting to merely sociable. 'After all, we've played together enough times in the dim and distant past for me to be sure you are not lacking some skill.'

This might have been very true. All the same,

when he steered her towards a corner table in the room set out for cards, where two gentlemen were already seated, she didn't suppose for a moment her skill at cards, or lack of it, had weighed with him. No, there had to be another reason for choosing her as his partner, she finally decided.

'Fincham, dear fellow!' Sir Willoughby greeted him cheerfully. 'Come to join us for a hand or two? And you've brought your delightful fiancée, I observe! Such eyes! Once seen never forgotten, eh?'

Had not Ben warned her of the baronet's penchant for wicked teasing, his remarks might have unnerved her somewhat. As it was, Georgiana merely favoured him with one of her most serene smiles, before seating herself at the table.

'I trust you do not object, Chard, to playing a hand or two at whist for very moderate stakes?'

Although there hadn't been so much as a hint of welcome in the baron's hard features, he sounded companionable enough as he said, 'As you're very well aware, I should welcome it, Fincham. I've been losing far too heavily of late.'

'What's this? What's this?' Clearly it was news to Sir Willoughby. 'Don't tell me, like our friend Gyles, you'll be rusticating too? Heard he's now kicking his heels in the country.'

'Might have to resort to that if my luck doesn't change, or if Fincham's here doesn't alter soon. He's been having the devil's own good fortune of late,' Chard revealed grimly, before concentrating on the cards in his hand.

After having listened intently to this little inter-change, Georgiana began to appreciate why she had seen so little of the Viscount since the evening of the engagement party. Initially she'd feared that he must be tiring of her company and the role he was obliged to enact. Then, of course, he'd gone out of his way to provide her with the perfect mount, and she'd begun to wonder if she'd misjudged him entirely. Seemingly, instead of squiring her about, he'd been spending his time at the gaming tables, relieving a specific person of his money. Was he now firmly convinced Chard was the guilty party? Had he been doing his utmost in recent days to persuade Chard to organise a further robbery in order to recoup his losses so that a trap might be sprung in order to bring him to justice? That could well be true. All the same, it was also possible that something might go drastically wrong, which might result in some poor unsuspecting soul being deprived of a fortune in gems!

She raised her eyes to find the Viscount's regarding

her steadily above the cards in his hand, his expression, as it so often was, totally unreadable. Little wonder he was such an accomplished gamester, she reflected. No one could ever be sure just what was passing through that astute mind of his. He might well have been attempting to convey some secret message about one or both their opponents, or merely silently advising her to concentrate on her cards.

She did her utmost to do so and was rewarded by helping to win the first game, though she was forced silently to own their success was mostly due to the skill of her partner. The run of the cards was never with them throughout the second. However, they won the third comprehensively and she decided it was time for her to leave while they were still ahead.

'If you will forgive me, good sirs, I have promised to partner one or two gentlemen in a dance, so I think it behoves me to leave you to your own devices,' she said, rising to her feet. 'No, please,' she added, when the Viscount made to rise also, 'I believe I've wits enough to find my own way back to the ballroom and shall have the pleasure of your company later in the evening, no doubt.'

'You may be sure you shall. And I insist upon the

supper dance,' he added, before gathering the cards together and shuffling them expertly. 'What is your pleasure now, gentlemen?'

'I'm happy enough to leave the choice to you, Fincham. But, given our mutual friend's straitened circumstances let us keep to moderate stakes, shall we?' Sir Willoughby suggested, thereby proving there was a considerate streak in his nature also.

'That filly of yours is really quite remarkable,' he added, after studying Georgiana's progress across to the door. 'Not in your usual style at all, I wouldn't have said.'

'You think not?' his lordship returned, recalling his good friend Charles Gingham remarking on much the same thing. 'Like yourself, I was first attracted by the eyes. And, in truth, I believe my tastes have changed. Fair and docile damsels no longer interest me. I like a girl with some spirit.'

The baronet chuckled appreciatively. 'Ah, well, you certainly have one there. And I must say, Fincham, you couldn't have chosen more appropriate gems to enhance that wonderful feature of hers. They must have cost a pretty penny. What say you, Chard? You're something of an expert when it comes to judging precious stones.'

'Oh, I wouldn't go as far as to say that,' he returned

promptly, while the Viscount, eyes determinedly lowered, concentrated on dealing out the cards. 'I'm sure our mutual friend here, being a sensible fellow, has them insured, no matter their worth.'

At this, his lordship couldn't forbear a smile. 'I assure you I've every intention of taking very great care of them. It just so happens I'm leaving London at the end of the week for that very purpose.'

'Not you, too!' Sir Willoughby exclaimed in disgust, while the gentleman seated opposite silently picked his newly dealt cards up off the table. 'First Gyles, and now you—there'll be no one left in town at this rate!'

'You exaggerate, Trent,' his lordship countered. 'Chard, here, will bear you company until the end of the Season, I'm sure.'

'Well, that's no good to me, if his pockets are to let,' Sir Willoughby pointed out peevishly.

'I'm not bankrupt quite yet,' Chard countered. 'Though I sincerely trust you'll offer me the opportunity to recoup at least some of my losses before you desert the metropolis for the wilds of Hampshire, Fincham?'

'You may be sure I shall,' the Viscount responded, staring resolutely down at the cards in his hand, his expression, as his fiancée often found it, inscrutable.

'As I mentioned before, I do not intend leaving until Friday afternoon. I have an appointment with my bankers in the morning.'

This captured Sir Willoughby's attention. 'You'll not make it home in the day, then, will you? Intend putting up somewhere?'

'I usually put up at the White Hart just a mile or so west of Liphook. I'll finish the journey the following morning, and cut down on time by taking a shortcut through Cheetham Wood. It's a nuisance, but I must needs ensure the ancestral pile is ready to welcome its future mistress. We've decided on a quiet wedding this summer, you see. All the same, there are—er—certain items of value I must take to Fincham Park in readiness for the event.'

After fulfilling her promises to those two gentlemen guests who had secured her for a dance, and partnering several others too, Georgiana was more than happy to return to the Dowager Countess's side in order to marshal her thoughts.

Silently she was obliged to own she was finding Fincham's behaviour increasingly puzzling— One moment so thoughtful and attentive, nothing being too much trouble, but for the most part seemingly happy to go his own way and ignore her very existence. Why, for instance, had he been on the watch for her, demanding her attention the moment she had arrived, only to allow her to leave the card room without so much as attempting to detain her? Furthermore, had his request for the supper dance been made to avoid suspicion, merely for the benefit of the other gentlemen present, or had he a genuine desire to bear her company later in the evening? Always where Fincham was concerned it was impossible to judge!

'Something appears to be troubling you, child.'

The Dowager's concerned voice succeeded in interrupting her disturbing thoughts. 'Yes, I do have one or two things on my mind at present,' she freely admitted, knowing her ladyship was far too astute to accept a denial.

'No doubt your fiancé will be able to alleviate any concerns you have, should you confide in him. He is an eminently sensible gentleman.'

Georgiana couldn't forbear a smile at this. 'You've clearly changed your opinion of the Viscount, ma'am,' she pointed out. 'He's positively spiralled in your estimation in the space of a few short weeks.'

'I sincerely hope, Georgiana, that I never become so vainglorious that I cannot admit when I have been in error. And I do believe I grossly misjudged

Fincham and that I was guilty of the sin of prejudging someone merely on the evidence of idle gossip. I shall endeavour never to do so again. Fincham is not only a person of immense character and astuteness, he is a gentleman of principle.'

At any other time Georgiana would have been elated to hear the Dowager say this, for she valued highly the elderly lady's opinion, but her own doubts concerning the Viscount refused to leave her and she decided finally to share them with her companion.

'I agree with what you say, my lady…at least up to a point. I just wish he would confide in me more with regard to any progress made regarding your son's death. Why does he refuse to take me into his confidence? He tells me nothing…or very little to the purpose.'

The Dowager gave vent to a wheezy chuckle. 'Ah, my dear child! I can only assume love is adversely affecting your judgement. You are not usually so imperceptive. I just revealed that, in my opinion, Fincham is a sagacious gentleman of principle. Perhaps I should also have added he's a man well able to take care of his own. And that is what you are, child. Hasn't he declared that to the world by decking you out in such fine jewels? He views you as his own property and is determined to protect you at all costs.'

Maybe so, but why then does he insist the jewels are retained in his possession at Berkeley Square? Georgiana wondered, gaining scant comfort from her ladyship's assurances. If he truly loved her, why had he never said as much?

It was unfortunate that at that precise moment, when she was no nearer unravelling her conflicting thoughts concerning the Viscount, that she should suddenly observe the gentleman himself weaving his way round the little clusters of guests towards her. Something in his expression gave her every reason to suppose that he had been regarding her for some little while, for there was an unmistakable enquiring lift to one black brow.

'You look unusually pale, Georgie. I think it behoves me to take you out on to the terrace for a breath of air, if her ladyship would forgive the desertion yet again?'

As his lordship, seemingly, could do no wrong in the Dowager's eyes, it came as no surprise that he quickly gained her ladyship's assent; the next moment Georgiana found herself being led inexorably towards the doors that granted access to the terrace.

Given that it had been the hottest spring day thus far, it was a little surprising to find the large paved area entirely deserted, a circumstance that caused Georgiana some disquiet, but appeared to have the opposite effect on the Viscount.

'Ah! A moment to ourselves at last. We rarely seem to attain that, do we, my love?'

'Hardly surprising since we rarely see each other nowadays!' she retorted, before she could stop herself, and then turned her back on him when an infuriatingly satisfied grin curled his lips.

'Do I infer correctly from that waspish tone that you have missed me, my angel?'

She resolutely refused to answer. She was in no mood for these cat-and-mouse games he seemed to enjoy playing with her. And that was precisely it, she told herself. She was like some plaything—the centre of his universe one moment, tossed aside, like some toy that has lost its fascination, the next. And totally forgotten no doubt! Why, if she'd a modicum of sense at all, she told herself roundly, she'd reveal their engagement was bogus to the world at large and have done with it!

The instant he placed his hand beneath her elbow, and turned her round to face him squarely once again, she knew she could not make public their secret, at least not yet, while there remained a real purpose for the deception. She must never lose sight of that fact, she told herself for perhaps the hundredth time. She must not allow personal feelings, or a bruised ego, to make her forget that one important objective!

'I'm sorry. I'm just blue-devilled. This whole business seems to be dragging on interminably.'

It wasn't an outright lie, and seemingly he believed her, because he said after a moment, 'It cannot go on for ever. Just be patient a while longer, then all the pretence will blessedly be at an end.' He raised his head momentarily, as though he'd detected a sound. 'But in the meantime we must both endeavour to maintain our roles, for I do believe we are no longer alone.'

Even before Georgiana could think of taking evasive action, she was already a captive within the circle of his arms. Yet no prisoner could have felt less desire to escape. The instant his lips touched hers no thought of breaking free entered her head. It was almost as if her mind had closed to coherent thought, and her body had taken control, a body that instantly responded to a masterly touch that managed to combine both gentleness and sensual expertise. As had happened before, she seemed to have no will of her own and was blissfully content to submit to his control, until he finally released her and common sense once again exerted itself.

Was it pure imagination or had that same husky timbre she'd detected on one memorable occasion in the recent past been back in his voice as he suggested they return to the ballroom? Georgiana was incapable of making up her mind as his lingering embrace had left her thoughts in turmoil. Notwithstanding, she still retained wits enough to realise, as she turned and walked with him towards the door, that, save for themselves, the terrace was deserted.

# Chapter Fourteen

By the time yet another week was rapidly drawing to a close Georgiana had decided that her pleasure in residing in the metropolis was assuredly waning. Not only had the week turned out to be a miserable one, as far as the weather was concerned, thereby denying her the pleasure of exercising her new grey mare, but also Lord Fincham had condescended to see her on two occasions only—once briefly at a party on Tuesday evening, when they had barely exchanged a couple of dozen words, and the day before when he had unexpectedly called at Grenville House to reveal that something had occurred at his ancestral home requiring his urgent attention, that he intended leaving town the following day, and would return as soon as maybe.

It was hardly surprising Georgiana felt scant enthusiasm for the new day ahead, when she rose from her bed much later than usual. Then she was pleasantly surprised to discover, as she padded across to the window, a city bathed in pleasant spring sunshine. The morning was all but lost to her, of course, but she was determined not to waste the sunny afternoon and sent word to the stables for her mount to be saddled, only to discover upon reaching the mews that her escort was to be none other than her ladyship's grim head groom.

'Where's Digby?' she demanded to know without preamble.

'Couldn't say, miss. Went off bright and early this morning, so 'e did, just after daybreak. Said 'e wouldn't be back for a day or two.'

Understandably miffed, she gave vent to a string of colourful invective, which rather amused the dour head groom, and which resulted in a partial thawing of his usual morose demeanour as they set off in the direction of the park. All the same, he was no Digby, and Georgiana continued to feel slightly resentful over what was tantamount to her servant's desertion.

Of course she could well appreciate just why he had abandoned her. Evidently his high-and-mightiness had decreed it and had required Digby to undertake some important task whilst the Viscount himself was out of town. It wasn't the fact that she would be deprived of her servant for a day or so that annoyed her so much as his lordship's high-handed attitude in assuming he could order her servant about without first consulting her. Furthermore, why hadn't he mentioned yesterday, when he had called at the house, that he would be requiring Digby's services? And why hadn't Digby himself said anything to her, come to that? To be sure, it was like some wretched conspiracy between the pair of them!

A vaguely familiar sing-song voice hailing her cheerfully succeeded in breaking into her irritating rumination, and she raised her head to see none other than Sir Willoughby Trent—of all people!— sitting beside the Duchess of Merton in her Grace's splendid open carriage. As the conveyance drew to a halt alongside, there was no mistaking the twinkling mischief in the foppish baronet's eyes and Georgiana prepared herself for some wicked bantering.

'I was just saying to her Grace, why, if it isn't Miss Grey out on her lonesome and looking so sad without her swain. He departed this very hour for the country and she is pining for him already. Or is it for those lovely sapphires that he's deprived you from wearing for the rest of the Season that has brought on such a bout of melancholy?'

'Pay him no mind, my dear child, he's nothing more than a wicked tormentor,' her Grace advised.

'Not at all,' Sir Willoughby countered. 'Fincham's only making ready at the ancestral pile for when the nuptials take place. Told me so himself only t'other week. But you had better warn him, my dear Miss Grey, when he does return to town, that her Grace's brother-in-law is like to beat him to the altar. He's only got himself in the coils of some young widow. And loving every moment of it, if his latest letter to her Grace is to be believed. And he a confirmed bachelor!'

'One moment, your Grace.' The duchess had been about to instruct her coachman to move on, but Georgiana had not hesitated to forestall her, for something the baronet had said had resulted in a tiny tinkle of alarm resounding in her head. 'Sir Willoughby, when precisely did Lord Fincham inform you of his intention to leave town? Was it yesterday, when he received news of some occurrence at Fincham Park?'

'Oh, no, no, no,' he answered, his thin brows drawing together. 'Not heard anything about that. Haven't spoken to him for several days, as it happens. Not since the night of the Radcliffe ball, now I come to think about it. So it must have been then… Yes, of course it was! I remember quite clearly poor Chard didn't want Fincham to leave town until he'd had a chance to recoup some of his losses. Fincham's been having the devil's own luck at the gaming tables of late, so I've been told. And poor Chard quite the opposite!'

'Don't look so worried, child,' the duchess advised kindly, after observing Georgiana's deeply troubled expression. 'Fincham will soon be back with you. And I know what it is to be deprived of one's jewels, even for a short time. But it is for the best. They'll be there, ready and waiting for you, when you enter Fincham's country home as its mistress.'

Georgiana didn't attempt to detain them further, and waited only for the carriage to move away before turning her mount and leaving the park, heading in the direction of Berkeley Square.

If the Dowager's groom was surprised by the route they were taking, he betrayed no sign of it. He even looked moderately pleased to be left in the mews to cast an eye over his lordship's fine cattle, the instant they had arrived, while Georgiana herself wasted no time in running her favourite butler to earth.

Her entry into the kitchen, by way of the door leading to the mews, naturally enough startled everyone present, not least of all Brindle, who hurriedly rose from the table, pulling on his jacket as he did so.

'Why, Miss Grey! We—er—didn't expect to see you today. The master has already departed, I'm afraid. Left about an hour ago.'

'Yes, I'm aware of that. He was seen. All the same, I'd like a word with you in the library, Brindle, if you'd be so kind.'

As always, where his future mistress was concerned, nothing was too much trouble, and he very willingly escorted her up the stairs and into the book-lined room. Georgiana waited only until he had closed the door before demanding to know just when his lordship had decided to pay a brief visit to Fincham Park.

'Was it a sudden decision? Did he, perhaps, receive a communication that persuaded him to go?'

'Oh, no, I do not believe so, Miss Grey. If my memory serves me correctly his lordship informed me of his intention to leave town several days ago.'

So, he'd deliberately misled her as to the reason behind his departure. Nothing untoward had occurred at his ancestral home. Georgiana began to pace the room, trying to recall in minute detail what Sir Willoughby had revealed not an hour since—his lordship openly revealing that he would be leaving town in order to take several items of value to Fincham Park, including the sapphire necklace.

As a further thought occurred to her she ceased her pacing. She had discovered the year before that there was a safe concealed behind a painting in his lordship's own bedchamber. A look in there might confirm her worst fears.

'Apart from the silver that I've seen about the place, does his lordship keep all his other valuables in the safe? Is the sapphire-and-diamond set stored there, for instance?'

'Oh, no, Miss Grey. His lordship has always taken great care of the family's heirlooms. The family jewels, for instance, are housed at the vault at his bank. He does keep a reasonable amount of money in the safe and one or two diamond pins for immediate use. And as for your sapphires, miss, as far as I'm aware they are still in the locked drawer in his desk. He thought they would be more secure there. Should anyone chance to break in, which is most unlikely with Ronan in the house, it would be the safe that was the main target.'

Going across to the desk, Georgiana soon located the drawer in question. 'Have you the key, Brindle?'

'Oh, no, miss. Only his lordship has a key to that drawer. He keeps it on his fob-watch chain.' He gazed across at her in a fatherly way, a touch of concern in his eyes. 'Is there something wrong, miss? You seem troubled about something. I believed his lordship must surely have mentioned to you his intention to leave town for a day or two, most especially as your own servant accompanied him.'

On discovering this alarm bells began to reverberate in earnest. 'Digby…?' She was mistress of her emotions again in an instant. 'Why, yes…yes, of course!' She seated herself at the desk, and took out a sheet of paper. 'I'll just leave a short note for your master, which I trust you'll ensure he receives directly on his return. I'll not detain you further, Brindle.'

Left alone, Georgiana wrote just two words in large and bold print, which adequately expressed her feelings at that moment, before folding the sheet of paper and sealing it with a wafer. Then, leaning back in the comfortable leather chair, she gazed meditatively at the lock on that particular drawer.

Her eyes narrowed. 'I wonder?'

Although not precisely basking in the sunshine of her approval at the present time, Digby years ago had been one of her favourite companions. Not only had he guarded her like some faithful dog, he had increased her knowledge of the world by teaching her things about which both her mother and grandfather had been sadly ignorant. His own misspent youth had not been in vain; one of Digby's most valuable lessons had been how to pick a lock. He used to sit and time her until she had mastered the art in under one minute. After all these years could she now put that tuition to good use?

Removing one of the sturdier pins from her hair, she fashioned it into that long-remembered certain shape, and then inserted it into the lock. She could no longer achieve her objective in under a minute. All the same, it was not long afterwards when she detected that rewarding click, and opened the drawer to discover a velvet-covered square box. Moreover, its contents were intact.

So, he hadn't taken any valuables with him to Fincham Park, and possibly had never intended to do so. But he had revealed that that was his intention, and he hadn't said it for Sir Willoughby's benefit. Other things that had puzzled her suddenly became clear—his neglect of her had been for some purpose; he had been spending more time at the gaming tables, relieving Chard of his money. He had deliberately proposed she wear the sapphires at the

Radcliffe ball in order to dangle temptation before the baron's eyes. Then he had declared his intention of going out of town in order to give Chard time to organise the robbery. Furthermore, his reason for keeping the jewels in his home was now abundantly clear also—he couldn't risk her donning them, when they were supposed to be on their way to Fincham Park.

Tears stung her eyes, but she refused to give way to emotion. All at once bringing Chard to justice was not important to her; Fincham's safety was everything, as was the well-being of those who had accompanied him. He was putting his life at risk for her, in order to assuage her thirst for revenge. She might be unable to stop him now; he was a man of strong determination. But she refused to remain in the safety of the metropolis, while he was in peril. There wasn't a moment to lose!

Discovering Brindle in the act of placing a vase of flowers on a table in the hall, she didn't hesitate to inform him that she'd found that particular desk drawer open. 'I can only assume his lordship forgot to lock it,' she lied without suffering a qualm. 'I would suggest you place the sapphires in the safe, until your master's return.'

Understandably he was shocked. 'I shall do so at once, Miss Grey.'

'Before you disappear, Brindle,' she said, regaining his attention. 'As his lordship left rather late, and it takes a full day to reach Fincham Park, I assume it is his intention to put up somewhere for the night and finish the journey in the morning.'

'He always puts up at the White Hart, just west of Liphook, and then takes a short cut on a road that traverses Cheetham Wood.'

Oh, God! Georgiana groaned inwardly. He must surely have been planning this for some little time. He'd considered everything. A wood—the ideal terrain in which to conduct a robbery! Without a doubt, at some point during recent days his lordship would have made that fact known. If Chard had mobilised his forces, then the Viscount was deliberately heading into a trap of his own contrivance!

Again leaving the house by way of the door leading to the mews, Georgiana was about to remount her mare when a soft whinnying broke into her agonising reflections. His lordship's favourite mount had poked his head over the stall. Instinctively she acknowledged the greeting by raising her hand to stroke the bay's fine head, and as she did so a seed of an idea, nourished by renewed hope, began to develop rapidly.

What she had viewed as her most besetting problem was how to reach his lordship in time. If by some chance she did manage to hire a carriage that afternoon, his lordship would still have several hours' start on her. She could never reach the White Hart by nightfall, and he would possibly have departed long before she arrived the following morning. Her mare, though admirable in most every way, was nowhere near strong enough to undertake such an arduous journey. But this powerful bay was, most especially if he was allowed to rest at frequent intervals. The only problem that she could foresee was that the bay, if memory served her correctly, had never experienced the side-saddle and might very likely react negatively if one was set on his back. So it wouldn't be wise for Miss Georgiana Grey to attempt to ride him. Her eyes narrowed. But there was nothing to stop Master George Green from doing so!

Smiling faintly, she disappeared into the large stable to converse with the young boy left in charge in the head groom's absence.

After enjoying a leisurely dinner, eaten in the secluded comfort of a private parlour, Lord Fincham went in search of his two courageous henchmen, both of whom were well aware of the dangers they might face in the morning. He ran them to earth in the tap and ordered them to remain seated as he approached their table.

'I shall join you, if I may?' His lordship then called across to the landlord and ordered three fresh tankards of home-brewed ale and three glasses of rum. 'We may as well sleep well tonight, gentlemen, and just hope that Lady Luck favours us on the morrow.' He looked from one to the other. 'It isn't too late for either of you to back out. I shall think none the less of you if you do. As I've already mentioned there's no guarantee the militia, although alerted to be stationed in the wood, will reach us in time if we are held up. The road through Cheetham Wood runs for a good two miles. The attack might take place anywhere.'

Both the head groom, Perkins, and Digby voiced their determination to remain with the Viscount. 'Besides,' Digby added, 'the young mistress would expect it of me. Given 'alf the chance she'd be 'ere with you 'erself.'

A ripple of alarm stole across his lordship's features. 'You're sure she knows nothing of this?'

'She's learned nothing from me, m'lord,' Digby confirmed. 'I left bright and early this morning, without seeing 'er. Thought it 'twere for the best.

She's a way of wheedling things out of you, so she
'as. Though I did leave 'er a note with the scullery
maid, just to say I were on some errand for you for
a day or two. Just 'ope the scatty wench ain't forgotten to give it to the young mistress, that's all.'

Reaching for the glass of rum the landlord had
just placed before him, Digby downed the contents
in one swallow, much as his friend Jem Fisher had
done when visiting his lordship's house not so very
many days previously. 'Miss Georgie's a downy one,
and no mistake. Don't want 'er going round asking
too many questions. She just might find out what
we're about.'

Although his lordship understood the loyal retainer's fears, he took a more realistic view. 'Well,
even if she should find out, I doubt there's much she
can do at, this, the eleventh hour, except mentally
rehearse some blistering tirade with which to greet
me upon my return.'

Digby's appreciative chuckle faded as he chanced
to glance through to the coffee-room in time to
catch a glimpse of a slight figure, swathed in a
voluminous cloak and wearing black buckled shoes
and a tricorn hat, pass the open doorway.

He shook his head and considered the empty
vessel still clasped in his large hand. 'Not that I

don't think that there rum must 'ave gone straight to me 'ead!' he declared. 'Best 'ave n'more!'

As luck would have it the landlady of the White Hart was a kindly soul, with a distinctly motherly nature. She had taken pity on the weary youth who had arrived late in the evening at her inn. Allocating a clean, airy bedchamber, overlooking the courtyard at the front of the inn, she had even gone so far as to send a substantial supper up on a tray, and had been only too willing to provide a hearty breakfast in the same fashion the following morning, the youth being somewhat shy and not wishing to partake of meals in the coffee-room. Which, as it just so happened, could not have suited Georgiana better.

Luck had favoured her thus far. The journey from London, though tiring for both rider and sturdy mount, had passed quite uneventfully. She'd even been fortunate enough to catch not so much as a glimpse of his lordship or the servants when she had arrived at the inn, and she was determined to do all she could to ensure her luck held. She'd already discovered from one of the inn maids that the Viscount had bespoken the only private parlour, and had ordered his breakfast for eight o'clock sharp.

Therefore he would be eating now. So there wasn't a moment to lose!

After gathering together the few necessities she'd managed to bring with her and thrusting them into a small leather bag, Georgiana made her way down to the coffee-room, while all the time keeping a sharp eye out for a certain tall, striking aristocrat.

The landlord was only too willing to look after the leather bag while the young gentleman was about on an errand in the locale, most especially as he was offered sufficient inducement to do so. The young ostler, who had been only too happy to look after the fine bay the evening before, was more than content to continue caring for the horse until the young gentleman returned, when he too was tossed a shiny gold coin. No sooner had he happily pocketed the unexpected largesse than he was called to help make ready his lordship's carriage.

Georgiana then wasted no time in secreting herself in the darkest corner of the large barn, from where she could view proceedings undetected. Without doubt this was the most hazardous time, when her presence might be discovered by either Digby or Perkins, both of whom were very likely busily preparing for the departure.

Through the open doorway, she watched as his

lordship's prime horses were harnessed to the carriage. Then she saw Perkins scramble up on to the box. Not long afterwards Digby joined him on the seat, and the carriage then was tooled slowly to the front of the inn. Leaving her hiding place, Georgiana moved stealthily across the yard to the inn's front wall in time to see his lordship leave and walk the few steps to his carriage. Then he was safely inside, and Digby, having jumped down, was letting up the steps and closing the carriage door. It was now or never!

Darting forward, Georgiana hurriedly perched herself on the dummy board at the rear of the coach. Thankfully the conveyance's rocking must have been put down wholly to Digby returning to his seat, for the carriage moved out of the yard without further ado and they were soon on their way.

Of course, Georgiana wasn't so foolish as to suppose her presence would go undetected indefinitely. Unfortunately she was discovered rather sooner than she might have wished. Digby, alighting to open a gate, almost sent her in to whoops by his expression of shocked dismay. Raising her hand, she placed a finger to her lips. Evidently he was too dumbstruck to say anything to her. He regained the power of speech quickly enough, though, for she clearly heard Perkins cry a minute later, 'Oh, my gawd!'

The Viscount heard it too and let down the window. 'Something amiss?'

'Er—no, m'lord,' Digby answered. 'It's just that we can see the outskirts of the wood.'

'Of course you can. I'm well aware of it. Keep your eyes open, both of you.'

He had sounded irritable. Georgiana knew, however, this stemmed only from concern for the servants' welfare.

And he had good reason to be anxious, for no sooner had they entered the wooded terrain than a shot rang out. A cry of pain quickly followed, though whether it was Digby or his lordship's head groom who had taken the shot, Georgiana could not have said with any degree of certainty. Nor did she attempt to discover which of them had been injured. The instant the carriage had drawn to a halt she slipped from the perch and secreted herself beneath the equipage.

By this time all was confusion. Shots had rung out from left and right. She could see three figures on the ground, two writhing in agony and one deathly still. Then a rough voice, clear and carrying, demanded his lordship drop his pistol.

'Do as I say or your other servant gets it.'

The pistol hit the ground with a thud not a yard from where Georgiana lay. Seemingly, the last of the highway robbers couldn't detect her from where he sat high on a bay horse. The advantage was hers. But for how long? How long before one of the wounded noticed her?

The conveyance above rocked as the Viscount obeyed the rough command to alight. 'And now, milord, I'll relieve you of the trinkets you be carrying.'

His lordship's response to this demand was to attempt to satisfy his curiosity, 'Would I be correct in thinking you and your fellows are the very ones who relieved the Earl of Grenville of a fine diamond necklace many moons ago?'

'Knows about that, do yer?' A sinister chuckle followed. 'Yeh, if you must know. Not that it'll do yer no good.'

'And was it, perchance, you personally who put a period to his existence?' his lordship enquired, sounding sublimely unconcerned at having a pistol levelled at his own chest.

'It were. And I'll be more than 'appy to dispatch you the same way, iffen you don't 'and over them there sparklers o' yourn.'

'Loath though I am to disappoint you, but you were sadly misinformed. Apart from my purse, I am carrying nothing of value, except perhaps my pocket-watch. Will that assuage your desire for bloodshed?'

'Quiet!' the highwayman bellowed to his injured compatriot who was doing his level best to impart that something untoward was lurking beneath the carriage. 'I'll not warn 'e again, m'lord.'

Georgiana waited no longer. Rolling out from her hiding place, she fired the pistol she had had the forethought to bring with her with unerring accuracy, and the robber's own weapon flew from his hand. For a second or two he remained seated on his horse, stunned, just clasping his injured wrist; the next he was being hauled to the ground by his lordship, who then proceeded to render the villain unconscious with a powerful blow to the jaw.

'Damned fine shot, Miss Georgie!' Digby approved, while his lordship appeared as though he were doing his utmost not to succumb to an apoplexy.

'I'll give her good shot!' he hissed between clenched teeth, while at the same time retrieving the highwayman's pistol from the ground. He then checked on the other three, moving their firearms out of harm's way as he did so. 'How the deuce did you get here?' he then demanded to know before rounding on the hapless Digby. 'Were you party to this?'

'Of course he wasn't,' Georgiana assured him, not hesitating to come to her servant's defence. 'The first he knew about it was when he got down to open that gate back along the road and saw me perched on the rumble seat.'

His lordship took a moment to consider. 'You couldn't possibly have left London with us.'

'Of course not,' she confirmed. 'I didn't leave the metropolis until mid-afternoon. I rode to the White Hart…on your bay, as it happens.'

Just what his lordship's reaction to this piece of downright impertinence might have been had not his attention been claimed elsewhere was anybody's guess. Not only was the militia rapidly approaching on horseback, but Digby had at last drawn his attention to the fact that his head groom had sustained an injury.

'It's naught but a scratch,' Perkins assured them all, as he obeyed his master's command to hand the reins to Digby and get down from the carriage.

Not wholly convinced, his lordship insisted the wound receive immediate attention and left

Georgiana to deal with the injury, whilst he exchanged a brief word with the officer in charge of the militia. By the time he returned to the carriage Georgiana had made a pad with her own handkerchief and was binding the wound up deftly.

'It is, indeed, little more than a scratch,' she confirmed, 'but it should be cleaned properly. And it goes without saying he's in no fit state to tool the carriage. He'll set the arm bleeding again if he does.'

'I'm quite capable of tooling my own cattle, Perkins,' his lordship assured him, cutting across the head groom's protests. 'The Major is happy to deal with things here, leaving me free to return to town. And I must get back before nightfall. There's the other members of the organisation to take in to custody, remember? We can, none the less, call in briefly at the White Hart in order to get that wound cleaned properly.' He favoured Georgiana with a darkling look. 'Besides which, I'm obliged to call back at that inn in order to collect my prized bay!

'And don't think you're getting away with that piece of gross impertinence so easily, my girl!' he added for good measure, before slamming the carriage door closed and clambering up on the box seat.

\* \* \*

Although his lordship proved to be highly competent at tooling a carriage and four, it was evening before they arrived back in the capital. Consequently, farewells were not protracted, with Georgiana just raising her hand in a final salute, as his lordship moved away from the Grenville town residence, and then letting her hand fall with a heartfelt sigh.

Digby was not so concerned by his young mistress's unusually sombre state as he was by her indecent boy's attire, and took it upon himself to enter the house first, by way of a side door, and make sure the coast was clear before ushering his subdued mistress up the back stairs to her room. Once there Georgiana didn't delay in donning more appropriate raiment, then wasted no time in searching out the Dowager Countess.

Anything but gratified by this unexpected appearance in her private apartments, the Dowager dismissed the maid before favouring Georgiana with a severe look. 'I assume you have come in order to offer a reasonable explanation for your departure from town, at least one that is more satisfactory than the one contained in the brief note you left for me?'

Although perfectly understanding her ladyship's

annoyance, Georgiana was too consumed with her own miseries to attempt to placate her. Throughout the long journey back to town she had been given ample time to consider her future, and from every angle it looked bleak indeed.

'It's over, ma'am,' she said softly. 'It is…all over now.'

Only a fool could have missed the desolation in the voice, and the sorrow flickering in blue eyes, and no one could ever have accused the Dowager of being dull-witted.

Rising from her dressing table, she led the way into her private sitting room. 'I think you had best sit and tell me all about it, my dear child.'

'No doubt Lord Fincham will furnish you with a full explanation of events, ma'am. Suffice it to say that he made it known that he was leaving town with the sapphire-and-diamond set he presented to me on the occasion of our engagement. He chose to put his life at risk in order to bring the ringleader to book for his crimes. I discovered what he was planning to do and followed him from town. The robbery was foiled, and those involved…those who survived were taken up by the militia. The other members of the gang are, no doubt, being taken into custody as we speak. The ringleader is none other than Lord

Chard, although of course he played no part in the robberies themselves. The man directly responsible for your son's death is now in the hands of the authorities and will stand trial for his crimes.'

'You took a grave risk,' the Dowager pointed out, a touch of admiration in her voice. 'You must indeed love Lord Fincham very much.'

Georgiana stared down at the empty hearth. 'I've always loved him, as I imagine you suspected all along. And I always will. And that is why I must leave London again tomorrow.'

'I do not perfectly understand you, my dear.'

'The engagement, my lady, was a complete sham from the first, instigated by his lordship in order to bring the guilty man to justice. He put it to me that working together would more likely lead to a successful outcome. What he intended, of course, was to undertake the investigation on his own and exclude me as much as possible.'

The Dowager could not forbear a smile at the disgruntled tone. 'If that was indeed his intention, he was not wholly successful, as you succeeded in discovering his plans.'

'Yes, that does afford me a modicum of satisfaction, but it is scant recompense for what I must now do.'

Georgiana took her bottom lip between her teeth in an effort to stop it trembling. Now was not the moment to break down. Time enough for that in the weeks, months…years ahead, she told herself.

'The reason for the engagement no longer exists, therefore I must do the honourable thing and terminate the union, for I'm very sure Lord Fincham would not do so.'

'Which might suggest, might it not, that he possibly has no desire to do so?' her ladyship pointed out, not unreasonably. 'Might he have had another purpose for proposing marriage?'

'Because he is in love with me, you mean.' Georgiana's shout of laughter was mirthless. 'If only that were so! But he has never said as much, ma'am,' she revealed. 'And he wouldn't if it was not so. I'm afraid the love is all on one side, though I've done my utmost to conceal that from him. The last thing I want is for him to feel honour-bound to wed me.'

She rose to her feet and went over to the door. 'I have much to organise if I wish to be gone by morning.'

'But, child, where do you intend to go? Wouldn't it be best if you discussed matters with his lordship?'

Georgiana, resolute, shook her head. 'My mother possessed strength enough to give up the man she loved. I can only hope I'm equal to doing the same. But I need time for some quiet reflection. Besides which, I dare not come face to face with his lordship, at least not yet. He might so easily weaken my resolve.'

## Chapter Fifteen

It was as the late May evening's light was rapidly fading that Lord Fincham arrived on foot at a much-admired residence situated, like his own, in one of the most-favoured parts of the city. He had called at the property on numerous occasions in the past. His association with Lord Chard went back many years, before the time of the late Lord Fincham's tragic and unexpected demise. All the same, even though he had never looked upon the baron as a particularly close friend, he gained scant satisfaction from what he felt obliged to do now.

Ignoring the two men loitering on the opposite side of the street, avidly watching the house, his lordship mounted the steps. After gaining admittance, he was very soon afterwards being shown into the book-lined room situated on the ground floor, where Lord Chard, betraying a marked degree of surprise, and a suspicion of wariness too, it had to be said, rose at once from behind an impressive mahogany desk.

'Why, when my servant informed me you had called, I was inclined to consider the wretch had been helping himself to the brandy!' The jocular greeting was not in keeping with the baron's normally sombre manner, and something in Lord Fincham's mien must have revealed that he wasn't deceived by the false display of bonhomie. 'Forgive me if I'm wrong, but wasn't it your intention to leave town?'

'It was, as you well know,' his lordship returned. 'So let us not attempt to prevaricate further. I know you are the brains behind certain jewel thefts that have taken place during the past couple of years or so. I know it was you who marshalled the gang that attempted to rob me early this morning. You must now fully appreciate they failed. Those members who survived the attack are now in custody, as are your other co-conspirators.'

Lord Fincham held up one long-fingered hand against the denial about to be uttered. 'It will avail you nothing to plead the innocent, Chard. Your steward, Ivor Hencham is, as we speak, in the hands of the authorities. How long do you suppose it will be before a confession is drawn from him? If for no other reason, he will undoubtedly reveal all in an attempt to save his own neck from being stretched. I am here in order to spare you that indignity, too, should you choose to avail yourself of the opportunity that you ill deserve, in view of the fact that your determination to maintain your lifestyle brought about the death of an innocent man, one of your fellow peers.

'No, I'm afraid there is no escape,' he continued, when Chard, attempting no further denials, went over to the window. 'As you can see, across the road are two employees of Bow Street. No doubt there are others watching the rear of the property. They have been following your every movement since my meeting with a well-known personage connected with maintaining law and order.'

His lordship sighed deeply, and there was no mistaking the genuine regret contained in the sound. 'In deference to those closely connected to you, and innocent of any wrongdoing, I was permitted to see you before you are taken into custody. I do not believe you would want close members of your family to suffer further humiliation by a long and highly publicised trial, where every last detail of your life and marriage will come under public scrutiny. Better, surely, to spare them that and put a period to your own existence?'

'I might ask why you became involved, but of course I believe I know the answer—your fiancée, Miss Grey,' Lord Chard at last remarked, breaking his silence. 'I believe someone mentioned once she was very close to Grenville.'

'He was like a father to her, yes,' his lordship confirmed softy. 'And, of course, what adversely affects her now very much concerns me.'

'It was never my intention to harm anyone, Fincham. I hope you believe that,' the baron said, returning to his desk with a distinctly purposeful stride, as though he had come to a decision. 'I'm afraid, though, that since my marriage I've grown accustomed to every creature comfort, and when, owing to my excesses, the money began to run out, I had no intention of altering my lifestyle, if I could possibly avoid it, even if this meant putting more lives at risk…I was even willing to risk yours in order to get my hands on those sapphires.' He laughed hollowly. 'Yes, a despicable fellow am I not?'

Opening a desk drawer, Lord Chard stared down solemnly at its contents. 'I think you can appreciate why I have no desire to prolong this interview. It

only remains for me to say…thank you for showing me more consideration than I deserve…and
goodbye.'

His lordship had no desire to remain, either, and
left without uttering another word. He had reached
the street and had turned in the direction of Berkeley
Square when he detected the two men watching
the house begin to cross the street. He didn't look
back.

When he related all to the Dowager Countess of
Grenville late the following morning, she betrayed
little emotion, least of all gratification. In fact, several long moments elapsed before she eventually
spoke.

'I owe you a debt of gratitude, Lord Fincham, that
I could never hope to repay. I recall dear Georgiana
revealing something shortly after she had returned
here yesterday that, now, I can fully appreciate. She
said she no longer sought revenge. And I can perfectly understand that sentiment also. It will afford
me no gratification whatsoever to see Lord Chard
dangling from the end of a rope. I am not sorry you
offered him the opportunity to take his own life.'

'Whether or not he chose to avail himself of it,
ma'am, I have no notion. If he did not, he is most

definitely now in the hands of the authorities. There was no possible escape for him.'

She was not a female given to smiling too often. Lord Fincham, however, was the recipient of one of those rare displays of absolute approval. 'And what are your plans for the future now that you have succeeded so admirably on my behalf? Do you intend to remain in London, as do I and my granddaughter, and enjoy what is left of the Season?'

He smiled ruefully. 'I am no longer able to consider only myself, ma'am. Much will depend on my fiancée, though given the choice I would not delay too long in tying the final knot.'

Again the Dowager smiled, only there was a suggestion of satisfaction in it this time. 'I did not believe my judgement could be so flawed.'

It wasn't so much the admission itself as the tone in which it had been uttered that aroused his lordship's suspicions. Something was wrong… Yes, something was decidedly amiss.

He cast a frowning glance towards the door. 'Where is Georgiana? Is she, perchance, out visiting with Lady Sophia?'

'My granddaughter is, indeed, out paying morning calls,' the Dowager confirmed, before revealing what he most wished to know. 'But I regret to tell you that Georgiana is not with her. She left town first thing this morning in a hired carriage.'

'The devil she did!' he cursed, his perfect manners forgotten, and was on his feet in an instant. 'Where the deuce has she gone?'

'That, I'm afraid, I am unable to tell you,' the Dowager responded and, ignoring his fulminating glance, also rose to her feet and went across to the mantelshelf, from where she collected a glittering object, which she subsequently placed into the palm of his lordship's right hand.

'What the deuce does she mean by it?' he demanded to know, staring down almost in disbelief at the sapphire-and-diamond ring.

The Dowager regarded him in some exasperation. 'For a highly intelligent man evidently you can be remarkably obtuse on occasions, my lord. What on earth do you suppose she means by it? She is releasing you from the engagement she believed all along to be a mere contrivance to obtain an end… Was it a sham, my lord?'

He shook his head. 'Not as far as I was concerned, it wasn't,' he admitted softly.

'No, I thought not. All the same, I never attempted to set her straight on the matter. I believe she needs to hear it from you, personally. She is under the impression, you see, that all the love is on her side. I know you are not a gentleman to wear his heart on his sleeve. But did you never once admit your feelings for her?'

A moment's silence, then, 'Not in so many words, no.'

The Dowager sighed deeply as she returned to her chair by the hearth. 'I once interfered in matters of the heart…I vowed never to do so again. I am prepared, however, to make this an exception. If you take my advice, my lord, you will locate the girl you desire so much to wed and tell her of your feelings without delay.' She sighed again. 'I only wish I could inform you where to look.'

Again he regarded her in silence for a moment. 'And you genuinely have no idea where she might have gone?'

'I would tell you if I had,' she assured him. 'I think Georgiana appreciated that and therefore chose not to confide in me. All I can tell you is that she left London early this morning in a post-chaise. I cannot imagine she would be so foolish as to return to her home in Gloucestershire, or take refuge in my private residence in Bath. She would consider they would be the first places one would look. Perhaps the only clue she gave was to reveal that she was going to seek shelter with someone whom she knew would be kind and offer her a retreat from the world for as long as she craved sanctuary.'

'In that case, ma'am, you must forgive me if I leave you now. It might be difficult, but not impossible to discover the precise road a lady travelling alone left London on early this morning.' He paused as he reached the door. 'She did leave alone, I take it?'

'She took only her belongings with her. But not Digby.'

'In that case, ma'am, I shall run him to earth without delay.'

Using the journal she had pored over at the breakfast table, Georgiana sat by the open French windows, fanning herself. June had arrived with tropical fury, and the sun's merciless heat showed no signs of abating.

'Truly, Eleanor, I'm so glad I left the capital when I did. It must be absolutely oppressive there now.'

The lady, sitting serenely on the sofa, raised her eyes from her sewing. 'Are you so very glad, Georgie? Wouldn't it have been better to have spoken to Ben first, instead of what was tantamount to fleeing from him a second time?'

Since her arrival at Lady Eleanor's charming home

the week before, Georgiana had been granted ample opportunity to confide all, and she had, leaving out nothing, not even that very first encounter with the Viscount. Like kindred spirits they had laughed and cried together in turn, but even so, close though they had become, nothing Eleanor had said had persuaded her guest to write to his lordship.

Georgiana shook her head. 'I like to think I am my mother's daughter, unselfishly releasing the man I love from an engagement for the very best of reasons.' She smiled wryly. 'But I'm not so very sure I possess her strength of character. Your brother-in-law can be very persuasive, as you know. He is also very honourable and would have married me.' She raised her hand in a helpless little gesture. 'Oh, he's fond of me, right enough, very fond, I like to believe. But that doesn't alter the fact the real love on his side would have been missing from the union. No, it is better this way, and in time I'm sure he'll come to appreciate it too.'

Rising from the chair, she went to stand beside the window to attain the benefit from what little breeze there was. 'Did you read that obituary in the morning paper?' she asked, changing the subject from one that was still too painful for her. 'It strongly suggests that Lord Chard died as a result of an accident while cleaning his pistol. No doubt out of consideration for the immediate family the authorities have decided not to reveal what they know.'

'But it could be true,' Lady Eleanor pointed out, having been in possession of all the facts herself for several days, but Georgiana was sure it was not so.

She shook her head. 'No, unless I'm much mistaken Ben persuaded Chard to take his own life. He was in a strangely subdued state throughout the journey from Cheetham Wood back to London that day. We hardly exchanged a couple of dozen words. Not that we could do a deal of talking. He was tooling the carriage for much of the time.'

'Besides which, he was no doubt furiously angry with you for following him from town,' Eleanor pointed out, thereby eliciting a tiny gurgle of mirth from her very welcome visitor.

'He was as mad as fire,' Georgiana confirmed. 'If you could have seen the look on his face! I think he could quite cheerfully have strangled me.'

Her smile faded as she detected a distinct sound. 'Was that a carriage I heard…? Are you expecting visitors today?'

'Not that I'm aware of, my dear. Possibly one of my neighbours paying a call.'

'In that case, I'd best retire to my room. It wouldn't do for anyone to know I'm— Oh, good gracious me!' she exclaimed in alarm, after catching sight of an unmistakable tall figure making his way towards the house by way of the rose garden.

Eleanor watched in some dismay as the morning journal was tossed in the air and her endearing houseguest raced from the room in blind panic, knocking an occasional table over as she did so. Even though Lord Fincham's appearance in the doorway a moment later was not wholly unexpected, she still managed to let her sewing slide from her fingers to the floor as she rose to her feet.

'Oh, God!' Eleanor muttered for want of something more appropriate to say by way of a greeting.

'Not quite, merely your brother-in-law.' He felt for his quizzing-glass, and through it surveyed the bits and pieces littering the floor. 'Dear me, my unexpected arrival does appear to have had an adverse effect.'

'Not at all, dear brother,' Eleanor assured him, though still clasping her throat with one hand, like a Drury Lane actress performing in some Greek tragedy. 'It is always such a pleasure to see you. Can I offer you some refreshment?'

'No, thank you, Eleanor. I have no intention of taking up more of your time than I need do, and so shall come to the point of my visit—where is she?'

'W-who?' she managed faintly, and his smile in response was not pleasant. 'Oh, my daughter, you mean,' she continued valiantly. 'Why, where you would expect her to be—upstairs with her governess.'

'So, it is to be that way, is it?' So saying, his lordship did no more than give an ear-piercing whistle. A crossbred pointer appeared in response and went padding round the room, sniffing excitedly at the various items of furniture as he did so. 'Picked up the scent already, have you, boy? Good lad! Go and find her,' he ordered, after obligingly opening the door.

'Oh, this really is too bad of you, Benedict!' Eleanor admonished, though not at all convincingly. 'Not that I hadn't considered writing to you on several occasions during recent days. The poor girl is so desperately unhappy, and doing her utmost not to show it. It is all so very sad.'

'No, it isn't,' he countered at his imperious best.

'It's all so damnably unnecessary. And the little madam has put me to the trouble of organising everything myself. Still,' he continued, sounding and appearing well pleased with himself, 'if she isn't satisfied with the arrangements, she's only herself to blame.'

He raised a finger as a series of enthusiastic barks from above reached his ears. 'Ah! Sounds as if Ronan has run the quarry to earth. If you'll excuse me, Eleanor, there is a little matter on the floor above requiring my immediate attention.'

He turned, about to leave, when he bethought himself of something else. 'Perhaps in my absence you would care to get yourself and your daughter ready. Our wedding will be taking place in my local church early this afternoon and I should like you both to attend.'

Leaving his sister-in-law to gape after him with a look of astonishment, not untouched by admiration, Lord Fincham bounded up the stairs two at a time and along the passageway to that bedchamber from where a deal of excited yapping was still emanating. He paused on the threshold, surveying, with a deal of pleasure, the fond reunion taking place in the centre of the chamber. How typical it was of Georgie to take the time to return the affection by kneeling down and stroking the dog so tenderly! She could so easily have locked Ronan in some room and attempted to make good her escape.

The look he received was anything but affectionate when she chanced to raise her head and saw him standing there. 'Involving Ronan was damnably sneaky of you, Fincham!' she told him sternly.

'Damnably astute, I should say,' he countered, strolling languidly into the room. 'Saved a deal of time, what's more. Which reminds me—we haven't much left to us. We're due in the church in a little under two hours.'

'No!' The refusal, clear and carrying, held a strong note of determination, but did not leave his lordship visibly crestfallen. He merely called Ronan to heel before sensibly shutting him out of the room, then assisting Georgiana to her feet.

The instant she had gracefully risen, she attempted to withdraw her hand from his clasp, but he held fast, and even went so far as to capture the other. 'Now, so that we do not misunderstand each other further, I shall take leave to inform you, young woman, that I never for one moment considered our engagement a sham, simply because I love you…I love you even when you're impertinent enough to leave curt missives with my butler, denouncing me as a deceitful wretch… I've always loved you, and I cannot envisage the day will dawn when I do not love you.' He drew her unresistingly closer. 'Why, I even loved you—God help me!—when you were a boy.'

This drew forth a decidedly watery chuckle, and his lordship, exhibiting great presence of mind, took immediate steps to prevent the touching little sound from becoming an inexhaustible torrent of emotion.

When finally he had left her breathless and clinging to him for support, he settled her next to him on the chaise longue, content in the knowledge that she couldn't possibly now doubt the depth of his feelings. He received immediate confirmation of this when she slipped her hand shyly into his and confessed that she was very glad that he had found her.

Then something occurred to her and she raised her head briefly from the comfort of his shoulder. 'But how did you know where I was? I didn't tell anyone.'

'I discovered that for myself on the morning of your flight, when I called at Grenville House. Which reminds me, I have your engagement ring about me, which I shall return to you when I have placed a gold band on your finger first. But I digress…

To continue—on discovering that you intended to seek refuge with someone you could trust, I first supposed you just might have gone to Charles Gingham to seek his aid. So I immediately set out for Deerhampton. I needed to visit Charles to inform him about his cousin being taken into custody. You were not there, of course. But Charles's uncle still was. Which was most opportune, as far as I was concerned. Charles's uncle is a bishop, you see, and I was able to obtain a special licence from him.

'Charles, of course, was only too happy to accompany me back to town in order to help in the search. Fortunately, whilst I was absent, Digby managed to discover by which road a young lady, travelling quite alone, had left town in a hired carriage.'

He slanted her a mocking glance. 'I'll take leave to inform you, my girl, that not too many people can afford the luxury of travelling in a hired carriage, and those who can usually have conveyances of their own. Furthermore, not too many young ladies set out on journeys without so much as a maid to bear them company.'

'No, I suppose that was foolish of me,' she acknowledged after a moment's consideration. 'But I've never employed a personal maid, and I could hardly abscond with one of the Dowager's.'

'Well, you have one now, and she's awaiting you below,' he informed her, much to her surprise. 'Brindle managed to find a suitable young woman before we closed the town house and left for Fincham Park. Charles is there, ready to act as my grooms-man, and the Dowager and Lady Sophia are also staying at the house as our guests for a few days.'

He rose to his feet, smiling at the look of shocked disbelief flitting over her lovely features. 'So it only remains for you to get ready for our wedding.' He consulted his fob watch. 'And you have a mere half an hour, my love, before we must leave for the church.'

Any slight suspicions that he wasn't being totally serious left her in an instant. 'Oh, this really is too bad of you, Ben! I have absolutely nothing suitable to wear.'

'I'm certain you and your new abigail will come up with something appropriate.' He sauntered across to the door, but turned back to add with a challeng-ing gleam in his eye, 'Or do I take you as you are? Be very sure of one thing, my girl, I leave this house in half an hour, and you will be travelling with me to the church.'

Violet eyes glinted in response. 'You may be sure

of it, my lord. But now go away, do, and send up that abigail. If I'm to appear halfway presentable for my own wedding there isn't a moment to lose!'

\* \* \* \* \*

# HISTORICAL

## Large Print

## MISS IN A MAN'S WORLD
### *Anne Ashley*

Georgiana Grey disguised herself as a boy, and became handsome Viscount Fincham's page. Having come home love-struck, she must return to London for the Season. When she comes face-to-face with him again, her deception is unmasked…

## CAPTAIN CORCORAN'S HOYDEN BRIDE
### *Annie Burrows*

Aimée Peters possesses an innocence which charms even the piratical Captain Corcoran. Then he discovers the coins stitched into her bodice—what secrets does Aimée hide behind her naive façade?

## HIS COUNTERFEIT CONDESA
### *Joanna Fulford*

Major Falconbridge can see that Sabrina Huntley is no ordinary miss! With their posing as the Conde and Condesa de Ordoñez, he doesn't know which is worse—the menace of their perilous mission, or the desires awakened by this tantalising beauty…

## REBELLIOUS RAKE, INNOCENT GOVERNESS
### *Elizabeth Beacon*

Despite hiding behind shapeless dresses, governess Charlotte Wells has caught the eye of notorious Benedict Shaw. Charlotte declines his invitation to dance—but this scandalous libertine isn't used to taking no for an answer!

 MILLS & BOON

# HISTORICAL

## Large Print

## MORE THAN A MISTRESS
### *Ann Lethbridge*

Miss Honor Meredith Draycott knows she doesn't need a man—but society takes a different view. Meeting Charles Mountford, Marquis of Tonbridge, she discovers he's more than happy to make her respectable…but only if she acts privayely as his mistress!

## THE RETURN OF LORD CONISTONE
### *Lucy Ashford*

Lord Conistone vowed to look after Verena Sheldon. Now, her beloved home up for sale, she needs his help even more. But his dreams of holding her are shattered every time he imagines her reaction should she learn what he has done…

## SIR ASHLEY'S METTLESOME MATCH
### *Mary Nichols*

Determined to overthrow a smuggling operation, Sir Ashley Saunders will let nothing stand in his way—until he runs up against Pippa Kingslake! She's careful to protect her own interests…but could her independence end Ash's case—and his rakish ways?

## THE CONQUEROR'S LADY
### *Terri Brisbin*

To save her people and lands, Lady Fayth must marry Giles Fitzhenry, the commanding Breton knight. The marriage is as unwelcome as the deep desire which stirs each time she looks at her husband's powerful, battle-ready body…